Acclaim for Lisa Samson

"At the same time funny and meaningful, this is a beautiful gem.... The characters shine from the page with amazing insight and reminders about what's important."

—*RT Book Reviews*, 4 1/2 stars, TOP
PICK! review of *The Sky Beneath My Feet*

"The sweet truths of the gospel emerge not only through the pain and heartache, but through the healing that eventually comes."

—*Christianity* magazine,
review of *Resurrection in May*

"Samson is bold as ever, exploring big questions through her vivid writing and memorable characters."

—*Publishers Weekly* review
of *Resurrection in May*

"Samson spins a convincing tale about the plans we make for our lives and how God often has other ideas. Well written and enjoyable, this title will appeal to readers who appreciate intelligent fiction with a spiritual element."

—*Library Journal* review of *The
Passion of Mary-Margaret*

"Quirk works; this is a deeply engaging book deserving of a broad audience."

—*Publishers Weekly* starred review
of *The Passion of Mary-Margaret*

"*Quaker Summer* speaks to the heart of women. It just might set you free in ways you've never imagined."

—Mary Graham, Women of Faith

"It's not often that I say, 'This book changed my life' but in the case of *Quaker Summer* I shout it with a hearty amen. Samson weaves a compelling, surprising, faith-awakening story with the deft skill of a writing artisan. Her characters partially materialize in the room when you're reading, wooing you to consider their lives, struggles, and questions. Samson puts a human face on consumerism, compelling the reader to consider Jesus' radical call, but she does so with candor and grace. A highly recommended book."

—MARY DEMUTH, AUTHOR OF *WATCHING THE TREE LIMBS* AND *WISHING ON DANDELIONS*

"*Quaker Summer* is a perfect example of the life-changing power of fiction. . . . [Samson] manages to call into question the state of the North American church and challenge the reader to consider what life would look like if we took Jesus' example seriously. I was entertained, but I was also given a glimpse of the church doing what it should be doing—and it's changing the way I view my own spiritual walk."

—ALISON STROBEL, AUTHOR OF *WORLDS COLLIDE* AND *VIOLETTE BETWEEN*

"[A] staggering examination of the Christian conscience. [Samson] paints an emotionally and spiritually luminous portrait of a soul beckoned by God."

—*PUBLISHERS WEEKLY* REVIEW OF *QUAKER SUMMER*

Runaway Saint

Also by Lisa Samson

The Sky Beneath My Feet
Resurrection in May
The Passion of Mary-Margaret
Embrace Me
Quaker Summer

Runaway Saint

LISA SAMSON

THOMAS NELSON
Since 1798

NASHVILLE   DALLAS   MEXICO CITY   RIO DE JANEIRO

Published in Nashville, Tennessee, by Thomas Nelson. Thomas Nelson is a registered trademark of HarperCollins Christian Publishing, Inc.

Thomas Nelson titles may be purchased in bulk for educational, business, fundraising, or sales promotional use. For information, please e-mail SpecialMarkets@ ThomasNelson.com.

Library of Congress Cataloging-in-Publication Data

Samson, Lisa, 1964-
    The runaway saint / Lisa Samson.
      pages cm
    ISBN 978-1-59554-546-6 (pbk.)
    1. Runaway women—Fiction. 2. Sisters—Fiction. 3. Alienation (Social psychology)—Fiction. 4. Missionaries—Fiction. 5. Families—Fiction. 6. Domestic fiction. I. Title.
    PS3569.A46673R86 2014
    813'.54—dc23

                    2013037441

            Printed in the United States of America
        14 15 16 17 18 19 RRD 6 5 4 3 2 1

For Rhonda Roberts and Elysa MacLellan, the Mississippi Mamas who read every single word.

"Happiness as a goal is a recipe for disaster."

Barry Schwartz

1.

Happy Birthday to Me

I'm thirty years old and I still believe in ghosts. I believe in ghosts because I have one. He's like an imaginary friend, only with a bit more heft. Unlike an imaginary friend, he doesn't go away when I don't need him anymore and surely, at my age, I don't.

Today is my birthday.

My mother, Rita, has arranged a birthday lunch, a typical mother-daughter activity, which is weird in and of itself. I'm meeting her at Grove Street Artisan, a bakery two blocks down the street. It is March, forty-five degrees and ready to rain any second, but she's sitting outside at one of the round, black iron tables, the chairs chained together like petals around it. Her bike leans, chained, against the iron railing surrounding the patio. What looks like a crumpled ball of paper tied with twine sits perfectly centered over the umbrella hole. She's a beautiful fifty-something woman, her long white hair, having begun graying in her early twenties, a little ghost unto itself when viewed from behind. This morning that hair is contained by a long braid wrapped twice around her head. My mother's features are delicate, unlike my own, which match my father's.

She sleeps year-round in a tent on an organic farm where she works and lives.

It's fine. Go ahead and let that sink in.

"Don't open it here," she says, indicating the present. She rises from her chair to kiss either side of my face. "You're all by yourself, I see." She pinches the side of my hair close to my head between the blades of her index and middle finger. "I like the cut. Makes you look like a pixie. But the color is new, isn't it?" She sits back in her chair, the thick fabric of her baja bunching around her middle. There's not much of a middle. "I got it!" She snaps her fingers. "Baby, most people *go* blond, they don't cover it up with red! *That's* what feels so different here!" She places her left work boot, complete with the steel toes necessary for chores like chopping wood or digging fence posts, on her right knee, then gasps. "What if the Universe gave you blond hair for a reason, and the reason happens tomorrow?!"

The Universe.

This from the woman who taught me that a TULIP wasn't just a flower but a system of theology worth dying for.

Well, we don't believe everything our parents tell us, do we? But sometimes they leave an unwanted residue.

"Mom, I've always wanted red hair, so at least I'll have one more item off my bucket list before I kick that bucket."

"Baby, death is a misnomer."

I pivot one of the petals away from the table and sit down, noting everything seemingly corporate and industrial-complex about my jeans even though they're fair trade and cost me a fortune. "It's just me today. Finn has done a runner right on the morning of the big 3-0. No coffee. The sheets on Finn's side of the bed cold. He left early without leaving so much as a note. It's some kind of birthday mission," I tell her. "He was dropping hints all night, but I couldn't get him to spill the secret."

She smiles.

"You know, don't you?" I ask.

She nods. "And that's how it's going to stay."

I rest my chin in my hand. "I figured. So, ready to eat?"

"I was going to order, but it would be better if you picked out what you want. I don't want to lay that on you," she says, leaning forward across the table and taking my hand in her small, well-muscled one.

Honestly, though. You just can't help but love someone that earnest about individual freedom, both yours and hers. Hers first, of course.

We head inside to the counter together, her homemade drawstring pants, a touch too short, flapping around ankles encased in high-quality woolen socks. She may not have much, but what she has will last the rest of her lifetime and probably mine.

We cast our eyes over the pastries under glass, each one carefully composed and artful. I love this place. When our turn comes, Mom orders a piece of cake and a café latte, which she insists on having made with coconut milk instead of the real thing. "Poor cows," she says, watching the counter-girl put a hefty slab of carrot cake on a plain white plate. "Not that the rest of the cow is any better." She takes the plate as it's offered. She sure didn't feel the need to change her sweet tooth all those years ago, and I'm glad. "If human beings would stop drinking cow's milk and eating their bodies, the average life span would rocket up to a hundred and fifty. Not to mention how much better it would be for the cows themselves."

I can see her logic, but as for me, "I don't want to live in a world without hamburgers, Mom."

"Baby, even not considering the cows, it's time to start valuing yourself more. That's the way the Universe works, you know. It won't look out for you if *you* don't start looking out for you first. It all works together. You and God. God and you. All together in one big Universe."

Mom is a big believer in the Universe. Manifestation. Think and you will become.

Finn calls her the Buddha of Baltimore, and it all sounds fine coming out of her mouth, but Finn hasn't known her as long as I have. The only side he's seen of my mother is this free-spirited, crazy person who doesn't want to get involved in such a way that might actually affect his life. He's good with that. And when we visit her at her tent, it's Finn who takes creek walks with her and helps with the meals on the camp stove.

The Grove Street Artisan opened up maybe six months ago. My clothes all seemed to fit a little looser back then. As it is, the bakery sits aside the path I walk every day from home to work and back again. The owner, Madge, copper-skinned and freckled, comfortably plump, vivacious, always ties back a headful of tiny, honey-brown braids that go down almost past her knees with a sky-blue scarf. It's one of my favorite color combinations.

"Oh, this weather, yeah, Sara?" Madge calls across the counter, rubbing flour-caked hands on the front of her apron as Mom pays for our breakfast, pulling a small cloth change purse, probably from Peru, from her pants pocket. Madge has the loveliest lilt to her voice, like she learned English in a *Masterpiece Theater* boarding school but spent her holidays in a Caribbean shantytown. Apparently everybody in Trinidad speaks that way. "You think it's gonna stay like this, all gray and depressin'?"

"Better not. It's my birthday," I say.

"Well, happy birthday, Sara. At least *that's* not depressin', yeah?"

She has no idea.

Madge's former position as a baking instructor at the French Culinary Institute ensures our neighborhood not only these decadent butter croissants fresh every morning but breads and pastries, some of them fancy enough to be served at Baltimore's best restaurants. But she's our best-kept secret. I save her croissants for a special treat, because otherwise I'd send Finn out for a batch every morning until my clothes stopped fitting. But it's my birthday. I take one back to an inside table with me, along with my coffee.

Mom bites into her cake, pronounces it a work of art, and then starts poking it apart. Something's on her mind.

"What is it?" I ask, knowing better. Why do I do that?

"Nothing," she says. "Have you heard from the Old Man yet today?"

Ugh.

Her lips turn down. "Of course you have. You probably had a card from him yesterday."

I don't tell her she's right about the card. "Not today, not yet."

Ever since she left him, she's called my father, a professional calligrapher in a world that's gone digital, the Old Man. In her mind, everything about him is unliberated, chained down, and suffocating. He's lived his life looking backward, with a sense that the more we progress, the more we have lost, while Mom fancies herself a progressive thinker, anticipating and embracing whatever is next, even if it means going back to the past as long as it's a past she can relate to. Dad, however, is her last holdout in her journey to accept all things and all people that the Universe brings her way. Wu wei, she calls it. I have no idea what that even means, but I think it's from the Tao Te Ching or something like that.

All I can say to that is, thank God somebody was stable.

"Oh, I'm sure he will," she says with a magnanimity born of a sudden sense of superiority. "I've got a rad new idea for a T-shirt, baby. Do you think you could help me with the design?"

"What will it say?" You just never know with Mom.

"Wherever you go, there you are."

"Mom. That's been done before."

Her eyes widen. "Really?"

"Yes."

"But that's so Zen! Really?" She seems delighted. "I just tapped into something bigger all on my own? Don't you just love it when that happens?"

"I think I'm too busy for that sort of cosmic symbiosis to occur. Plus, I'm not sure if God really works that way or not. I mean, yes, truth is truth. But it has to come from a reliable source to mean anything, doesn't it?"

"Then, baby, if it's not happening, you're just too busy."

"I'm happy with my life the way it is, Mom."

"You know something, baby? We tell ourselves we're happy, when what we really are is content. Contentment is nothing but the conviction that things are 'good enough,' and we let our fear convince us that if we try to make them better, we risk losing everything. Well, I don't believe that, Sara. We tell ourselves the only reason to make a change is because we're miserable. But change is the natural order. The people who realize that and embrace it, *they're* the ones who discover real happiness."

"You mean living like a hermit in a tent in Baltimore County?"

She gazes at me with imperturbable serenity. I really wish I could perturb that serenity once in a while. That's our mother-daughter dynamic in a nutshell.

"If that's what it takes, yes," she says, letting the subject drop.

I finish the last of my croissant, licking the shiny residue off my fingertips.

"So what's next on your special day, baby?"

"After this, I'll probably check in at the office, even though I promised myself a day off. Don't worry. I won't do any work—I won't even sit down at my desk. I'll just banter a little bit with Huey, see how the new posters are coming out, then make sure Diana knows who to call about securing the booth at the Wedding Expo, since I have a feeling Finn won't have passed along the info. Maybe I'll chat with Madge a little and take a bag of croissants into the office with me. No, wait, I'm not even supposed to go into the office today."

"There's something we need to talk about, baby," Mom says.

The somberness of her tone sets me off guard.

She glances out the window at a woman passing on the sidewalk, a mother in tight jeans and high boots with a phone pressed to her ear, pushing a big-wheeled stroller loaded with twins. Her brow furrows, leading me to imagine all kinds of possibilities: she's been diagnosed with cancer, she's filing for bankruptcy, there's another lawsuit, or maybe even a new man.

"Mom, what's wrong?"

She gives an eloquent, helpless shrug. "I don't know how to break it to you, so I'm just going to say it. Bel is back."

———

Bel is back. Belinda. Aunt Bel. My mom's baby sister, a missionary in Kazakhstan who dropped off the map about fifteen years ago after my grandparents died.

To understand the importance of her return is to understand my family, something I'm not able to do. I would look at her photo on my grandparents' mantel when I was a kid. Aunt Bel gazed at me with hooded eyes, as if she concealed some secret understanding, her full mouth upturned slightly at one corner, like the cryptic women of Renaissance art. She was a blond and beautiful teenager, her chin tilted in defiance at whoever was taking the picture.

My grandmother organized her church's missionary conference every year, so you can imagine how they felt about their younger daughter. Growing up, I knew Bel was the favored one, the holy one, the Mahatma Gandhi if they would dare to even bring up someone from, gasp, India of all places. She was part of God's plan to save the elect from the fires of hell, and if that isn't the mission of all missions, nothing is.

"First I got this strange postcard in the mail," Mom says. "There was a picture on the front, one of those churches with the golden onion domes. The postmark was from Romania, and it said she was thinking of me and thinking about home. I didn't recognize the handwriting at first and she didn't sign the card, but I knew it had to be her. After all these years. So weird."

"She's here in the States?"

Mom nods. "She got back over the weekend. As soon as she got to your father's house, she called the farm and left a message saying she wanted to see me."

"Wow," I say. "She's at Daddy's?"

"Yes, if you can believe that. Apparently they've kept in touch all these years. Just every so often, but still. That was news to me."

"Where else is there to go, then, I guess."

"I guess. It's been so long. This will sound terrible, but I kind of thought of her as if she were dead."

"It's not like she kept in touch," I say.

"Of course you were too young to understand what was happening at the time, but the whole thing was *very* traumatic. I mean, you don't go overseas for the summer and then decide you're never coming back. That's crazy. She was only nineteen. Your grandfather was going to fly over there and get her, whether she wanted to come or not."

This is more info than she's ever given me. "Did he go?"

She shakes her head. "Your grandmother laid down the law, the way she does. As far as my mom was concerned, Aunt Bel was a saint. She could do no wrong. And having a missionary in the family? Over the moon. It was because Aunt Bel gave her so much trouble as a teenager. When she straightened herself out, when she became so devout, well, that was Mom reaping her reward. 'Train up a child in the way she should go.'"

"Did they ever see her again?"

"No. And even so, Aunt Bel was golden in her eyes." The bitterness in her tone comes as a surprise. Not that she feels it, but that she's allowing herself to express it, and me to see it. "Anyway, I think it was me who finally convinced him not to go. Just wait, I said, and Bel would come home on her own."

"You were right."

She laughs. "I guess I misjudged how long it would take her. Do you remember much about her?" she asks as if she hopes the answer is no.

All I can do is shrug. My actual memories of my aunt Bel are all mixed up, just a fuzzy set of half-remembered sensations. She'd left for the field when I was four. I have some warm but vague recollections from family Christmas parties, Aunt Bel always my biggest fan, throwing me in the stroller to go hang out with friends. I seem to recall a tall, lissome girl sitting on the floor, holding me in her lap as I opened presents. No word she ever spoke to me is preserved in memory. Only a vague aftertaste of her presence, the sweetness diminishing each year, but never fully gone, remains.

"Here's the thing," Mom says. She's done with her cake, but uses her fork to tap the empty plate. "I don't think she's here for a visit. She plans to stay for good. She doesn't have a job, obviously, and I doubt she has much money, though she's living on something. She's going to need a place to stay. Walter doesn't have the room."

She shifts the crumbs on her plate here and there, long enough for me to see where this conversation is leading.

"What about *your* place?" I ask. "She's *your* sister."

She raises an eyebrow. "I don't think she had living in a tent in mind when she got on the plane to come back, baby. But I figured *you* might want to put her up, since you and Finn have a lot in common with her, you know. Being religious, I mean."

For Mom the word *religious* means signing on the dotted line of conformity that you will hereby cease and desist all autonomy and free-dom. That all decisions have been taken out of your hands and into the grips of prideful old men with loads of money—if not their money, yours. Mom is very spiritual, as she's quick to point out, but not at all religious.

I'm not sure how I feel anymore about all of that. Really. If Aunt Bel seems mysterious, Jesus is even more so. He seems so different from all the ways God has been presented, and while I've rejected the notion that he was hanging on the cross with just a few people in mind, I just can't see him as anything else. I've never had one of those experiences where Jesus came into any kind of focus. So I just trust that he's like Finn says, full of grace and truth, whatever that even means.

"And you have so much more room," she adds. "At least I guess so."

"Finn won't go for it."

"Baby, he'll go for anything you want. That boy is putty in your hands. Compared to him, you're a rocket scientist, and yet he's smart enough to know that!" She seriously thinks she's giving us both a compliment.

"Thanks a lot."

"Besides, it's your birthday. He can't say no to you, today of all days."

"Yay. Happy birthday to me. So this is my present? You're dumping your sister on my doorstep?"

She slides the garbled paper ball across the table. "No, *this* is your present. Your Aunt Bel is just the icing on the cake."

I walk home in a state of mild ambivalence, unwrapping my birthday present on the way. It wasn't a crumpled ball at all, but a carefully folded sphere because, I'm assuming, Scotch tape would be an extra possession in my mother's eyes. Inside the paper, in a tuft of white cotton, nests a vintage cocktail ring of my grandmother's, a big blue sapphire circled with tiny diamonds.

I admit, I'm touched.

About a year before she died, my grandmother started giving away possessions almost willy-nilly. Walk in the door, you were sure to walk out with something, whether you were a relative, a friend, or the mailman.

Somehow Mom secured the prize: the ring I always tried on when Grandmom let me play in her jewelry box.

I slip the ring on my finger. It fits.

Thank you, Universe, for looking out for me just this once.

It begins to rain.

2.

The Iron Maiden

Way back in the city's past, maybe as far back as the days when Edgar Allan Poe roamed the cobbled streets, the Old Firehouse really was a firehouse, a modest fire station executed in utilitarian brick, though it looks ornate by modern standards. Over the years, the building has been gutted and repurposed a number of times, until it was finally left abandoned for a decade or so, tagged with spray paint, its windows busted out, rendering them sightless eye sockets looking out over Patterson Park and remembering the good old days.

Then Finn's brother, Chris, stepped in. He bought the Old Firehouse and fixed it up the way he'd rehabbed a half dozen other properties, a minor player in the Patterson Park renaissance. Real estate is a Drexel thing—Finn's brother and father are always buying and renovating and selling. Property is in their blood. We snagged some studio space in the Old Firehouse at a great price, on the condition that in return Finn wears the hat of property manager, seeing to the other tenants' needs so his brother doesn't have to. From home to work is just a ten-minute walk.

Honestly, it just couldn't be better.

Three years ago I quit my job at a big Baltimore creative agency and married Finn, one of the freelancers I used to contract. Together, we started an agency of our own with a sideline in letterpress printing. The official name on the business cards is DREXEL PRESS AT THE OLD FIREHOUSE, but we just call it "work," and the office we've dubbed the "studio." While I design for clients and produce a line of cards and stationery for retail stores, Finn designs their websites and runs our print shop, devoting his spare time to renovation projects at home.

Was it the great Chinese philosopher Confucius who said, if you choose a job you love, you'll never work a day in your life?

He was so wrong.

Loving the job means you *have* to work. You never neglect what you love. Everyone who knows me thinks I'm living the dream. But they also say I work too much, so go figure. Like my mom, I do what works best for me. And working hard works best.

How much time I'm going to have for mysterious Aunt Bel from Kazakhstan is already wearing on my mind. Will she need entertaining? A crying shoulder for the adjustments she'll need to make?

Spare me, Lord. I'll go to the dentist instead if you think that would be a fair trade.

The stable-sized doors in front of the Old Firehouse have been replaced with plate glass, flooding our studio with light. The front of the space is reserved for the printing presses—we have a Vandercook and two tabletop presses, a Pilot and a freshly restored Sigwalt—so people passing on the street can see us at work. Huey's in action, pulling prints off the Vandercook and holding them up to the light. He sees me outside the glass and gives me a wink.

Can I just say here and now that I love Huey? I did from the moment he walked in two years ago and told us how badly we needed him at our studio.

I push through the front entrance and down the hallway to our door, which opens into the back of the studio, where the open-plan cubicles are separated from the presses by a long counter. My desk, along with Finn's and a conference table for spreading out paper samples and meeting with clients, furnishes the stark white room, the walls displaying our best work.

"I thought you weren't coming in today," Diana, one part pin-up and two parts Rosie the Riveter and an extra 10 percent punk rock if her tattooed sleeves have any opinion on the matter, says from her swivel chair behind the counter. To one side of her large-screen Mac, she's inspecting the colored edges of some duplexed business cards that have to be picked up later this afternoon.

"You're supposed to say, 'Happy Birthday.'"

"Happy Birthday. Do you feel old?"

"I do now. How do the cards look?"

"Perfect. I can't believe how clean he gets the edges. Huey's the man, even if he does say so himself. I'm about to box them up. Ooooh—I like your ring. Birthday present?"

She takes my hand, gripping the back of my hand with fingers tipped with nail polish so deeply red it borders on black, to examine the cocktail ring closer.

"Present from my mom," I say. "Any sign of Finn?"

Diana shakes her head, but not too convincingly, because her bouffant hairdo barely moves. Whatever the surprise is, she must be in on it.

I help her box up the business cards, reminding her about

confirming the booth at the upcoming show. As I suspected, Finn hasn't forwarded the e-mail from the organizer, so I plop into his cubicle chair and do it myself. Then I walk up front to interrogate Huey, an angular black man in his late forties with a thing for wearing boiler suits with his name embroidered on the chest.

"I haven't seen Finn," I tell him. "I think you know what's going on."

"Not me, Boss. I keep myself to myself."

"What do you think about the new poster?"

He pulls one of the prints off the drying rack, handing it over. "It's not my thing, personally, but I think we'll sell a bunch."

"Wow." The idea was Finn's, but I ended up doing all the research and figuring out the design. It's a chart depicting a grid of coffee cups in profile, with the correct proportions of coffee or espresso, milk, and foam for making twenty different drinks. The background is bright orange, the coffee inky brown, the milk tan and creamy, the foam white, the text red. Every color represents a separate pass, except for white, which is the Mohawk paper showing through. Framed, the poster will look striking above any coffee shop bar, or on the kitchen wall of a home espresso enthusiast. "You're good, Huey. They look amazing. Has Finn seen them yet?"

"Not yet."

"So he hasn't been in this morning?"

"If he has, he snuck right by."

I examine it some more, finding no imperfection to the naked eye. Huey's that good.

"Can I tell you something?" he says. "This whole infographic kick, it leaves me cold. I understand the theory—people like this stuff, and it helps get our name out there—but to me, it's like opening up the *USA Today*. It's just not beautiful."

"I'm doing my best."

"It's not you that's the problem, Boss. It's the idea. 'Everything we do here has to be in good taste.' You made the rule, not me."

"Infographics are hot on the Internet. If you create a good one, it can go viral and that brings a lot of traffic to the site. People buy the prints, and we get to pay the bills. I can't help it if you don't like coffee."

"The caffeine makes me jittery," he says. "And what you're describing is being a trend-hound, not having good taste."

"And if you ask me, this is beautiful, whether you see it or not."

"I'm looking right at it, and I don't know."

Channeling Mom, I say: "You've got to look with your eyes open, my friend."

He shakes his head. "Thank you. I'll give that a try."

"One thing I'd love to see, though, is a deeper impression. You're keeping it light again, Huey. I want the plates to bite into the paper."

"Yeah, yeah," he says, waving me off. "You're listening too much to those hipster types. Now back in the day—"

"So what are your plans for the day off?" Diana interrupts just in time to abate the upcoming lecture. "You did the big birthday dinner last night, didn't you? Anything special coming up?"

"The point of a day off is that you don't have to plan. But I would like to know where Finn disappeared to."

"Have you tried calling him?"

"I'm trying not to."

As I'm standing across the counter from her, Diana sneaks a look at her phone, which I pretend not to notice.

"I guess I'll take off," I say.

"You should stick around for a few minutes."

"How many minutes?"

She checks her phone again. "Maybe ten?"

"Is a camera part of the surprise here, because if it isn't . . ."

"Stick around anyway."

"Drat."

The big red pickup rolls to a stop right in front of our window. I can't tell one truck from another, but I recognize this one. It belongs to Finn's older brother, Chris, who slides down from the driver's seat, taps the glass, and waves. Finn exits from the passenger side and circles behind the pickup, examining the rain-slick plastic tarp that covers and conceals their cargo. The shape underneath is suggestive, tall and square like an old arcade game, and it's so heavy that the truck's rear wheels are half hidden.

"Look at that!" Diana coos in mock surprise.

Now Finn is tapping on the glass, beckoning Huey to come out. Huey strips off his latex gloves—he's been cleaning the Vandercook—and rests his hands on his cocked hips, watching the men outside with no indication that he's about to join them in the rain.

I push through the door and into the corridor, leaning outside for a better look.

"What have you got there?" I ask.

My husband comes around to the front of the truck, smiling broadly, his copper-brown curls dripping wet. He rubs his gloved, greasy hands together in anticipation.

"Hey, hon, look what's out here. You want to come and see?"

"I'll get all wet."

"It'll be worth it," he says. "Come have a look."

It's not that camera. For sure.

As I venture into the rain, Chris, same hair as Finn, but with a shorter and stockier build, lowers the tailgate and growls out a greeting: "How's it hanging, birthday girl?"

"All right, I guess."

"The suspense is killing her," he says, laughing.

Finn leaps into the bed of the truck and starts working on the guide ropes and bungee cords that crisscross around their cargo. The truck groans under the weight.

"What's under there?"

"Can't you guess?" Finn says.

The problem is, I *can* guess. I just don't want it to be true.

He loosens the ropes and starts working the back of the tarp up, revealing in stages what I've already guessed. "A Chandler & Price!"

Full-size.

"Look, hon," he says, pointing at the wavy spokes on the flywheel indicating an Old Style press, from back in the 1800s. "Once this is restored to working order, this beautiful old machine will be virtually indestructible."

Right now, however, its surfaces are pitted with rust, the moving parts seized up.

"Wow," I say. "Look at that. What barn did you find that thing in?"

The light of happiness glows in his greenish eyes. Oh, Finn.

"It's just what you wanted, right? A full-size press?"

The legs are bolted down on a wooden pallet, which is good, but the foot treadle is still in place, meaning the press was never fitted with a motor back in the day. Which is bad. Very bad.

He lays a hand on the rusted iron. "No, I know, I know, it's a little rough, but give me and Huey a couple of days, and we'll have it running like new. Imagine this thing front and center in the window. It'll be amazing. I was thinking we should paint it fire-engine red—or maybe British racing green, I can't decide. It'll be your choice, whatever you like. Happy birthday, hon!"

He hops down and puts his arms around me, leaning into a kiss. I kiss him back because it's the thought that counts, and we love each other, and even when he screws up and bites off more than he can ever chew, Finn can't help being cute about it, and charming. It always comes from a good place inside him.

"Are we bringing it inside?" Chris asks.

Finn releases me. "We need Huey. Go tell him to get his butt out here, baby."

Diana raises her eyebrows as I pass.

"It'll look nice once it's all fixed up," she says.

When I sidle up alongside Huey, who is still contemplating us through the window, he cuts me a sideways look.

"You *asked* for one of those?" he mutters. "It looks like jungle rot to me."

He's not wrong. It's true that I have had feelers out for a while, looking for a proper full-size press since the Vandercook, technically speaking, is a proof press, easy to use but not really made for doing high-volume jobs. I speak in low tones. "What I had in mind was a Heidelberg, if we could find one at a bargain basement price."

He nods. "The C&P Old Style is a platen press, just like the tabletops we already have. Maybe in perfect shape, and fitted with a motor . . ."

I take a deep breath. "In a few days, Finn says the two of you will have that thing working just like new."

"Is that right?" Huey says. "Well, isn't he the prophet?"

"Don't pitch a fit on my birthday."

"Me pitch a fit? Don't even think about it, Boss." He makes his way toward the exit—taking his time, though, in no rush to get wet.

Diana rolls her eyes at me once he's gone. "Oh man. Things are gonna get pretty interesting around here."

It takes the men about a half hour to agree on how to get the press indoors, then Huey disappears for another half hour, returning with a borrowed pallet jack. In the meantime, with Diana's help, I've cleared some space in the studio.

"Maybe they should bring it down to the basement," Diana says. "If they have to take it apart, won't all the pieces kind of get in the way?"

"I don't know how we'd get it down there. And besides, one of them might end up crushed at the bottom of the steps."

The glance Diana throws me assures me she believes that to be all too possible. Diana and I see ourselves as the women of the studio. Huey and I see each other as the practical people. And Diana and Finn look at Huey and me as hard-ass overachievers. It works.

With a lot of grunting and a few choice epithets, Finn, Huey, and Chris manhandle the press onto the curb and through the front door as my heart races. I realize my stress doesn't make the process any safer or easier, so I keep my mouth shut, but man, every cell in my body is screaming.

I can barely watch the progress down the sidewalk, and the small crowd of neighbors that has gathered is getting an eyeful of why I'm glad I'm a woman.

At the door to the studio, the men argue over whether the flywheel has to come off to get the press through. Huey wonders aloud if we have a sledgehammer, and I can easily picture him going all Paul Bunyan on the cast iron, pounding away till our ears split from the noise and pieces are flying straight into our eyes.

"You'll be thanking me one day," Finn says to Huey, who doesn't even dignify that with an answer.

In the end, Chris takes the door off its hinges, giving them just enough room. Good man.

Finally, they heave the press past the counter and into the center of the studio, where it towers in rusty steampunk magnificence.

I feel like we've just come safely to the bottom of the mountain after skiing a double black diamond. Not that I ski.

"Your wish is my command," Finn says, flourishing his hand. It's true, I wished for a press like this. Just not this one. In this way. Right now. Right here. But other than that . . .

"That thing weighs a ton," his brother adds. "No, two tons."

Diana comes over to inspect the hulk. "Let's see. That would mean each of you were responsible for almost seven hundred pounds." She tries the lever, but it's stuck fast. "I can't believe you guys even got it in here. It's like a work of art, though. Like a piece of sculpture."

Chris rubs his lower back. "Or a medieval torture device. The Iron Maiden."

"Reminds me of an idol," Huey remarks, chuckling to himself. "Made of metal and just as useless."

Finn winces. I feel sorry for him.

Huey taps the flywheel. "Well, I guess we better get used to moving around the thing. It's gonna be here awhile."

"I found a great way to get the rust off," Finn explains, guiding Huey to his computer so they can review some YouTube videos that will walk them through the process.

The eager innocence in his voice is painfully familiar. It's the same tone I remember from the morning he decided to replace the tile in our upstairs bathroom. Four hours later we had a gulf of gray dust and jagged grout between the bathroom door and the toilet, and Finn had given up on the job, explaining that he'd need to address the subflooring before going any further. That was months ago.

Knowing how handy his father is, how handy Chris is, I always figured that if Finn got in over his head on a renovation project, he'd just call for help. But the manly code of the Drexels does not allow for such shows of weakness. After screwing up the tile, the last person in the world Finn would call is his brother, who'd never let him hear the end of it. I've learned to adapt.

His short-lived enthusiasm, however, isn't his sole characteristic. Finn has a way of giving people a break, of cheering them on, greater than anyone I've ever seen. He's amazing. He's really good in bed too. And he's a good cook and doesn't mind doing the dishes.

Yes, I hit the mother lode. I still don't know why he looks at me like he does, as if I'm not the slightly frumpy young woman I am. He says I have the sexy librarian look. I tell him beauty is, quite obviously considering the work I do, in the eye of the beholder.

"I'm going to head home," I tell Finn, running my hand through his damp hair. He pulls away from YouTube long enough for a peck on the cheek. "When you get home tonight, I have a favor to ask."

He smiles. "Anything you want. It's your birthday, after all."

"Anything?" I whisper in his ear.

"You want to go home right now?"

I laugh. "Get your work done. I'll be there all night."

"Be thinking about what you want."

"All right," I say. "I'm gonna hold you to that."

I'll make sure to ask him about Bel *after* playtime in the bedroom. Wouldn't want to miss any of that for the sake of my mysterious aunt. I didn't grow up thinking missionaries were saints just because.

3.
Good Taste

"So your aunt the nun wants to move in with us? And you think it's a good idea?"

"First off, she's not a nun, she's a missionary."

"Same difference."

"No, not really. And she isn't doing the asking. It's my mom."

We're sitting downstairs in front of the flat screen, eating leftover birthday cake with our feet up on the coffee table. Finn has found a way to spread himself so flat that he can rest his plate on his chest, lifting his head to take a bite. The copper stubble on his chin is flecked with icing.

"And that's the favor you wanted?"

I nod. "My mom dumped it on me this morning. I was, like, whatever, at first—but the more I think about it, the more intrigued I get. I mean, I wonder what she's even like."

"Is she old like your mom?"

"Aunt Bel was a teenager when I was born," I tell him. "So I'm thinking she must be . . . I don't know, midforties? Not that much older than us."

"Speak for yourself. I'm still in my twenties, you cradle-robber."

On the table next to the remains of the cake rest a few more presents Finn brought home with him: a DVD of the *Helvetica* documentary (which I love), a striped sweater he located by clicking through my Pinterest boards (shows initiative), and best of all, a vintage Minolta Autocord, one of those cool medium-format film cameras with the viewfinder on top, perfect for the kind of portrait and street photography I'm always daydreaming about getting into. A Japanese copy of the famous Rolleiflex Automat, only the copy improved on the original, and is a lot cheaper on the secondhand market.

"It's serviced and ready to go. The guy at the shop showed me some pictures it took, black-and-white stuff, the real deal. The depth . . . well, they're completely amazing."

"You're completely amazing," I say, bestowing a kiss. "Sometimes I have my doubts, then you do something like this and I think, 'He really knows me.'"

"Of course I *know* you." He gives me his squinty, uncomprehending smile. "I was thinking, you know the half bath in the basement? It would be the easiest thing in the world to blow out the side wall, build it out, and put a worktable in there. You could have your own private photo lab for developing your pictures. You'd like that."

"Maybe," I say, envisioning the half bath with no wall, the project abandoned in midstream until he can replace, say, the copper pipes. "We'll see. I can always have them developed professionally for the time being."

We watch eating shows on TV. My favorite, chain-smoking chef travels the world, drinking to his heart's content and showing us his hangovers. Now that's entertainment. Finn stares over the top of his cake and I watch through the Autocord's viewfinder, letting the camera dangle around my neck by the strap, fiddling with the silky focus lever until the picture looks razor sharp. After a while, I run upstairs to change into comfy clothes, sweatpants and my favorite T-shirt, a dark gray one a few years old. It fits like a second skin, only this skin comes from my babyhood, it is that soft. On the back in white Futura lettering it says GOOD TASTE. Coming down the stairs, the camera still dangling, I notice a little hole in the shirt, just over my left hip.

"Look at this," I say, plopping onto the couch.

"Stop picking at it or you'll make it bigger."

It looks big enough for my pinkie finger to pass through. Sure enough, I try it and succeed. A vague memory from this morning surfaces. As I made my daily hop into the upstairs bathroom, I bumped the doorjamb and there was a tiny tearing sound. At the time I didn't know what had ripped—now I do.

"This sucks. It's not on the seam or I could sew it back up."

"Can't you . . . I don't know, weave it back?"

I laugh. "Right, I should have thought of that. I'll get out my spinning wheel and fix it right up. I can patch it, or do a Frankenstein stitch, but it'll look ugly."

"I'll get you a new shirt."

"I like this one," I say.

"Then leave that hole alone." He reaches across the couch and pulls my hand away. "Seriously, babe. You're just going to make it worse. Here, play with your camera some more."

"All right."

He turns up the volume on the show, then starts talking over it. "I don't think Huey's very happy with me at the moment. He was kind of sulky all afternoon. You know how he gets. Over polite, and then he starts doing *exactly* what you tell him, being super literal about every little thing. I think he's ticked off because I didn't consult him about the press."

"Hmm," I say.

"Every time he had to move past it, he would knock up against it and kind of stagger back, making a big show. It was cracking Diana up, but seemed a little dramatic to me. And not in a good way."

"So what do you think about Aunt Bel?"

"You mean the Nun? I don't know. You think she'd want to stay very long? More than a couple of days?"

"I have no idea. According to my mom, she has nowhere to live, no money, no job."

"And you think it's your responsibility?"

"Not per se. But she's family."

"And a missionary to boot."

"I didn't know your family was big into missions."

He waves that away. "They weren't. But your grandparents were. Right?"

He remembers everything. "Yes. Mom feels like she was always a disappointment."

"But they loved you a lot, right?"

"Definitely."

"Well?"

Things are so cut and dried with Finn.

"Mom doesn't want her around," I say. "That much is clear. And she made it seem like something funny's going on with Aunt Bel and my dad."

"Is there?"

"Finn, Aunt Bel is almost as much of a mystery to me as she is to you."

He sits up, puts his plate on the coffee table. "Okay, so let me get this straight. Bel ran off on a summer missions trip and never came back.

Your grandparents worshipped her, and your mom has never forgiven them, or her sister, for that. Is that about right?"

"As far as I can see. If there's more, I almost just don't want to know about it."

He makes no comment, but I can guess what he's thinking. If this were *his* family, we wouldn't be in this situation to begin with. The Drexels don't turn up on your doorstep asking if one of their middle-aged siblings returning from overseas can move in with you for a while. For one thing, I don't see many middle-aged Drexels resurfacing after twenty years. They're a sensible breed, always looking and planning ahead, aware of their responsibilities and quick to fulfill obligations, not to unload them on others. They exude competence, especially when you stack them up against the Crazy O'Haras.

"This is what you married into," I say, the thought that a good part of him actually fits in better with my family than his own remaining in my head, and at this moment I want to crawl over there and smother it with affection.

"No, it's not that. I was just thinking. The spare room upstairs, if we blew out the closet wall and refinished the hardwoods . . ."

Saturday morning I wake up to the smell of coffee. The sheets on Finn's side of the bed are still warm. I roll over into the heat and breathe deeply of his scent, brushing the hair from my face and stifling a yawn. Padding into the bathroom, I check the mirror over the sink. I rub my eyes. I hear the beat of a pounding hammer downstairs.

I slip on my sweats before going down. The hole in my T-shirt looks bigger to me, but maybe I'm imagining things. In the empty kitchen, I pour myself some coffee and nibble on a piece of toast from the stack Finn's left on the table. The silver lining when you're married to a morning person is that breakfast is ready and waiting, more often than not, even on weekend mornings when you're supposed to be on duty. The hammering sound comes from under my feet. I follow it down the steep basement steps, ducking my head to avoid a collision with the low-hanging bulb.

In the back corner of the basement, illuminated by shop lights, the head of a ball-peen hammer keeps poking through the wall of the half bath. Each crumbling hole spits a cloud of bone-colored dust into the air.

"Finn," I say.

The hammering stops.

His tousled head appears in the bathroom doorway. "I figured I'd get an early start. The darkroom won't take long to frame out, then I'll run out and get some drywall. With any luck, I'll have everything but the painting done by lunchtime tomorrow. You can pick the colors. I called Chris and got the number of a guy who'll rent me a sander."

"A sander for what?"

"The floor upstairs," he says. "I'll get it sanded down this afternoon, and then we can refinish. It'll need to dry overnight, I'm guessing. If you come to the hardware store with me, you can pick out the stain."

I stand at the foot of the steps in my bare feet, munching toast and sipping coffee, just looking at him, not saying a word.

"What?"

"Nothing," I say. "I'm going upstairs. You should be wearing a mask to do that."

"Are you gonna run to the hardware store with me?"

"I'll let you know."

You have to love that kind of optimism or it will drive you crazy. And the man looks extra cute with tools in his hands. Is it wrong that I pray the number for the guy with the sander was written down wrong?

In the kitchen, I finish the toast, pour myself more coffee, and start on the weekend edition of the *Sun*. The hammering continues for another fifteen minutes, then I hear his footsteps ascending.

"Come to think of it," he says, setting the hammer on the table, "before I go any further on the darkroom demo, I should probably frame out the walls first. Get some two-by-fours and lay out the new perimeter." He sits at the table and frowns at the empty toast plate. "Although, really, we might want to start with the floor upstairs and see how long that takes. I've never actually done it before, but I found a video online."

He throws on some clothes and heads out in his ancient pickup truck to collect the rental sander. When he's gone, I dial my father.

"So, you're entertaining strange women from foreign lands, I hear," I greet him.

He laughs, and I can picture him leaning back against his kitchen counter, the spiraled cord of the telephone attaching him to the wall by the refrigerator. He's probably wearing gardening clothes as it's Saturday, his yard day. And one item is plaid, the other either khaki or navy.

Yes, he has a yard day. A grocery shopping day. An errands day. And an ex-wife living in a tent. Sometimes it's just too easy to figure out what went wrong in a marriage.

"Somebody has to, Sare. And she helped out on laundry day, so it could be worse."

From what I remember, Dad and Aunt Bel got along famously.

"Where's she sleeping?"

"On the sofa."

After the divorce, he built his home himself, just enough for himself, and nobody but himself.

"Can I talk to her?"

"Why do you want to do that?"

"To invite her over."

"Are you sure about that?"

"Yep."

"Well, just so you know, it's on your head if something goes wrong."

"I know."

"I'll let her know. Your mother's coming by tomorrow to pick up something of hers from the storage shed. I can get her to take Bel over in my car. Would that work?"

"If you want. Or I could come get her. I haven't visited in a while."

He falls silent a moment. "It would be simpler if Rita just brought her over. It's a little insane here right now. Bel's a little . . . off."

"What do you mean, off?"

"Nothing serious, Sara. Don't sound so worried. She's not certifiable or anything—"

"That's supposed to reassure me?"

"No, no, no," he says. "It's the whole family dynamic, you know. I've got a ton of questions, and I'm afraid Bel, she just isn't talking. I don't think she's going to either, but that's just my take."

She's just as big a mystery as before. Drat.

"I have to say, doll, that if you took her off my hands, I'd appreciate it. I've been a bachelor now for so long, having a woman around . . ."

"Say no more, Daddy."

He sighs with relief. "You're an angel."

"I learned from the best," I say.

"Speaking of angels, any announcement from you and Finn yet?"

"Daddy . . ."

"Hey, now. You're my only chance at grandparenthood. I hear it's a lot easier than parenthood. I'd like to give it a try."

"I'm sorry I was such a burden."

"You have no idea, Sare." He chuckles and I can't help but laugh. Only my father can get away with this.

"How about this? I'll take Aunt Bel off your hands and that counts as having a baby. I can only add to the fold at my house so quickly, you know?"

"Ha! You got it. For the meantime. Until you're adjusted, of course."

"Deal." Good. Maybe it'll buy me another year.

"Hey," he says. "I'm making my hot milk cake today, doll. I'll send one over."

"Thanks. It'll last about five minutes unless I hide it from Finn."

"You have my express permission to do so. How is that boy?"

I catch him up on the general scoop, the birthday surprise, my new camera. He's delighted about everything, promising to come over and watch *Helvetica* sooner rather than later. Seems we just have a love affair with letters, my father and I.

We ring off and I'm already making a mental list for Aunt Bel's arrival. I've got to get a lamp for that room and wash the sheets for that bed. I wonder what kind of milk she likes? Whole? Two percent? Orange juice or grapefruit? Will she take long showers and hike up our hot water bill? Will she teach Finn to make Kazakh food?

Outside, the city is still on the gray, rainy cusp of spring. According to the forecast, the sun will creep out in the early afternoon, giving the park and the surrounding blocks the brightly scrubbed luminescence that sometimes follows a good drizzle. A nice day to be out on the streets, trying out my new camera, getting the hang of shooting film. I dress upstairs, donning my gray jeans and the striped gray-and-white sweater Finn gave me for my birthday.

Since it's still wet outside, I trade my usual leather boots for some green wellies and put my raincoat on over my sweater. Then it's out on the streets, past the colorful row houses and the bakery, past the garage that's now a bicycle shop and the deli with hand-painted windows. Before we moved into the city, Finn and I lived in a small apartment in the northern suburbs near Cockeysville, where Chris and his parents reside. Out in the country. Nobody in their right mind would ever dream of moving to Patterson Park, which they associated with drugs and street gangs and drive-by shootings.

But they were wrong about our neighborhood. It isn't spic-and-span. There are still derelict houses, still patches of pavement cracked to hell and back with grass growing up through the gaps. But it isn't what it *was* by a long shot. The houses have been reclaimed, restored. People are raising their kids here, starting businesses, living their lives. We have our fair share of hipsters. (You can always tell because, when you use the h-word, people don't reject it, they simply introduce so many shades of variation that you're left with the impression you don't know what you're talking about.) Don't get me wrong. Patterson Park isn't exactly a hipster mecca like Brooklyn, but we do have an open-air market and more tattoo shops than tanning salons, and microbrew pubs, bike transportation groups, and—did I mention?—a letterpress shop. It's a good place, too, for an aspiring street photographer. Always something interesting to see.

My first capture: a weathered old black man sitting on his front porch.

"What you wanna take my picture for?" he asks, sitting up straight.

"You look cool," I say.

This makes him smile. "You that little girl over at the old fire station?"

"Yes, sir."

"You sure prettied up that place."

"Thanks. Don't look friendly," I tell him. "Look severe."

He laughs, then gives me a scowl. I fiddle with the light metering app on my phone, then make the adjustments and snap away.

"Perfect."

"Go on, now," he says, shaking his head in baffled delight. White people.

As I turn the corner in the direction of the park, a lanky kid on a BMX bike pedals along in the opposite direction, his body slumped back, hands hanging at his sides. He's already past me before I can get him in focus, but I swivel and snap the picture from behind. The Autocord has to be advanced after every shot by a hand-crank of the right side of the camera. I turn the crank and shoot him again, but he's half a block away by now.

Using my digital camera, I always feel self-conscious taking pictures in public. The clickety-clack of the shutter, the big telephoto lens. Way easier than the manual film camera, but more ostentatious, making me feel like a poseur. The Autocord, because of its leatherette panels and its Flash Gordon–looking double lens, gets a friendlier reception. Instead of aiming the camera at people, looking at them through the camera, I'm resting it against my breastbone, gazing down into the viewfinder. Less intrusive somehow.

"That old thing still *work*?" a woman in a seersucker housedress of multiple sherbet colors, clearly not one of the newer residents of the neighborhood, calls out from her stoop.

"Yeah," I say. "Can I take your picture?"

And just like that, she raises her cigarette to her mouth and smiles. Perfect.

By the time I reach the park, a light rain has begun. Faint drops hit my face every now and then and create the occasional pockmark on standing pools of water left from the rain overnight. Over at the basketball courts, some guys play pick-up games, shirts and skins, the squeals of their rubber soles shooting directly from the wet pavement and up my spine. Standing on the edge of the game, I take a few pictures. Once they become aware of me, everybody who gets the ball runs it in for the shot.

"Look at that." A man on the sidelines comes over, leaning down to stare into the lens. "Is that 3-D or something?"

"No, but it's film." I shield my eyes from the emerging sun. Sun and drizzle. I've always loved that combination, as if the weather itself is saying, life isn't always either/or, sometimes it's both/and.

"So really, you have no idea what your pictures are gonna look like. Not till you get 'em developed. Like in the old days. Huh."

"Pretty much. Isn't it a little wet and cold to be playing basketball?" I ask.

"Never," he says, trotting back to the line.

Arriving home midafternoon, I'm welcomed by the sound of whirring and scraping upstairs. The air in the house tastes gritty. When I reach the top of the stairs, I open the door to find Finn sanding away in the spare room, no mask on.

Before he sees me, I snap his picture. Evidence.

"You think this is a good idea?" I ask.

"What?" He points to his ear.

"I'm not going to shout."

He cocks his head, then shuts the sander off.

"You're supposed to be wearing a mask, aren't you?"

Ever since I can remember, safety has been important. That imaginary friend of mine? He was a real stickler. I heard his voice every time I climbed the sliding board or dove off the high dive at our neighborhood pool. And don't even get me started about wearing socks on wooden steps. I feel the need to police everybody else's well-being. Almost needless to say, I was not the most popular kid on the playground at school.

He steps away from the grinder, brushing sawdust off his forearms. "Don't worry. I rented a machine that sucks up almost all of the dust. But I've been thinking. Maybe this *isn't* a good idea. Moving the Nun into this room, I mean." He moves toward me, resting his hands on my hips, pulling me close until my camera pokes his chest. "When you stop and consider, you know what this room should be? Don't look at me like I'm crazy."

"You're getting dust on my lens."

"Is that a metaphor?" he says, using what he thinks is his sexy voice.

I look at him like he's crazy. Finn isn't exactly precise with his metaphors. "No, really. Let me put the lens cap on."

"I'll put your lens cap on—"

"Ooh, baby. I have no idea what that entails, but I'm willing to give it a try." Imprecise metaphor be hanged.

We laugh.

"But you get what I'm saying, right, hon? She can come if she wants, that's fine with me. We just need to put her somewhere else. I could build out the room in the basement. That could be nice. Like a mother-in-law suite."

"Finn, no way. She's coming tomorrow."

"Wow. That soon?"

"Daddy's dying over there."

"No prob, then."

Finn should have been their child, someone more able to bend in the wind.

"Besides, I'm not sticking my aunt in the basement. What's wrong with here? If you stop shredding the floor, it'll be just fine."

"Okay, but . . ." He makes a frame with his outstretched hands, forcing me to see the room through his fingers. "Wouldn't this make a great . . . nursery?"

I blink. "We don't need a nursery, Finn. Not unless you know something I don't."

"I'm just saying." He pulls me back into his arms and nuzzles my cheek. "Maybe it's time. You're not getting any younger, after all."

"Oh, that will convince me." I push away from him.

"What? You *do* want kids?"

"Not this minute. Not . . . for a while. What brought this on all of a sudden?"

"Nothing brought it on. We just need to talk about it, that's all," he says, following me across the hall into our bedroom. "We've been avoiding this discussion for years. Sort of."

"Look, you married me without the kid commitment, remember? Remember? I said, 'I don't know if I want kids or not,' and you said you were marrying me for just me. Remember?"

"You've made sure of it."

"What is it today? First Daddy, now you?" Suddenly I don't want to be in the bedroom with him. My heart speeds up as I circle around him back into the hall, then close the bathroom door behind me. My shoe catches on the edge of the no-man's-land where Finn ripped up the tile, pitching my body forward. Landing on my hands and knees, coming an inch away from banging my head on the edge of the tub, I feel like I'm going to cry. Instead, I slap the side of the tub hard enough that it hurts.

"Are you okay?" Finn calls, tapping on the door.

"I need a second. Can you just leave me alone?"

"Are you sure? I didn't mean to upset you."

"I'll be out in a minute."

After a pause, I hear his feet scrape down the hallway, down the stairs. I lift myself up, sitting on the lip of the tub, resting my head in my hands.

Why does the thought of having a child upset me like this?

It's a bit too much, that's all. He deserves to have kids, though, and for the life of me, I don't know why I think I don't.

4.
Bel and the Dragon

Just after eight the next morning, Finn tromps down the stairs, already half dressed and carrying his acoustic guitar, the outside of its black case covered over with travel stickers from places he's never been. I've downed two glasses of orange juice and made the hole in my T-shirt even bigger, all in fifteen minutes. Go me.

"You coming with me?" he asks, leaning the guitar in the corner, looking bleary-eyed from the big clean-up of the sanding experiment. No stain yet.

"Not this morning, I don't think." I'm sipping juice and thinking about all that needs to be done with the house. So much potential = so much work, and don't let anybody tell you differently.

He's driving up to Timonium today, to our old church, where he still plays in the band despite having cut all his other ties. The Community, as it's called, is a big suburban megachurch now housed within a former manufacturing park, the miles of parking lot all around packed full every Sunday by affluent suburbanites. Finn has a love/hate relationship with the place. On the highway map of divine history, The Community and churches like it represent for Finn a tragic wrong turn, so shallow and superficial, all the ancient power of the faith hollowed out, leaving behind just a glitzy, entertaining husk with glorified babysitting.

They tried to teach me a little more about what God is like, but at the end of the day, I never fit in. God can be a little more friendly-like, but if his people are busy trying to fill up your schedule and make you feel like you're a second-class woman if you haven't opted for motherhood, you still have to wonder about him.

At the same time, Finn grew up there. It's home. It's where the Drexels are married and if not buried, well, they will be someday. So far he hasn't made it an issue if I don't go. So I'm not going to. Plus, it was Pastor Rick at The Community, Finn's former men's pastor, who passed along to him his Big Idea.

"What about tonight?" Finn asks. "You're not bailing?"

"I don't know yet. My mother's dropping Aunt Bel off sometime today."

"Has she called yet?" There's hope in his voice, like maybe she won't.

"Not yet. Give her time."

While he finishes dressing and carries his guitar out to his truck, I make breakfast and try to ignore the frenetic energy that follows him room to room. After yesterday's outburst on my part, I realize I have to come to grips with the kid issue. I just . . . can't. Not today. Not yet. Aunt Bel is coming; I've got things to do.

I've made the bed in the spare room, put new towels and a spare set of sheets on the dresser, and dug a ceramic-shade lamp for the nightstand out of the attic, trying to make Aunt Bel's space appealing. I even rolled up the rug from the living room and carried it upstairs to cover the grooves left by Finn's sanding, but I was hoping to run down to Grove Street and get some of Madge's finer offerings for dessert tonight.

He kisses me on the forehead before leaving. "What's wrong?"

"What do you think?"

"I don't know. That's why I asked."

"I'm nervous. I haven't seen her in twenty-some years. I have no idea what's going to happen. I have no idea what she will think." The panic in my voice surprises me.

"Who cares what she thinks? Come on, Sara. Don't get worked up over this."

"But what if she hates me?"

Finn screws up his face. "*Hates* you? For what?"

I blink. "Well, I don't know. I mean. No. I don't know why I even said that."

"You're just nervous, babe. Everything's gonna be just fine. You'll see. You'll do great with her even if she is as nuts as your dad says she is."

"Well, compared to who I work with . . ."

"See? Now I gotta run."

One of the great things about Finn—and I mean this sincerely—is that no matter how much a situation bothers him, when he realizes that I'm bothered too, he calms down. He soothes and comforts me, and really means it. No one has ever believed in me the way he does. As a designer, an artist, and even a human being. The whole course of my life changed when he entered it, because he never thought that any of the things I was afraid of doing were impossible for me. Whatever the challenge, in his open-eyed, insistent way, he puts his hand on my shoulder and he says, "Of course you can." And he's usually right.

Mom calls just before eleven. She's frazzled, I can tell.

Driving a car, oh dear. Dad's cell phone, oh man.

But first and foremost: estranged sister. Oh great.

"Where do you people even *park* here? I've been circling your block for ten minutes!"

My mom using the term *you people* is like Catherine of Siena yelling a string of epithets.

"I'll come outside," I say, hanging up the phone. It's cool and sunny outside, a gentle breeze stirring the leaves of the tree outside our house, its roots forcing squares of sidewalk to slope upward.

She's right, the streets are packed even more so than usual, cars parallel-parked bumper-to-bumper in a way that incoming suburban-ites can hardly fathom, accustomed as they are to sprawling parking lots and two-car garages. A woman fresh off the farm? Doubly daunting.

A blue Camry hums down the street, pausing before me. My mother's window whirs down. She's looking frantic, woodland animal frantic.

"What should I do, baby?" she says.

Next to her in the passenger seat, a woman's silhouette blocks the light. I glimpse the shape of her head, a short and angular bob, and then the Camry lurches forward. Another car rides my mother's tail, the driver urging her forward with none-too-friendly gestures. Resisting the urge to yell at him, I jog down the sidewalk to keep pace with her, but she freaks a little and guns the engine, making another circuit around the block. When she comes back around, I motion her to stop.

"Just double park. They can still get around you."

The driver behind jams on his brakes and throws up his hands.

She throws the car into park and gets out. "Good idea. Wow. What a downer that was."

I wave Mr. Merry Sunshine around.

Mom opens the trunk and pauses. After about two seconds of glassy-eyed staring, she shakes herself a little and turns to me with a sunny smile. Which is very sunny because the white hair surrounding her face sifts the rays spilling through the tree nearby. My mother is beautiful. Clueless, but beautiful.

I stand on the curb, waiting expectantly. Do I go to her and help, or welcome my aunt—who doesn't seem to be leaving the car?

I lean through the open driver's door.

"Hello," I say.

Aunt Bel blinks as if noticing me for the first time. "Hello."

She doesn't seem to hate me.

The photograph that once sat on my grandparents' mantel did her no justice. My aunt, like my mother, is physically beautiful. But where my mother is soft, with the faintly sculpted lines and rounded symmetry of a pre-Raphaelite model, soft and hard all at once, Aunt Bel has had the softness sanded down by what I can only guess was a spare existence in Godforsakenstan. She is thinner, leaner than in the photo, which lends her face and throat and arms a delicate impression, as if they might break with use and are best admired behind glass. She looks at me with wide and innocent eyes, the golden brown of a panther's, and seems as entranced by my sudden appearance as I am by hers.

"Bel, come get your bag," Mom calls.

My aunt's mouth curls at the corner—the smile from the photo. Before moving, she glances at her seat belt buckle and at the door handle, as if plotting her course, deciding in advance how to navigate unfamiliar devices. She loosens the seat belt and lets the tensioner pull it clear before laying her hand on the door latch, which releases with a click. Aunt Bel turns to me, eyes sparkling, as if to say, *See, it works.*

Aunt Bel walks around one side of the car and I go round the other, meeting Mom at the trunk. My aunt's blond hair is cut quite short in back, down to her chin on one side and barely lower than the ear on the other. Her bangs are cut short too, awkwardly so, as if she might have done it herself. She's the same height as my mother, just shy of my five foot five, but her body is all angles—hips and elbows and shoulders—making her seem rather taller. She wears a navy flower print dress that stops short of the knee and a mossy cardigan with the sleeves pushed up her forearms.

"Thrift store chic," I say. "Not bad for a missionary. On me it would look ridiculous—but on you . . . And you have the figure to carry it off."

I only realize I'm babbling when she fails to respond.

"There's just one bag," Mom says, indicating a green nylon duffel with bellows pockets on the side. Aunt Bel lifts it by the shoulder strap, her body arching under the weight. When I go to take it from her, she shakes her head.

"Is that everything? Let's go inside."

She follows me onto the curb, but the sound of the slamming trunk breaks our stride.

"Aren't you coming?" I ask Mom.

"I'd better not block traffic," she says with an apologetic laugh, though there aren't any cars behind her. "I'll let you two get reacquainted. If you need anything, leave me a message at the farm."

Despite my pleading looks, my mother gets in the car and pulls the door shut. She smiles back at me and then frantically pulls away.

When I turn to Aunt Bel, she is staring up into the tree, as if she hasn't seen one before.

"Want to come in?" I ask.

She smiles at me—a wide, almost grinning smile, not the Mona Lisa side curl.

What you would never guess from a photograph is how expressive she is, her whole face—no, her whole body—contorting itself to convey her meaning. The sort of skill a woman might pick up if she found herself alone in a foreign country, unable to communicate via words. Come to think of it, she's only uttered a single word in my presence, when she said hello.

"Can I please take that for you? It looks heavy."

Aunt Bel regards the bag, her eyes following the line of the shoulder strap—again, as if my saying something has called her attention to a previously unremarked object. She shrugs the strap off, testing the duffel's weight in her hand, then passes it to me, radiating gratitude the whole time. Does she not talk? I feel a sudden panic. Maybe in all those years overseas, she's lost her ability to speak English.

"Aunt Bel, is everything all right?"

She looks herself over, as if checking. Then nods.

"You're sure?" I ask, willing her to speak.

She nods again, then adds a single word: "Yes."

Relieved, I escort her inside—even though a confirmed vocabulary consisting only of *hello* and *yes* is not much to be relieved over. No wonder Daddy wanted her out of his cottage. It must have been like trying to entertain a rock. My voice blathers on autopilot, down the "welcome to your new home" highway, ushering us all the way to the stairs before I realize she's not with me. Aunt Bel stands just inside the threshold, taking in the house: ceiling, woodwork, floors, furniture, everything waiting its turn to be noticed.

"You can come in," I tell her.

She takes a step or two, then stops. "Lovely."

"You have to use your imagination. I know it's a bit of a dump right now, but we have big plans, and I think the fundamentals are good, the bones of the structure—"

"Lovely," she says again, meaning it, and suddenly I feel ashamed for making excuses for the place, for deflecting a heartfelt compliment and revealing my insecurity in the process.

And compared to Kazakhstan? Even in my eyes it looks better.

I set down her bag at the foot of the stairs and walk her around the ground floor. Right away she notices the maple floors with inch-wide strips of inlaid mahogany about eight inches from the baseboards. "They're my pride and joy," I tell her.

She runs the tips of her fingers around the swirl at the top of the newel post at the bottom of the steep stairs, which I'm sure aren't up to code these days. "Oh, Sara." The light coming through the two windows, tall enough for me to stand on the ledge and still have a good two feet of space above the top of my head, shines in her eyes.

And once again, I see my home in a new light. Not the Sara-you-bit-off-more-than-you-can-chew light, but the one that says, in Aunt Bel's tone, "Lovely." Because it is.

"As annoyed as I get at Finn, he's really the only one who's trying to love this house like she should be loved, even though he might seem to be the Casanova of renovation."

Aunt Bel just nods.

Unfortunately we hit the kitchen and I have to bite my tongue. Aunt Bel takes it all in, her eyes darting, and while she says nothing, she gives the impression of barely contained pleasure, as if the stripped-away suspended ceiling and the flicking overhead lights are right up there with the Hall of Mirrors at Versailles, the nooks and crannies of our hundred-year-old house a source of limitless wonder.

Is she simple? I find myself wondering. Is that the problem? Has something happened to her, some kind of emotional-growth-stunting trauma? Because she doesn't just look young for her forty-odd years, she seems childlike.

I'll ask Finn when he comes home if it seems like she's been the victim of some past head trauma. He can spot that sort of thing a mile away.

I escort her up the steps and down the hallway to the spare bedroom, pulling the empty dresser drawers out so she can see where her things are meant to go. The conversation is so one-sided I find myself overexplaining things, and using the tone of voice you'd use with a grade-school kid.

"The upstairs bathroom is just across the hall, but you have to be careful just inside the door, because we haven't quite fixed the tile yet."

She puts a hand on my wrist, pausing my monologue.

"Sara," she says, turning her voice up at the end, introducing doubt.

"Yes."

"Do you remember me?"

Her first complete sentence, pronounced in a tone of great intimacy, as if we're about to confide our secrets to one another.

"Of course. Aunt Belinda."

"Do you actually remember? Can you remember anything about me?"

"Yes," I say, but now I'm turning my words up at the end, making them into questions.

"You remember what I was *like*?"

"You were . . . nice?"

As she considers this, her whole expression changes. The smile fades and the eyes cast inward, as if she's gazing into the past and seeing— what? Lines emerge on her placid skin, the crease of etched smile-lines like parentheses around her mouth, deltas opening around her eyes, as if whatever she sees is aging her in real time. As if she's staring into some kind of black hole, an abyss.

"Aunt Bel, are you okay?"

"I was nice," she says, the darkness lifting. "Yes, I suppose that is true."

"I'll let you settle in," I tell her, backpedaling toward the door.

Aunt Bel pulls open one of the side pockets of her duffel bag, removing something wrapped in fabric.

"Here," she says, holding it out. "Because I was never there when this would have made sense to you."

I take the object and unwrap the folded material. Inside is a doll about the length of my hand, made of porcelain with glistening glass eyes. It has red, curled hair that looks like a young child has brushed it well past its expiration date and cheeks painted hot pink. A coarse lace dress that would serve equally well for communion or burial swaddles around—I lift up the dress—a rudimentarily carved wooden body.

"The woman who gave that to me had carried it with her as a girl, when her family was deported to Kazakhstan. Stalin deported a lot of people there. She was my friend. My only friend for the longest time, the only person I could talk to. You should have it."

Objections come to mind—it's too precious, too laden with sentimental value, and way too creepy by half, the kind of doll that watches you when you sleep, the kind you throw away only to wake up and find it perching on your chest.

"Thank you," I say.

Aunt Bel approaches me and takes me by my forearms. "You know you're a good person, don't you, Sara? Did you ever feel like you weren't?"

I stare into her eyes, and I see in them a brave resolve and acceptance I could only dream of having. I can't help but say, "Yes. I try not to think about it. But doesn't everybody feel that way?"

"They do."

As I descend the stairs, the click of her door shutting hits my eardrums and relief ripples over me. What just happened? I place the doll on the table downstairs in front of the television, then collapse on the couch, exhausted. Being with Aunt Bel is like being in the presence of a light that burns too bright. Something about her makes you put up your guard, and then she finds her way underneath it despite your careful engineering.

I'm not sure I like such intuitive candor around my house. Bare bulbs? Fine. Suspended ceilings? No problem. Soul-probing questions? Sorry. Wrong number. Call again.

But it's too late now. Aunt Bel is in the house, one more person to worry about. She will not be unobtrusive. Like the rusty hulk at the center of my studio, she will be unavoidable. We will bump into her wherever we try to go. And in my heart, which forms its intuitions without hard evidence and yet is rarely wrong, I am convinced that in giving Aunt Bel shelter, I have made a mistake I might soon regret.

5.

A Stranger Here Myself

The Aunt Bel who drifts down the stairs, the childlike Aunt Bel, seems so different from the serious woman who saw deeply into my soul an hour ago. I can't help questioning whether I understood her right. Uncertain how to proceed, still nervous from earlier, I play hostess—but badly. *Can I get you something to drink? Are you sure? And have you eaten? You really must be hungry*—Until she finally agrees to hot tea, at which point I'm forced to confess to not being sure we actually have any.

"That's okay," she says, watching me closely, like she's not sure what I might do next but knows it is certain to be wonderful.

It makes me uncomfortable, that look, giving me her full attention.

I could be the only other person in the world, not just the room, judging by those eyes. A part of me has gone through life thinking all I wanted was the world's undivided attention—its praise, its love, its undying admiration. Paying attention to all the work I do, the things I make, even my thoughts and opinions for the admiration of others. But here I am getting a taste of the real thing, the full attention of just one person, and I'm not sure I want it anymore.

It feels like being wrapped in a quilt knitted of candy-coated claustrophobia.

Whatever it is, I already know I can't live up to it.

"Let's get out of the house," I suggest. Finn, who has yet to meet the newest member of Drexel's Curiosity Shop, went to the studio to work on the Iron Maiden after church.

In the open air, the strength of Aunt Bel's presence is somewhat diluted. She has other things to occupy her: kids chalking pictures on the still-wet pavement, a couple of neighbors inspecting the portable grill on their stoop to figure out why it won't light, the coming and going of Lycra-clad cyclists in twos and threes on the opposite side of the street. She knots her fingers together, taking everything in.

"How are you adjusting to being back?" I ask her.

"I don't know." She wriggles from the bottom up, loosing herself from an imaginary net. And her eyes constrict the way they would if something cold and unpleasant had crawled across her bare skin. Her *I don't know* seems just a placeholder for other words she is unwilling or unable to utter.

"You've been away a long time. What was it like?"

Again she pauses, as if I've posed some unanswerable riddle. "Everything's changed," she finally admits.

"Well, maybe in the winter, when the heat is reliable, you'll feel differently."

"I can't say."

The Grove Street Artisan is my third place, the notch in my dial between home and work, the place I end up when I don't intend to end up anywhere, so that's where I take her, snagging the same table by the window that Mom chose on my birthday. I introduce her to Madge, which serves the added purpose of distracting her long enough for one of the girls behind the counter to make my latte. Despite having already eaten, Aunt Bel devours a blueberry scone, then returns to the counter and, after some indecision, brings back a mammoth sugar cookie.

The sweet tooth must run in the family.

"You don't have to talk about it if you don't want to, but I've always wondered what it was like, staying over there."

"What do you want to know?" She breaks off a piece of cookie and takes a bite. Her eyes grow large and she nods. "These are good."

"The story I heard was that after your summer trip, you liked it so much that you decided to stay. It's hard to imagine not coming back, though, at least to visit. You must have really . . ."

"Really what?"

I shake my head. "I dunno—found your calling? Loved being a missionary?"

Her mouth drops open. "Is that what they've always told you?"

"It's true, isn't it?"

She stares at the crystals of sugar that have fallen on her napkin. "I guess you could say I had a calling I needed to fulfill."

"Did you?"

"Fulfill the calling?" she asks.

"Uh-huh."

"There's only one person who can be the judge of that." She waves a fragment of sugar cookie in the air, dismissive. "What's a missionary, anyway? Everybody's a missionary, or nobody is. It's all the same, isn't it?"

"Wait. So you weren't a missionary?"

She shrugs. "Who's to say?"

Who's to say? What does that even mean in this context? Why would I be told she was a missionary if she wasn't? I'm confused, but observant enough to get the strong signal that she's not going to enlighten me further.

"Well, according to Grandmom and Grandpop's definition, then." Believe me, that definition made me decidedly *not* want to become one, and that definition always made me question my own dedication. It still does despite hundreds of sermons to the contrary, sermons about the spirituality of a life well lived, about calling and giftedness.

The Mona Lisa smile returns. "Sara, there isn't a missionary alive that's a missionary by their definition."

I laugh with relief. "You're not what I expected," I tell her.

"Were you thinking Saint Francis?"

"Maybe Judson Taylor." My grandmother actually had a framed picture of the famed missionary to the Chinese people in her prayer closet, the place she went for at least an hour each day to pray over all the prayer cards she collected at the missions conferences she attended over the years.

"Oh, Lord!" She barks out a laugh. "Heavens, no!"

"My husband, Finn—who you'll meet—he was calling you the Nun. I don't know, I guess when I think of somebody who's been a missionary for twenty-some years, I imagine she'd have her hair up in a bun, with no makeup and a big denim skirt."

"Sorry to disappoint you." She smiles.

"I know it's an unfair caricature. I guess what I'm saying is, I don't know anyone like you."

"What am I like?"

Someone prone to asking uncomfortable questions?

I veer away from any answer that might have some depth. "You know, you're stylish. I mean, look how you dress. It kills me you can wear what you wear and look great in it. I'd look like such a poseur," I say. "Like I was dressed by the Internet."

She looks at her clothes, as if noticing them for the first time, and I can see that she's surprised by what I've said.

"I'm not stylish," she says. "I just wear what I like. Things that come to me."

"That kills me even more."

"The dress I found in the hallway of my apartment building. I never knew if someone dropped it on their way back from the laundry or threw it out." She places a hand up to her mouth and stifles a laugh. "I never had the nerve to wear it over there. I've had it for ten years too!"

"That's insane!"

"What? No. I just didn't want—"

"No. I don't mean that you're crazy, Aunt Bel. The situation is. Don't be offended. It just means I find it all so . . . unusual. I can't relate."

"Oh." She nods once. "Okay."

"What about the sweater?"

"This sweater, my friend Katya gave it to me." She pinches the fabric between her fingers, remembering. "That makes it special. I think of her."

"The friend who gave you the doll?"

"Oh, no," she says. "That was someone else, a long time ago."

"Well, maybe Katya can come and visit you sometime."

"No," she says. "I don't think so."

"Do you think you'll ever go back?"

"I will never go back."

That has an air of finality. "Never?" I ask.

She shrugs. "I don't want to talk about me, I want to talk about you, Sara. We have so much catching up to do. But not all at once." She clenches her hands together, the tips of her fingers squeezing against the backs of her hands ever so slightly.

"Are you all right?" I ask. "It can't be easy coming home after so long. All the people you left behind back there, twenty-some years of work . . . ?"

As I say this, Aunt Bel starts looking over her shoulder, scanning faces at the other tables. Is she worried about being overheard? She leans forward a little and under her breath asks, "Is it okay to smoke in here, or is that not allowed?"

———

When Finn walks up, I am sitting on the stoop next to my missionary aunt, who is on her second cancer stick since we left Grove Street. She holds it delicately between two fingertips, resting her elbow on her knee, and when she blows smoke she tilts her neck back, releasing it toward the sky. If you put a gif of it on Tumblr, it would probably go viral. My husband pauses on the sidewalk, giving me a *what's this?* grin. I can tell as he approaches that he hasn't put two and two together yet.

"Hey," Finn says.

"Hey, yourself, Mr. Fix It. How did it go?"

"Oh, there's plenty of time to catch up about that."

Is there something in the water around here?

Aunt Bel glances up, then flicks her cigarette to the curb before standing. They must be as casual about littering in Kazakhstan as they are about smoking.

"This is my aunt," I tell him. "Aunt Bel, this is Finn."

"You're—" he begins, then stops himself.

"You can say it." Aunt Bel laughs. "The Nun."

I can't believe it. She's making a joke. And he's most likely thinking that missionary aunts aren't supposed to be hot in their own special way. He's shifting gears in his mind, but being an aesthete like I am, I know what he's thinking: *Better this than what I was picturing. Old lady brogues. Gray hair in a short, mannish do. Definitely not those gorgeous legs.*

Finn puts the guitar down and reaches his hand out, then seems to decide that long-lost aunts probably merit a hug. I almost stop him, thinking Aunt Bel might shrivel at the touch, but she hugs him back, and by the time we're up the stairs and inside, I find myself envying Finn's easy way with people, free of the constraint, the uncertainty I can never seem to shake.

The questions I've been reluctant to ask he poses right off the bat, and instead of evasive monosyllables, he gets answers out of Aunt Bel. Of a sort.

"So what's your plan?" He pulls out a kitchen chair for her. "You're starting all over, is that the thing?"

She nods her thanks and sits down. "Oh, I have a lot of plans. Nothing *but* plans. I don't know what half of them are yet, but I could do anything, be anything. That's how I feel."

"Well, that's a fantastic place to start." He pulls out a chair for me. "I guess you have people to touch base with. Supporters, that kind of thing. I know a lot of missionaries come back on leave, raising funds before they go back. That's not what you're doing—or is it?"

"Deputation," I say, marveling at how easily the term jumped up from its seat at the back of my mind.

"Nothing like that," she says. "I told Sara. I won't be going back. This is the beginning. There is no one to see or touch base with. A fresh start."

Unlike me, Finn doesn't seem to find Aunt Bel's intensity draining. Instead, she injects air into the fire of his own intensity, which comes out blazing.

"Wow," he says. "That's pretty brave. Do you have any ideas as far as work goes, the job market?" He grabs the kettle and begins to fill it.

Good luck with that tea, dear heart.

"Lots of ideas," she says. "I thought of being a painter."

"You mean, like houses?" He gives me a look.

"Painting pictures."

"As in—art? That's more of a hobby than a job, though. Unless you're like Picasso or something. You're not a Picasso, are you?" He reaches into the cabinet and pulls down the tea tin.

Really? How did I not see that earlier?

"I don't know what I am anymore. We'll have to see."

They're like two gamblers at the poker table, raising each other's bets.

My cell phone rings. Dad. "Excuse me," I say, heading into the living room.

"You surviving, Sare?" he asks.

"You're right. She's a little . . . unusual."

He barks out a laugh. "You asked for it."

"Mom did, actually."

"Look, the couch here isn't the best of situations, but if you ever need to get away–"

I laugh. "I thought you were going to offer to have Aunt Bel return."

"She's all yours. By the way, how's that pound cake?"

"What pound cake? Mom must have driven off with it."

"Big shocker there." He pauses. "Well, at least I can still do something right."

"Daddy, you do most things right."

"Thanks, doll. So do you."

He's wrong, but I don't mind one bit that he believes it.

The kettle is screaming when I hang up. From the hallway, I watch as Finn lifts it off the burner and pours it into a French press we use for tea, all the while describing to Aunt Bel our little creative agency and telling her that if she's serious about painting, he could introduce her to some people. I have no idea who he means, but Finn's circle is much wider than mine, thanks to his role at the Firehouse.

And, let's face it, his general easygoing, caring, confidently friendly personality goes a long way too.

I listen unbeknownst to Aunt Bel, who fiddles with her pack of smokes. "What I really want is to know Sara more. I've wanted to meet her a long time. Living over there sometimes, I would imagine all this, what her life must be like."

"And how does it compare to what you imagined?" Finn asks.

"I don't know yet," she tells him. "I only just arrived. But so far so good."

I make my entrance and sit at the table.

Finn drops some shortbread on a plate and sets it down in the middle of the table. "Are you coming tonight?" he asks me.

"Aunt Bel's probably tired, and I don't want to leave her on her own."

"What is tonight?" Aunt Bel reaches for a cookie.

"Church," Finn says.

"Oh, I'd like to go."

"It's not like normal church," I blurt. "You might not be—" I struggle for the word and end up with: "Comfortable."

Aunt Bel narrows her eyes. "I don't want to be comfortable."

"Then you're going to love this." Finn grins and starts his well-rehearsed missive about St. Rick, the Big Idea, and the Microchurch.

I know the story already, so I pour a cup of tea, grab a couple of cookies, and head upstairs to change my clothes. Why would anybody not want to be comfortable? Why would she say that?

At the door to the spare bedroom, I glance inside to see whether Aunt Bel has unpacked. She has. Two framed pictures rest atop the dresser too. Whose pictures would she have?

My curiosity propels me into the room.

The first one isn't a picture at all; it's a framed greeting card. A cartoon bird executed in shiny blue foil perched on a branch, with a speech bubble coming from his beak. Inside the bubble, the bird says, @TWEET, @TWEET.

Looking at the card, I get goose bumps. What is she doing with this? I designed it two, almost three years ago, the first card we managed to get into retail shops. Compared to the work we do now, thanks to Huey's expertise, this one looks a little crude, the kiss of the plate cutting deep but unevenly into the card stock. I pulled them all myself on the Pilot, and Finn helped me fold them. There were two hundred altogether, and I think half of those are still sitting in a box somewhere at the studio. How did she get her hands on this in Kazakhstan of all places? Daddy, I suppose.

Underneath the card, however, is a photo turned around. I peel it away.

It's my graduation picture. Now that probably did come from my father. But . . . why me? Why the fascination?

Next to the bird sits a framed black-and-white photo of a boy, about five or six years old, his back against a tree, with a leafy field over his shoulder. He might be at a park, or in a rural backyard. Features slightly out of focus seem burdened by a dull, almost sleepy expression, his eyes half closed. Only visible from the shoulders up, he appears to be wearing a T-shirt too large for his body. A contrasting color circles around the wide collar opening, revealing his clavicle and the right side of his neck. Honestly, he would be perfect on the cover of a memoir about a child-hood of deprivation, sorrow, and life in postwar poverty.

Only there's a certain little flame in his eyes as if to say, *I may look miserable to you, but I'm happy where it counts.*

I open this one too, looking for writing on the back. Finn's still talk-ing downstairs, which means neither one of them is about to walk in on me. This feels like a violation, but I do it anyway. The back of the photo is blank. Maybe it's from Kazakhstan, or maybe it's one she has kept with her since before she left. Hard to tell.

Sometimes I wonder whether a photograph stared at long enough can retain a kind of resonance. Like a battery soaking up and storing energy, the photo stores the emotion invested in it by the human gaze. Sounds silly, I know, but this boy's picture radiates sadness. He doesn't seem unhappy in the photo. If anything, he seems listless. But that's not what I'm feeling. There's something else, something the image itself does not convey, something coming from the gaze that beheld the image before me, not from the boy himself.

I feel like a voyeur all of a sudden, put the photo back in the frame, then scurry away to change. Finn enters our bedroom and closes the door behind him. He leans against it and shows me what he has in his hands: the porcelain doll I left downstairs.

"What's this all about?" he whispers in that "conspiracy of the odd" voice we get when we're talking to the person who doesn't get what we don't get either.

I shake my head. "She gave it to me. It has sentimental value."

"I sure hope so. Yeesh." He sits next to me on the bed, arranging the doll on my nightstand, back up against my lamp.

I don't want the doll there, but I ignore it. "What do you think?"

"She's not what I expected."

"You mean she's pretty."

"Well, yeah," he concedes. "Especially for a woman her age."

Good boy.

"And kind of . . . not all there? I guess I imagined her like one of those nuns who hits your knuckles with the ruler." This from a man who didn't grow up Catholic and, as far as I know, has never met a real nun in his life. "Instead, she's kind of cool, but kind of spaced out, you know? But I like her. I think. She did ask me if it was okay to smoke in the bedroom."

"What did you say?"

"I didn't know what to say. We haven't had that conversation. I told her you were in charge of things like that. You didn't tell me she smoked."

"How was I supposed to know? I didn't think missionaries were allowed."

"Maybe she was like some badass, twisted missionary."

I lean over and rest my head on his shoulder, sighing. "A twisted missionary. I am sure that's *not* allowed."

"How much time before we have to leave?" he asks.

"Enough," I say, turning to face him and pushing my fingers into his curls. Realization strikes. "Wait. We're not alone in the house."

"Oh, baby. Really?"

"Really. Look at it this way, she won't be here forever." Not like kids are. Chew on that a little bit.

"Where's she going to go?" he asks.

"I think that's up to us to help her find out."

"I'm on it."

6.

Microchurch

Behind the studio, at the very back of the Old Firehouse, a long narrow room runs the length of the building, open all the way to the ceiling but without any windows along the outside wall. To bring in light, Chris had his contractors put in a row of skylights and turned the room into a gallery. As the building manager, one of Finn's jobs is to recruit local artists interested in showing their work. He's a natural-born networker, so fresh pieces are installed every couple of months. Thanks to the ethereal mood created by the high ceiling and the skylights overhead, the gallery was also the perfect space for Finn to realize his Big Idea.

It came to him one weekend when I was out of town. After playing in the band at The Community, he had gone home with Pastor Rick and his wife, Beth, for lunch. And Rick started telling him about this revelation he'd had after locking himself in his backyard shed for a month, or something crazy like that. People had nicknamed him St. Rick, because some painter had used him as the model for a church mural. A Catholic church mural. So we're not talking something worthy of a dilapidated Greek diner or a Sunday school room. After the shed episode, he decided to leave his job at The Community and start some kind of inner-city church—or maybe it was a halfway house. I've heard a couple of different versions.

Anyway, Finn hears all this, and he feels his chains fall off. That's how he described it afterward: iron hitting the floor. Here's this authority figure in his life, this guy who was his youth pastor and then became the men's pastor at the church, and Rick's telling him that the way they're doing things just doesn't make sense.

"I already knew that," Finn said, "but hearing it out loud made the difference."

So my husband starts thinking, if the problem with The Community is how big it is, how bloated, how out of touch with anything the early Christians might have recognized as church, if it's what people call a "megachurch," then the solution is to cut off the prefix. Lose the mega.

"The megachurch is like Budweiser," he tells St. Rick. "Nobody drinks that unless they don't know any better. What they drink is a microbrew—assuming they care anything about beer. So apply the same logic to church. If you care anything about church, what you want is not the Budweiser. You want the Microchurch."

That was his Big Idea.

What makes St. Rick different from the people Finn usually advises is this: instead of running with the idea, Rick told him, "*You* should do this."

He didn't mind helping, didn't mind throwing his weight behind the concept, but Rick thought that since Finn had had the vision, it must have been meant for him.

This was almost seven months ago. Finn drove me up to Towson for dinner with Rick and Beth. We met their boys, we took a tour of the famous shed out back and even walked over to the Catholic church where Rick's face was commemorated on the mural. To my surprise, he wasn't the only saint in the picture. Everybody on the wall had a halo too, and there were plenty of them.

"After that," I tell my aunt as we walk to the Old Firehouse, "Finn did what designers do. He started making posters. He put them up around the neighborhood and started opening the gallery late on Sunday afternoons. I don't know if you'd call what we do a church service, but it begins in the daylight and ends when the sun goes down."

"I want to see this," she says.

"You will."

About a block ahead of us, Finn is double-timing so he can open the doors. There are usually a couple of people waiting on the street. He doesn't like to keep them out there too long.

"It's beautiful," I tell her. "The only light in the room by the time we finish will be the art lights hanging over the paintings. Just being in the space feels really different from what people are accustomed to. It feels sacred and set apart."

"And you, Sara? You believe in this—in what you're both doing?"

"Finn's the one doing it, with Rick's help. God is God no matter what. I don't have to have the perfect experience. Because, let's face it, I'm not the perfect Christian. But I do know what happens here isn't for show. There aren't any microphones or flat screens, there's no production value at all. It's the church unplugged, I guess."

"Unplugged?"

Okay, that expression sure got deep into the vocabulary quickly, didn't it?

"Nontechnical?" I supply.

"Like it used to be." She nods.

"Maybe," I say. Although how far back she's taking "used to be," I don't know. Acts 2? Well, there's always that hope.

We enter the Old Firehouse through the back, just as Finn turns on the art lights. The whole gallery is flooded with soft gray light from above, the evenly spaced paintings, colorful abstracts, popping against the dark walls like tiny jewels. A rustic farm table holds down the center of the gallery surrounded by a large semicircle of stamped aluminum chairs—very trendy of Chris to have chosen, but not especially comfortable. "You said you didn't want to be comfortable," I whisper to Bel. "No problem there."

Finn sits on the edge of the table and starts picking out a tune on the guitar. Sounds don't exactly echo in the gallery, though they take on a metallic edge and tend to seem farther off than they are, as if the waves rise upward instead of out.

People wander in as Finn plays, moving their chairs around, nodding silent greetings. Once six or seven of us have arrived, Finn starts to sing. His singing voice matches the space, simple and bright but with no extra embellishments. I love hearing him sing.

He'll have chosen the verses beforehand, a few lines from one of the psalms, and come up with a simple tune to accompany them. As he repeats the refrain, the rest of us join in. Next to me, Aunt Bel coos the words. When I glance over, she appears to be crying. I can hardly carry a tune, so I contribute my rhythmic whisper:

> Let the words of my mouth
> and the meditation of my heart
> be acceptable in your sight, O Lord,
> my rock and my redeemer.

The words are like water washing the outside world away. When I look up, fourteen of us have gathered, including Rick, who holds a thick hardback book in his lap and has brought one of his sons with him—the younger one, I think. The guitar stops and we all keep still, waiting and praying. Rick speaks quietly into the silence, praying the Lord's Prayer, after which Finn leads another psalm.

"I have something a little different tonight," Rick says when we're done singing. "I thought I'd read you a story."

"Didn't have time to prepare anything?" somebody jokes, and the rest of us laugh.

"It's not that," Rick says. "It's not *only* that." He smiles.

"This is a favorite of mine," he says, opening the book on his lap. "The first time I read it, I went a little crazy. But I'd been holed up on my own for a while."

That gets a smile from those of us who know his biography.

Without further preamble, he plunges right in, reading the story in a slightly higher pitch than his usual voice, and with a Southern inflection that seems to go with the material. It's the story of a man named Parker, a navy vet covered in tattoos, who finds himself unhappily married to a fundamentalist preacher's daughter intent on watching his every move, suspicious of sin. Parker lies to her about the old lady he works for, describing her as attractive in hope of making his wife jealous. What frustrates him most, though, is that she has no appreciation for his many tattoos, which for him are a source of wonder and always have been since he first glimpsed a tattooed man at a county fair.

So he concocts a plan to foil his wife. He's going to go into town and get a tattoo on his back—the only space he has left—and the subject will be Jesus Christ. His wife won't be able to hate this tattoo. It would be tantamount to hating God.

I glance over midstory to gauge Aunt Bel's reaction. She listens intently, though with a slightly confused expression. Either she is not quite following the narrative or she can't figure out why Rick thought a story about a foul-mouthed, tattooed sailor would make a good substitute for a sermon.

"I've always wanted a tattoo," Aunt Bel whispers.

When Parker goes to the tattoo artist, he flips through a book of religious subjects that are arranged by period. Working his way from the back, he passes up the warm and fuzzy Jesus pictures, the quaint Victorian representations. The further he goes, the scarier and more awe-inducing the images of Christ become until he comes upon "the haloed head of a flat stern Byzantine Christ with all-demanding eyes."

Rick pauses here and passes a piece of paper to Finn, who looks at it and sends it around the circle. When the paper reaches me, I find a color print-out of a "flat stern Byzantine Christ" staring down from the top of a painted dome, probably somewhere in Greece. I hand the picture to Aunt Bel, who gazes at it a long time.

I continue to stare at it. I don't know this Christ. But my eyes won't leave the page. The beautiful story turns into a Rick-toned thrum as Christ's eyes bore up into mine. He's saying something.

"It looks like the sun has set," Rick interrupts. "Why don't we pray?"

Yes, please. Let's just pray.

After we finish, as people chat and catch up on each other's lives, Aunt Bel asks me what the name of the story was.

"Let's find out," I say.

I introduce her to Rick, but before I can ask about the book, Finn starts telling him about Aunt Bel's twenty years of mission work in Kazakhstan, so eager to impress his mentor that he overdoes things a bit. Conscious of Aunt Bel's embarrassment, Rick takes her by the elbow and guides her over toward his son.

"Don't talk her up so much," I whisper to Finn.

He shrugs. "I didn't mean to."

"Grab your guitar and let's go. I'm starving."

On the way out, I ask Rick about the story. "I'd love for Diana to read it—my in-house tattoo geek. I wouldn't mind having the upper hand on Huey either, since he's always referring to books I've never heard of and acting like my bachelor's degree should be revoked on account of my ignorance. No matter how many times I tell him there's not a lot of time for reading in college, he never seems to understand: 'What's the point, then?'"

"Here, you take it," Rick says, handing me the book. "That's the Library of America edition, and it has everything in it—all her fiction."

I check the cover. Flannery O'Connor. Good Irish Catholic name, as my grandfather on my dad's side would remark. A toothy, sideways-looking woman with cat-eye glasses and flipped hair.

"I can't take your book."

"It's one of my missions in life, spreading the word about her. You take it. Believe me, I have plenty more."

On the walk home, I hand the book to Aunt Bel, who flips through the pages absently despite the impossibility of reading by streetlight. Finn is lagging behind us now, as he tends to do after our evenings in the gallery, lost in thought. I know he's asking himself what kind of Christ he's always imagined. Like he thinks it should be the flat, stern Byzantine Christ, when in reality, Finn's Jesus is truly the most loving of friends. He's so lucky he gets to have this Christ.

"That man in the story," Aunt Bel says. "He really suffered."

"Parker? Well, he wasn't very nice to begin with."

"No," she agrees, "he certainly wasn't."

"*A flat stern Byzantine Christ*," I call over my shoulder, so Finn can hear. "I absolutely love that line."

Next to me, Aunt Bel hugs the book to her chest. "I know," she says. "It's a good line. Is that your Jesus?" she asks me.

"I don't know who my Jesus is, Aunt Bel."

Let's hope she's not thinking she moved from one mission field to another.

"Do you know who your Jesus is?" I ask Finn as he pulls off his clothing down to his boxers.

"What do you mean?"

"Is he the flat, stern Byzantine Christ?"

"Uh . . . nope."

"I didn't think so."

"What about you?"

I sit on my side of the bed and reach for my nail file. The scratch-scritch takes away some of the drama here.

"I don't know. I remember one time I let a college acquaintance talk me into attending church with her, one of those crazy holy-roller places. Not my scene, I had tried to explain, which only egged her on. Afterward, she looked devastated and told me how sorry she was I had to be there for the guest preacher."

"Were *you* sorry?"

"Not really. I could tell the sermon had horrified her, as it had quite a few others."

"What was he talking about? Tithing?"

I laugh. "He talked about the violence of Jesus, how he'd made himself a whip and used it to clear out the temple. This man had a way with words, and if he had been talking about one of those other Christs from the Flannery O'Connor story–the Smiling Jesus, for example–his listeners would have left in a warm and fuzzy frame of mind. But the Christ he brought to life that night wasn't smiling. He wasn't gazing down coldly from on high. No, he was right behind you, breathing hard, putting all his strength into the swing of the lash, cutting your skin with his indignation."

"Sounds a little scary, don't you think?"

"'What if that was the only Jesus you knew?' the preacher asked. 'What if you were living back then, and your only contact with the man was that one time, when he'd beaten you? What would you think about him then? What sympathy could you muster for that man's suffering?'"

Finn slides into the sheets on his side of the bed and picks up his book. "It's an interesting thought, though, right?"

"I have never heard another sermon on the beating Christ gave to those money changers. I've never heard anyone try to dramatize the scene, let alone defend Jesus from the assault charge. If it is mentioned at all, it gets glossed over, as if the most natural thing in the world for a man to do, if he's all loving and kind, is to make himself a whip and start flaying people raw in the temple, driving them out like they were subhuman swine. This is not the Jesus anyone wants, and so they don't dwell on the incident."

"So are you saying you want the Byzantine Indiana Jones Jesus or not?"

Oh, Finn.

"I'm saying it's all disturbing, this kind of Jesus. And that big wonky eye in the icon . . . it just stares at me and all I feel is reproach."

Finn shifts to his side to face me. "Yeah, that one eye is kinda disturbing."

"I don't like it, Finn. I don't want Jesus to be that way."

"He's not." Finn lays down his book.

"How can you be so sure?"

"Because he's never been that way to me. Has he been that way to you, Sara?"

I shake my head. "I don't know."

He turns back on his side to face me. "What's this about, really?"

"When I was a kid, the church Mom took me to had this Sunday school teacher. And I remember we talked about Jacob and Esau, and she said, with this strange sort of glee, that God hated Esau. That God hates some people. And it didn't sound like she was talking about hating their sin but loving the person."

Finn raises up to rest the side of his head in his hand. "Wait a sec. She said God hates people?"

"Yes."

"Sara, that is messed up. Believe me." And he lays flat again.

"That's it. You just tell me it's messed up and that's it?"

"Some things don't deserve any other sort of explanation, they're that absurd." He picks up his book again. "Sara, forget what she said. God loves everyone. Period. Because if he can hate one of us, he can hate any of us, and I can't live that way. None of us can. Not really."

Finn, the practical theologian.

"I love you," I tell him, still not necessarily sure about God and Jesus, but definitely sure about Finn Drexel.

7.
Bel Canto

The week after Aunt Bel's arrival, a new client walks into the studio just after opening. Right off the street, not even calling ahead. From my cubicle, I can hear her talking to Diana, saying all the things I like to hear. Could this finally be it? The ideal client who says things like, "Price is no object." Or, "Please, you're the artist. Do whatever you want."

Uh, most likely not. But stranger things have happened.

"I've heard some great things about you guys, and I'm looking for the very best. I need something different, something creative and outside the box. I really want to invest in something special, you know? Make it magical. I want to grab people by the heart."

I head over to the counter.

The woman dwarfs Diana and me, this blond, dressed in an expensive-looking short tailored jacket and dark jeans. She has an oversized leather purse over one shoulder that I'm accustomed to assuming is a knock-off, though in this case it probably isn't. If I had to guess, I would say she's about Aunt Bel's age, but in terms of conscious sophistication, she's the anti-Bel.

Her blond hair falls straight, a shining light down to the middle of her back.

She reaches over the counter to shake my hand. "You're Sara? It's a pleasure to finally meet you."

"Finally?" I say.

"I'm Holly. We have some friends in common."

These friends, it turns out, are from The Community, where Holly works as something called Director of Aesthetics. She knows Finn, she knows St. Rick, and is apparently best friends forever with Rick's wife, Beth. She explains all this as I lead her over to the conference table, and my heart starts to sink. Church work tends to be pro bono work. Not to mention most churches involve too many people in the decision-making process, which leads to every designer's nightmare: design-by-committee. Every time I do a freebie for some church group, I promise myself afterward I'm going to start saying no.

"I'm not wearing my Community hat," Holly explains, removing a file folder from her bag. "I'm helping my husband out. Eric Ringwald, the financier?"

She says his name like I ought to have heard of him, so I smile and play along. Doing work for a financier sounds a lot more promising than undertaking a job on behalf of The Community, especially given Finn's on-again, off-again relationship to that church.

"He left all that behind a few years ago," she says, "and now he's a full-time fund-raiser."

My heart can't take this. Fund-raising sounds like nonprofit, and nonprofit groups are right behind churches in the line for free stuff. Not to sound cynical, but when you have rent and employees and your own house payments to make, you start to resent people bringing you these pro bono opportunities, encouraging you to "give back," as if you've already made it and all that's left in life is to work gratis on behalf of others.

"This," she says, sliding the folder over, "is what he's working with now. He spent a lot of money a couple of years ago to have the organization branded, and as you can see, ended up with something so sterile and generic that it says absolutely nothing. Safe and corporate, but it has no soul."

Inside the folder, I find a stack of glossy four-color brochures, some invitations to events that took place last year and the year before, and a flat version of what appears to be a DVD cover, featuring some stock photo children riding bicycles through a park. I glance over the copy inside one of the brochures and come away none the wiser.

"What was all this for?"

"If you want people's money," she says, "you have to ask for it. These are some of the ways you ask. We mail the brochures, invite people to parties, show them videos of all the good work the organizations are doing—whoever Eric's raising money for at the moment—and then, once the groundwork is laid, Eric asks if they'll write him the check."

Unlike most clients, Holly knows exactly what she wants. Her husband is hosting a fund-raising event twelve weeks from now. She wants us to start with the invitations to the event, then redesign her husband's logo and website, along with all the collateral printed pieces, from stationery to the brochures. And she wants all of it designed, printed, and ready to go by the evening of the fund-raiser.

"We're picking up the tab on this, not the charities," she explains, "and I don't want to cut any corners. I want everything to be beautiful, and it should capture what his work is all about. The organizations Eric raises money for are really making a difference in the world, and people should know about it. That's what I mean when I say it has to grab them by the heart. They're not giving money to Eric, or to the charities even, they're giving it to *people*." She pauses, then smiles. "Okay, that's the end of my sermon. This is my budget." She hands me a piece of paper. "Now, is twelve weeks enough time?"

"We'll make it enough," I say. "We're gonna show you what we can do."

Oh yeah, we are.

It's the chance of a decade, the one I've been looking for.

I round everybody up immediately and explain the project, the reactions ranging from Huey's sigh at the deadline to Finn's boyish enthusiasm. "These are the kind of clients we've been dreaming of," he says. "The Ringwalds are loaded, and they know a lot of people who are even more loaded. If we pull this off, it could lead to big things."

"Sure," Huey says. "If we can pull it off."

"What do you mean *if*, Huey?" I ask. "I'm usually with you on the practical side of things, but look at who's sitting in this room? If we can't do . . . well, I just don't know. Can you let go of the curmudgeon act for just an hour and let me relish a little?"

Finn stifles a laugh with his fist.

Huey apparently didn't hear me. "We've already got more on our plates than we can handle, and that hunk of junk in the middle of the studio isn't going to fix itself. We need working presses here, not restoration projects."

"Whatever we can't do in-house, we can outsource," I say.

Huey glares at me like I've just suggested opening a sweatshop powered by orphan labor. "The whole point of being a printer is not having to send things out."

"Which is why you need to be on board one hundred percent." Looking for some way to motivate him, I say, "With the money from this project, we can buy a Heidelberg."

Finn sits up straight. "What do we need a Heidelberg for when we've got *that*? Am I right or am I right?"

We all turn to look at the rusted Iron Maiden dominating the center of the studio.

Huey stands. "Anybody want a cup of coffee or tea? This is going to be a long afternoon."

All three of us raise our hands.

He heads back to the small kitchen at the back of the shop. Finn, Diana, and I look at each other, the excitement foaming and frothing between us.

"This is gonna be good," I say.

"Oh yeah, you guys." Finn smiles. "Nothing Byzantine about this situation here, Sara."

Nope. Just a pie-in-the-sky, all-is-right-with-the-world thing going on right now and I'm not going to complain.

———

By the end of the meeting, I've worked out a plan. Diana and I will divide design duties down the middle. While I focus on Holly's job, she will handle the log of wedding invitations and walk-in design projects on her own, with help from Finn as needed. Once I have the invites for the fund-raising event done, Huey will print them, and then in the space, as I work on the brochure and other promotional pieces, Finn will build the website. Together, Huey and Finn will see what can be done with the Chandler & Price.

But right now, I have to do an immediate turnaround for the invitation to the fund-raising event. I told Holly I'd have a few design options tomorrow. Thank goodness she just wants something simple. Thank goodness we've designed more wedding invitations than I ever thought we would. I haven't pulled an all-nighter in a long time. Hopefully it won't come to that.

Taking me aside for a private consult, Finn makes a suggestion. "You know something, we could use an extra set of hands down here. For the time being, anyway. What about your aunt? You think she'd be interested?"

"Are you serious?"

Apart from devouring Rick's Flannery O'Connor book and smoking on the stoop, I'm not sure Aunt Bel has any interests. In the week since her arrival, she's gotten more reserved than on the first day, not less. All my conversations with her when I go home at night are one-sided, and Finn's efforts haven't yielded much more.

"You said yourself, you don't know what she even does with her time. Maybe she needs something to occupy herself."

"Other than smoking and reading Flannery O'Connor."

"Right. Plus, it might be good for her, you know, being around other people. I get this vibe off her like she's spent way too much time in her life alone."

"Maybe you're right," I say. "I just don't have time to babysit her here—there's too much to do."

"I'll do it, Sara."

"For real?"

"Yeah. It was my idea, so I'll be responsible."

"Finn, you know I love you, right?"

"How could you not?" he asks, grinning. Then he sobers, takes my face in his hands, and kisses me softly on the mouth. "I've always been crazy about you," he whispers almost inaudibly in my ear.

Sometimes, for the life of me, I can't understand why. But that doesn't mean I won't take it.

That night at dinner he floats the idea to Aunt Bel, who absorbs it in her ambivalent, noncommittal way. But the next morning she's dressed and ready for breakfast, walks with us to the studio without our asking, and seems in higher spirits than I've seen from her since day one. I'm about as tired after my late night as I ever want to be, but between Diana and me, we have three good designs for the invite.

True to his word, Finn finds little jobs around the office to keep Aunt Bel busy—stacking, folding, cutting—and from time to time gives her impromptu lectures on various things happening all around her. He parks her behind my desk as I go over the work on the fund-raiser invite, going on at length about vector art and the new platemaking process for letterpress printing. "Nobody uses lead type anymore, not for serious work. We send out the files and have polymer plates made." He digs some flimsy old ink-stained polymers out of the drawer and shows them off. Bel makes appreciative sounds, as she always does during Finn's instructional interludes.

Not that Finn is in her age range or anything, but there's an inherent sensuality about my aunt. It basically creeps me out thinking about that, but that doesn't change things. Some women just can't help it. They've got so much sexual energy, it just bleeds out of them whether they want it to or not.

I am not one of those women.

In thirty minutes I leave for a meeting with Holly to garner her approval of the invitation design. I'm nervous. I may not have a lot of sexual energy oozing out of me, but nervous energy? If you could hook up a backhoe to me right now, I'd dig you a pit the size of Kazakhstan.

After garnering a reaction from Holly only someone like Nelson Mandela deserves and a tour of her husband's office as well as lunch at the Nautilus Diner to celebrate the direction of the project, I find Finn and Aunt Bel standing over Huey's shoulder at the Vandercook. At the counter, Diana motions me to be quiet and listen, much as she would if she were observing wildlife and didn't want to spook them.

"Just wait," she says.

Finn is narrating Huey's every move like a color commentator, as if he expects my aunt to jump in and assist once she's heard enough. Judging by Huey's bristly, overprecise movements, I can tell he's about reached his limit. Sure enough, he starts offering his own counter-narration in between Finn's pauses, explaining what he's *really* doing on the press and how catastrophic it would be if anyone were to take Finn's explanations at face value.

"They're in top form today," Diana says, crossing her legs on her stool.

"Nice pumps," I say, pointing to black vintage kitten heel shoes.

"Thanks. So while you were gone, Finn announced he was going to get a start on the Iron Maiden this afternoon."

At Diana's elbow I see the Flannery O'Connor book. "What's this?"

"Bel brought it in. She wanted me to read one of the stories. Because of these," she says, lifting her arms to indicate her shoulder-to-wrist tats.

Noticing my return, Huey breaks off and comes to see whether the designs met with approval. I give him the thumbs-up. "She picked one and loves it. Now we need to knock them out."

"I'm ready whenever you are. Let's rock and roll."

"I'm all set up," Huey informs me the next afternoon. "You ready to print?"

"Is that a rhetorical question?"

Huey smiles and we head out to the print floor.

There's nothing like the whir of the Vandercook, the back and forth *ker-clunk, ker-clunk* of its cylinder, rolling forward to make the print, re-inking the plate as it travels back. Huey walks the cylinder forward, his hand on the crank, pulling the prints one at a time and handing them to Aunt Bel, who places them gingerly on the drying rack. The sound of progress, the smell of the ink, the whole process is all rather intoxicating, and wonderfully manual. The ink and paper, though fine to begin with, seem somehow ennobled by the energy of a human being powering the process. The invitations are invitations, yes, but they are also now a form of art.

All afternoon the work continues, and as Huey works the press, Finn turns his attention to the Iron Maiden. He drags a chair alongside, then dons headphones so he can watch his instructional videos yet again. I check on him whenever I take a break, and by the time the invites are done, he has set out several plastic tubs of water and is soaking some test parts to remove the rust via electrolysis. He's bought a battery charger especially for this. I can't watch.

———

Despite the influx of work, I stick to keeping our weekly staff meetings, a habit I carved out early on that gives me a chance to kick new ideas around and keep a finger on the shop's pulse. This time of year we're always brainstorming ideas for the retail business. One of our major retailers, the Brooklyn-based lifestyle store Katz Lime, wants a whole new greeting card line, something exclusive to them and edgy.

"You don't want me at this," Bel says, groping at the fabric of her skirt.

"Everybody's sitting in. You'll have fun."

We gather around the conference table, laying out notebooks and coffee cups and tablet computers. Finn brings a fresh carafe of coffee and opens a box of pastries fetched this morning from the bakery.

"All right," I say, reaching for a cream cheese danish. "Let's hear something edgy."

Crickets.

It's the same thing that happens if, out of the blue, you say, "Tell me something funny." Most people when they're put on the spot can't deliver.

We go around the table, starting with Finn, who throws out a few ideas without finishing any of them. Halfway in, he stops and says, "No, that's crap." Then he launches into a new one, only to pull up again.

"What about you, Bel?" Diana asks, then bites into an apricot macadamia muffin.

"I don't even know what 'edgy' means."

"Diana?" I ask.

The girl has a rockabilly thing she's always trying to channel into the product. I'm open to her vibe, but between us we've never figured out how to make it work tastefully. Judging from her start, we're not going to manage that today either.

"Think roller girls," she says. "But absolutely *covered* in blood—"

Finn cups his hands around his mouth: "*Next.*"

Diana throws one of her Altoids at him.

"Okay, here's mine," Huey says. "Listen up." He pauses over the legal pad where he's scribbled his ideas down, awaiting our full attention. "Here it is: first lines of famous books, with sarcastic comebacks inside. For example, on the front of the card, you see a bonnet and a big Victorian dress, and underneath is the opening line of *Middlemarch*. It says—" He consults the pad again. "'Miss Brooke had that kind of beauty which seems to be thrown into relief by poor dress.' Then you open the card and it says, 'What's your excuse?'"

"So the comeback is aimed at the reader, not the quote?" Diana asks.

"Yeah, exactly. So, like, this is the card you give the friend who doesn't know how to dress herself. It's a trash-talking card."

"I like that." Sassy.

"Here's another one. First line on the cover comes from *Anna Karenina*: 'Happy families are all alike; every unhappy family is unhappy in its own way.' You open it up, and it says, 'Thanks for keeping us so unique.'"

"That one needs work," I say.

"What's wrong with it?"

"She's right," Finn says. "What's the card for? You give it to your parents for making your life miserable?"

I flap my hands in the air. "Oh, wait, I've got it. This is the card you give your soon-to-be sister-in-law so she knows what she's getting into. It says, 'Welcome to the family.'"

"No, no," Diana says. "How about: 'Guess which one we are?' You know, you're marrying into it, and you don't know the dynamic. You get this sarcastic card from your fiancé's sister and you're like, *Okaaaay*, I'm going with unhappy."

"But at least they have a sense of humor," I say.

Huey goes back to the legal pad. "Next one. Jane Austen. *Pride and Prejudice.* 'It is a truth universally acknowledged, that a single man in possession of a good fortune must be in want of a wife.' I don't have anything for inside that one, but I was thinking, you know, you give it to your friend who's just announced her engagement to a guy you don't like."

"'His fortune better be more than good. Just sayin','" Finn says.

"Ha, ha, I like that."

Diana shakes her head. "How about, it's the card you give the hot guy who just moved into the apartment building. The line is: 'Welcome to the neighborhood.'"

Aunt Bel sits across from me with a baffled look. We might as well be speaking Swahili as far as she's concerned. "I don't get it," she says. "These sound kind of ... mean."

"That's the idea," Huey replies. "They gotta have some attitude. That's the humor. People think of these classics of literature as kind of stuffy and sacrosanct. So you make 'em catty and ill-tempered, and people love it."

"But why would you buy something like that? I wouldn't give somebody a card to tell them I thought they were choosing the wrong husband, or to warn her not to marry into the family. Would you?"

"It's meant to be funny. Like I said, it's trash talk. Riffing on lines from literature makes it snobby trash talk, which is pitching right across the plate for our demographic—right, Sara?"

"Pretty much," I say.

"Maybe I just don't understand. Could you explain why it's funny?"

Huey starts chuckling. "Bel, baby, explaining a joke is like coming home drunk at three in the morning with another woman's lipstick on your cheek. Nothing you say is gonna be good enough. Trust me, this is good stuff."

As Huey speaks, I notice Finn—who's sitting right next to Aunt Bel—start to wriggle with discomfort, puckering his lips in a way I recognize. He thinks we're patronizing her and doesn't like it. The next words out of his mouth are going to be in her defense.

"Maybe Bel has a point," he says.

I cut him off. "We need to refine the wording, but I think the idea itself is solid. I don't know how big the market for sarcastic greeting cards actually is, but I think they'll do fine as letterpress pieces—and this is the kind of concept that'll get us play on the blogs. I can see us posting photos of these, closed, then open. We'll be reblogged, reposted, repinned, retweeted, you name it. This is good stuff, Huey."

"Thanks," he says. "Got a few more. Here's *Fahrenheit 451*: 'It was a pleasure to burn.' Open it up and—" He drops his voice into the Barry White register. "'Let's do it again sometime, baby.'"

"Yeah," Diana says.

"Are you adjusting all right, Aunt Bel?" I ask.

She's been at the studio every day for a couple of weeks, watching and learning, helping out where she can. In that time, I have picked up on her method and come to understand her a bit better. Aunt Bel focuses on one person at a time, does what she can to win them over, then—once she feels things are stable enough—moves on. That first day with me, her attention was total. Now she remains polite but distant. She attached herself to Finn next, then Diana, and finally put some time into winning Huey over.

"You seem like you've made some friends," I add, realizing I sound like the school counselor talking to the troubled new kid.

"It's relaxing here," she says.

"You think so? It can get pretty stressful for me sometimes."

"Everything is clear, though. The steps to go through, the deadlines. Once you know what to do, you can tune things out."

"You mean *turn* them out? You can get a lot done."

"No, tune them out. Forget they exist. I like that, Sara. Very much. You can't do that with people."

"Finn thinks you should learn how to pull prints. He wants to start you on the Sigwalt, which is nice and straightforward. I'm not sure, but he thinks you're ready."

She shrugs, not seeming to care one way or the other.

"You don't have to," I tell her. It's painfully obvious she could take or leave this stuff. "But it's a good skill to have. I'd rather see you doing that than getting dragged into Iron Maiden duty."

The Maiden is now partially disassembled, the big flywheel flat on the ground taking up twice the space as before, the other pieces arranged in various heaps, the logic of their division known only to Finn. While the bulk of the pieces still need to be de-rusted, he has moved on to testing paint on the handful of restored parts, collecting votes on bright red versus a dark blackish green.

"You're very blessed to have this place. I am happy for you, Sara. It's not at all what I imagined, but I am happy for you."

"Well, thanks." I think?

While she heads off to the Sigwalt, where Finn stands waiting with a spare apron, I catch Diana's eye and beckon her over.

"What do you think about my aunt? Is she right in the head?"

"I think she's kind of amazing," Diana says. "I wish she was my aunt instead."

If I had more time, I would chew on that thought, but rebranding Eric Ringwald's website hasn't come as easily as the concept for the invitation. I've had to figure out not just his operation but the various nonprofits he regularly assists, haunted by Holly's desire to grab people's hearts—which is much easier to say than to translate into good design. Picture a cartoon hand closing around a cartoon heart. It conveys . . . nothing. Yet every sketch I make, every idea I kick around amounts to little more than that.

It's four in the afternoon. I have been pushing myself since lunch and have nothing to show for it. Holly calls—she touches base every few days— and of course she's wondering if I have anything for her to see. I'm in the middle of making excuses when I hear a scream from over the cubicle wall.

"Holly, I've gotta go."

The voice was Diana's, but she's not the one who's hurt. She's standing with her back slightly arched, hands over her mouth. I follow her line of sight to a huddle of bodies, Huey and Finn bending over a crumpled Aunt Bel, helping her rise to her feet. I rush over, my chest pounding. Her face twists in pain as she cradles her left hand.

"Give her space," Finn is saying.

Huey's arm supports her. "Come on, Bel, lemme take a look."

"What happened?" I say, but it comes out as a shriek. Finn stares at me, pale and petrified.

"It's all right," Huey keeps saying, in a tone that suggests anything but. Aunt Bel turns slightly toward me, and I can see the problem. Her left pinkie finger hangs at the wrong angle in relation to her hand.

I slam my hand over my mouth, willing myself not to throw up.

8.

A Holy Fool

In the clinic's crowded waiting room, we hem Aunt Bel in on either side, shielding her from feverish, germ-clouded kids, a potbellied man in a neck brace, and a grandmother whose hacking cough is so loud I can visualize the inside of her throat and let me tell you, it should belong in a commercial for drain cleaner. They should post a warning on the wall: *If you weren't sick before, you will be now.* Just across from us, a guy on crutches flips through a wrinkled auto magazine with the ease of a regular patient, his shoeless foot cocked to knee-level, the dingy white sock tugged forward on his foot into a little point.

"Maybe it's not broken," Finn says. He's been clutching at this hope ever since Huey put it into his head. "They'll just have to pop it into joint like Huey said. It's ridiculous how long it's taking. Are you sure you don't remember how you did it?"

Aunt Bel shrugs, keeping her hand aloft. "It happened so fast."

"I'm so sorry, Bel," he says.

I don't like waiting rooms. So much despair, so much fear and uncertainty has leached like smoke into the upholstery. You can't be in such a place without feeling it. I never can. The senseless waiting. The irrational first-come, first-serve order, ignoring each patient's level of need in favor of something as random as mere chronology. The clinic makes me feel insecure. Anything could go wrong here. I just want to leave.

"What's taking them so long?" I say.

Finn chuckles. "They don't call it the waiting room for nothing."

It's your fault we're even here, I think. If he hadn't become so enamored of my aunt, she'd be home getting cancer on the stoop.

When the nurse finally calls, I accompany Aunt Bel through the inner door, leaving Finn and yet another of his apologies hanging in the air.

"He shouldn't blame himself," Aunt Bel murmurs.

"Well, he should have been paying attention."

"You're angry at him? Sara, don't be. I was the clumsy one, not Finn."

She bears the pain with uncomplaining nobility. Only her ashen skin and the way she hunches her shoulders forward protectively betrays how much her finger must hurt. The nurse settles us into a small examination room.

"Sit up there and the doctor will be with you," she says, motioning Aunt Bel onto the paper-lined adjustable table.

Another nurse taps on the door twenty minutes later and takes Aunt Bel away—just down the hall for X-rays. Alone in the room, the curled corners of the anatomy charts—the human eye in cross-section and the cardiovascular system—and the gritty floor tiles do little to inspire confidence. I can feel my heart thumping with anxiety, and yes, with anger: at Finn for letting something like this happen, at myself for not putting up a fight when he suggested letting her try the press, for letting my busyness overrule my better judgment.

Aunt Bel returns with a different nurse this time.

"Everything okay?" I ask.

She shrugs. "They don't tell you anything."

We wait another half hour or so for the doctor to arrive, a tiny Asian woman in pearls and lavender scrubs who takes one look at the X-ray in her hand and says, "Oh yes, you did a number on yourself, didn't you?"

"It is broken?" I ask.

"In two places—here and, you see, right along here." She slaps the film against the light box on the wall, indicating faint lines bisecting the bone. "On a scale of one to ten," she says, "how would you rate your pain right now?"

Aunt Bel considers, then says, "Two."

The doctor glances at me, surprised. "She must be a pretty tough customer."

Either that, or her scale for pain is calibrated a little differently.

"What about this?" the doctor asks, extending my aunt's arm and manipulating the hand. "Does that hurt? And this? Okay, we're going to set this and get you going."

The doctor pulls a high stool next to the table, taking Aunt Bel's hand in her lap. She works quickly, setting the pinkie, staking it with a metal brace, and wrapping it tight against the ring finger. As she puts the final touches on the job, the doctor draws Aunt Bel's arm farther forward, then pauses to frown.

"Can you bend it?" she asks, meaning the arm, not the finger.

Aunt Bel's pale cheeks flush. "Not all the way."

The doctor folds the arm back and forth, rolling it in its socket, testing the range of mobility. "It wasn't properly set? How long ago was this?"

Aunt Bel winces as the doctor rolls her arm to the left, elbow out.

"We should get an X-ray of this," the doctor says.

But Aunt Bel starts shaking her head. "No, no, it's fine."

"I'd like to take a look. It hasn't healed correctly, and you may need to have it reset or you'll run into some problems—"

Sliding off the table, Aunt Bel clutches her bandaged hand to her chest. Before I can speak, my aunt slips through the door, disappearing into the corridor. The doctor looks at me, puzzled.

"Is she coming back?"

I don't answer this, but ask, "What's wrong with her arm?"

"Looks to me like it was broken, and whoever treated it didn't set it properly. She can't turn her hand all the way, and the arm doesn't extend fully. It isn't any wonder she was injured trying to use it."

The thought makes me queasy.

"She's been overseas. I don't know what the health-care options were like where she was."

She glances into the hallway, but Aunt Bel is gone. "It really needs to be X-rayed," she says on her way out.

And that's that. Both Finn and Aunt Bel are missing from the waiting room, so I assume they're outside. Finn heads me off halfway to the car.

"What's the problem?" he asks. "She's sitting in the car and she seems pretty freaked out. Is the break really bad?"

"It's not that," I say. "Come on, let's go."

Finn drives and I ride shotgun. In the seat behind him, Bel stares silently out the window. "What was that all about back there?" I ask, leaning over to look back between the front seats. "Running out on the doctor. When did you break your arm? She says you're gonna need to have it looked at."

"I don't want to talk," Aunt Bel says.

Finn turns in his seat. "You broke your arm?"

"I don't want to talk about it. I'm tired. I want to sleep."

"Aunt Bel, what happened to you?" I ask.

She gives me a solemn look, but says nothing.

"Let's take her home."

Once she's settled upstairs, Finn asks me for the whole story. By the end, I feel shaken and psychologically bruised, not so much by Aunt Bel's past injury as by her strange reaction, her refusal to talk, as if the improperly healed arm was not just an inconvenience but a source of shame.

"I think something happened to Aunt Bel," I say.

"Something like what?"

I shake my head. "Whatever it was, she's not ready to talk. But it does make me wonder why she suddenly decided to come home. Could she have been in an abusive relationship?"

"I hope not."

Neither one of us knows what else to say, so Finn puts his arms around me and we hug. We have let something into our lives, someone. And both of us have enough faith to know it was for a reason, but clearly not enough insight to know exactly what that is.

"Tell you what," he whispers. "I'll stay with her, see if she'll open up. You go back to work, okay? Let Huey and Diana know everything's all right. We should keep the arm thing to ourselves, though."

"Thank you," I say. "I'll call on my way home. And I think this needs to be the end of Aunt Bel's printing career."

He smiles. "Yeah, you have a point."

I pause at the door. "You know, if she really didn't want to be found out, she would have just made up some excuse about having an injury years ago on the field."

"But she didn't."

"No. She didn't."

On the way to the studio, I call Daddy and tell him what happened.

"Is she going to be okay?" he asks.

"Yes. She's in a lot of pain right now, but she's handling it. Listen, did she say anything to you about a broken arm?" I ask.

"No."

"So she didn't tell you about it when it happened?"

"No, Sara, I swear. I haven't communicated at that level with your aunt for fifteen years. We just sent a postcard to each other every year or so with the most basic of news: yes, we're all still alive. That sort of thing."

"I wonder why she wouldn't tell you?"

He sighs. "I don't know. I always proved trustworthy, or at least I tried to. Bel knew she could always count on me. It must have been bad."

That's what I'm afraid of.

Diana is easy to reassure. She takes everything I say at face value and seems genuinely relieved. Over her shoulder, though, Huey fixes me with that skeptical gaze of his, telling me he knows better but isn't going to call me on it. For now. They go back to work and leave me to settle at my desk, but half an hour later I hear Huey breathing over my shoulder.

"What?" I ask.

"That's just what I was gonna say. I can tell when you're holding back, and you were definitely holding back just now. Is the finger even worse than it looked?"

I shake my head.

"Good. I think she just lost her focus. Looked lost for a sec. You know what I mean?"

"Well, whatever's going on with Bel, she's not confiding anything in me. She just shuts down."

"You don't know how to talk to her."

"Is that right?"

"Really, Sara, I don't know what it is, but you're not yourself around Bel."

"Maybe you haven't noticed, but I've been a little busy." That came out a little too quickly.

"I think she'd like to be close to you, Boss."

"That's what she told you, huh?"

"Yes, as a matter of fact, she did."

"Huey, why are you giving me such a hard time?"

"I'm trying to help."

I cross my arms. "You were trying to help when you wanted to pop her finger back into joint, and if I hadn't stopped you, you would have made it much worse."

He holds up his palms in mock surrender. "If you don't wanna hear it, I got plenty of other things to be doing. But I'm serious here, Sara. You just don't understand her."

"And you do?"

"I'll tell you something," he says, settling down on the edge of my desk, folding his arms all contemplative like. "Know who your aunt reminds me of sometimes? She reminds me of ol' Prince Myshkin."

I give him a blank stare. "I'm supposed to know who that is?"

"Pardon me, Boss. I apologize for making a literary allusion in the presence of a college graduate like yourself, when all I ever managed to do was scrape through high school. I just assumed, you know, that in the oh-so-ivory towers of your university, they did still read—you know—books?"

"If you're going to educate me, Huey, just do it. We've already crowned you smartest person in the office. I've got nothing left to give you."

"Prince Myshkin," he says. "From the Dosty-evsky novel."

"*Dostoevsky*," I correct him, then wince at my own puniness.

"So you know how to say it, you just ain't read it. I guess that diploma was worth something. Anyway, this prince, he's what they call a holy fool. What people mistake for his stupidity or slowness isn't that—it's actually goodness, innocence. Only they live in a world so far gone they can't even recognize those things for what they are and have to twist them. I think Bel's a little bit like that. She's too good to be understood."

"You just think she's pretty," I say.

He gives me a sly smile. "She is too. But this other thing applies just as much. I think you'd see it if she didn't make you uncomfortable. And why is that?"

Huey can talk to me this way because he talks to everybody this way. Somehow he's earned the right by virtue of his persona. Observant and unpretentious, always quick to speak the truth even when it's uncomfortable—perhaps *especially* then. But he's pushing me harder than he's ever done before, hard enough to make me wonder if what he says might be true. She does make me feel itchy inside. And maybe I resent that a little. It is one thing to resent a mother who broke up your family, and quite another to resent an aunt who, before she was old enough to feel responsible for anything much, left on some altruistic quest.

"I don't think I'm holding anything *against* her," I say. "You say I'm different around her—maybe so, but she's different around me too. She doesn't talk to me the way she does to the rest of you."

"She doesn't feel the need to make such an effort with the rest of us," he says, patting my shoulder. "All I'm saying is, she's a pretty amazing lady, if you think about it. Me, I'm not religious by a long shot, but even I can appreciate that. So should you."

"Thanks," I tell him. "I'll try."

Part of me wants to open up to Huey, to tell him about my aunt's improperly set arm and see what he makes of that. But Finn and I agreed to keep it to ourselves. I see the wisdom in that. Family is family, and if Aunt Bel wants to keep things to herself, even if I don't like it, I have to respect that. But I wonder what else she's keeping a secret if the resentment in my mom is any indication.

"What's the name of this book?" I ask him, catching him as he walks away. "The Dostoevsky novel."

"It's called *The Idiot*—"

"Uh-huh."

"—and before you make fun, you oughta read it for yourself."

After he's gone, I look up the title online. Over six hundred pages. I'm going to have to save that one for a rainy day. But this notion of Huey's—the holy fool—appeals to me. Suppose Huey sees something I cannot, and Aunt Bel is a holy fool, her dunce cap actually a halo. Which would suggest that, like Prince Myshkin's detractors, I may be too far gone to recognize goodness when I see it. Or maybe I'm too scared to.

Before I start the walk home, I call to check on Finn. He and Bel are running errands, he says. She's feeling much better. With Huey's words in my head, I leave Diana to lock up the studio, going a few blocks out of my way to pass the camera store where Finn bought my Autocord and I dropped off my first rolls of film for processing.

"You haven't shot film before, huh?" the kid behind the counter asks. He hands me the square prints in an envelope, along with a disc containing the scanned negatives. If he's old enough to drink, I'd be surprised, despite the scraggly fringe of beard along his baby-fat cheeks. "You need to use a light meter, you know, to get the best results."

"I did use one," I say. "I downloaded the app for my phone."

The kid looks sideways and suppresses a smug grin. "I'm sure you'll get the hang of it. Practice makes perfect. You were getting there by the end."

On the way home, I flip through the prints. They're all under-exposed, more black-and-gray than black-and-white, giving the images a sinister film noir vibe. The old man on the stoop looks wraith-like; the boy whizzing by on the bike resembles the shadow of some monstrous bird. Even the basketball players appear ominous. Still, the results excite me a lot. The quality of detail, the depth—so much better with medium format than anything I could achieve digitally, or with 35mm. And the Autocord's taking lens is dead sharp, separating every subject from its background with beautiful precision. Even with the exposure problems, I can live with these images. The darkness lends a mood I find appealing.

As I reach the bottom of the stack, shots 23 and 24, the last two on my second roll of film, I don't recognize the subjects at first. Then I pause on the sidewalk.

They are pictures of me.

In the first one, I am sitting at the table in the kitchen, Finn facing me so that his back is just in the shot. I am talking rather intently, the camera capturing my mouth half open, eyes intense, one finger raised in the air. In the second picture, I am laying on the couch with my legs under me, my GOOD TASTE T-shirt pulled down over my knees, asleep in the glow of the television. Unlike the photos I shot, these are perfectly exposed.

Perfectly exposed, and also nicely composed. My sense of surprise at being photographed without my knowledge—followed by a flash of anger—quickly subsides, replaced by interest (these are really good) and eventually awe (better than mine). I don't like to see myself in photos—I don't have the kind of symmetrical features that photograph well, and the camera always seems to exacerbate my faults, capturing me mid-expression with my eyelids half closed.

But I do like these. The photos capture the way I look to myself, the way I look in the mirror to my own eyes—which I've never been able to get on film, despite trying, and had come to assume was uncapturable. Or perhaps unreal, just a trick my mind played on me, telling myself I looked better in real life than the camera could perceive.

Aunt Bel took the pictures. No one else could have. I'd left the Autocord downstairs, meaning to shoot the last frames on the roll, and she must have picked it up—two nights ago, three?—and done the work for me. I had no idea she knew her way around a camera, especially one so exotic.

I study the two pictures awhile, as people pass me on the sidewalk, until a drop of rain hits the back of my hand. The sky rumbles overhead, promising more rain, and I tuck the pictures away. The thought of Bel gazing at me through the lens of the camera, dialing me into focus, pressing the shutter release, preserving on a piece of celluloid the image of my true self—a more intimate bond between us than any moment we have experienced in the flesh. I feel a strange debt to her, for showing me myself.

———

The two of them have beaten me home. I put my things down next to the front mat, shrugging out of my coat and shedding raindrops everywhere. Finn comes in from the kitchen, the aroma of the chicken curry he's making for dinner comingling with his clothing and hair, and gives me an absentminded kiss.

"Where's Aunt Bel?" I ask, leaning down to dig in my bag. Then: "Did you know she took pictures with my camera?"

He looks to the ceiling, trying to remember, then smiles. "When you were sleeping? You looked so cute."

"Did you teach her how to use the camera?" I hand him the package from the camera store.

"She already knew," he says, taking the photos and flipping through them. "You should ask her for some pointers. I don't think your settings are quite right."

"Where is she?"

"Guess what? I took what you said to heart, and I think you're right. At first I wanted her to learn how to operate the press so she'd have something to do, a creative outlet. But that's not what she wanted to do— so we went shopping. Come down to the basement."

He leads me through the kitchen where the rice cooker is spitting and down the stairs, where he has draped an old waffle blanket over the hole in the half bath wall. Beside the wall, the worktable he assembled in anticipation of building my darkroom is now covered with oil paints and brushes and a pair of oversized Canson sketch pads, most of them still in the plastic. Aunt Bel hovers over the pile, her body swaying from side to side, a little step here, another there, examining and organizing, her bandaged hand tucked close to her chest like the wing of a bird.

For some reason, this touches my heart.

"Help me, Finn," she says, not noticing at first that I am with him. She holds out a set of paints, wanting him to help remove the packaging.

"Let me," I say.

She looks up, surprised. "Maybe this is silly." She smiles nervously, stealing a glance down at the pile of art supplies.

"But you were all excited at the art store," Finn reminds her.

"I think it's great," I say, inwardly muttering at Huey for always being right. "You might have some challenges, trying to paint one-handed, though. And the light down here is terrible. You should come upstairs."

"This is better. I like it here, and I don't need light." She looks at her wrapped finger. "And this! I have no idea what I'm doing, so I will learn to do it this way. I won't notice the difference. Maybe I can use my hand too, just a little. It's only the pinkie that hurts."

"You may not know how to paint, but you know all about photography."

For the second time today, I see her blush. "Not everything. But yes, I used to love it, a long time ago. I filled albums full of pictures."

"I would love to see them," I say.

She gives me an appraising look, trying to gauge my sincerity, and like it did on the day she arrived, her face darkens and ages.

"Yes," Aunt Bel says, her eyes clouded. "But they are all gone now."

"You can take more, then. You can use my camera anytime. Maybe show me some things. I have a lot to learn."

"If you would like that."

"I would."

From the foot of the stairs, Finn gives me an approving nod. We start tearing into the packaging, handing the paints to Aunt Bel, who organizes them by color. There's an easel too, which I help Finn assemble, and a pair of blank stretched canvases. I place one of them on the stand.

"All you need now is a beret," I say. "It looks like you'll have to prep the canvas first."

Aunt Bel shakes her head. "I had no idea."

"Don't worry." Finn digs through his jeans pockets and produces his phone. "I bet there's a video online explaining just how to do it."

I love this man.

And I keep my mouth shut about gesso. Finn's need to find things out is greater than my need, right now, to be a know-it-all.

9.
The Old Man

Holly is one of those people that you're glad is rich. That's because she knows how to be rich and still be nice. She knows how to have money without making you feel like you don't.

For our meeting, she has brought us all coffees from Grove Street. You gotta love that.

Holly leans over the conference table, her pale-pink, manicured fingertips touching the tabletop, nodding her head again and again, a smile bursting across her face. "This is *it*," she says, her blond hair curled and somehow looking longer than it did when it was straight, swiping either side of her face. "This is it. Just looking at it is giving me goose bumps."

She holds up her arm and slides up her sleeve. Yep, they're there.

"You like it?" I ask, already knowing the answer a hundred times over, still wanting to hear her say the words again. Why does Holly's approval excite me so much? Maybe because of who she is. A woman who has it together, a woman with taste.

A woman who wears wigs. That's it!

"I *love* it. Now—can we have the tri-fold printed before the event?"

On the opposite side of the counter, Huey beams with satisfaction. The logo Holly has chosen is the option he predicted she would, one of three concepts I came up with late last night after scrapping a week's worth of lesser efforts. He gives me a nod—*Good work!*—then saunters over to the Iron Maiden, where Finn is struggling to attach the new rollers. And doing it so earnestly. I don't know anybody with clearer, cleaner motives than Finn.

Unfinished projects be hanged, right?

I guide Holly over to my cubicle, pulling up artwork on the screen, my preliminary designs for the printed pieces. Now comes the hard part. Instead of the plain vanilla three-panel brochure she has in mind, I want to do something quite special.

The idea came to me as I watched Aunt Bel working on her canvas down in the basement. When somebody tells you they want to paint, you assume they know about painting. Not her. She scrapes paint onto the canvas with a palette knife, scratching up angles and ridges of haphazard color and then stepping back to stare at the result, sometimes smoking a cigarette (we decided to let the basement be the smoking section, which has kept me up at night wondering just how flammable oil paints are). Coming home laden with the stresses of the day, I find it soothing to watch my aunt's experiments with paint. One night, frustrated with a sketch she'd made, she ripped the sheet out of the ring-bound sketchbook, crumpled it against her chest (unable to use her left hand), then threw it to the ground. The mashed sheet landed at my feet.

As I picked up the page and started to unfold it, inspiration struck. I ran upstairs to retrieve the paper contraption my mother made to wrap my grandmom's ring for my birthday.

Holly wants a showstopper, I thought, and this would do it. Instead of a traditional corporate tri-fold, what if we folded the brochure in on itself, the panels interlocking like a camera's aperture, or like an origami flower? I grabbed a sheet of paper from the printer and tinkered with the folds until I had something that worked. Eric Ringwald's function is to bring the various pieces together. When you peel back those pieces, you find him underneath. The brochure would mimic this, each fold-over panel devoted to one of the charities he works with. As you open them up, at the bottom of them all—the foundation, so to speak—is the panel devoted to his work.

"That will be a nightmare to fold," Finn had told me, brimming with excitement. He is drawn to nightmare projects, after all. "It's brilliant."

But I'm not sure whether Holly will feel the same way.

"This is going to be hard to visualize," I say, "so I'm just going to have to show you."

I open my desk drawer and remove the prototype, a big sheet of Twinrocker heavy text paper pre-folded and hand-lettered in ink, panel by panel. Taking the piece from my hand, Holly opens the panels one by one, as if plucking petals off a rose, breathing silently.

"I've never seen anything like this," she says.

"We've never done anything like this either. No one who receives this is going to just throw it away, which is what happens to a lot of brochures."

"No," she says. "They'll keep it. It's like . . . a work of art."

"So you like it?"

"When you pulled it out of the drawer, I got chills, Sara. I absolutely adore it. You have a gift, you know that? You take things and you make them . . . beautiful. I am in awe. Really, I am."

No matter how old you get, no matter how far from the princess daydreams of childhood, there's a part of you deep down that still thrills at being told you are beautiful. Finn says so from time to time, and while I don't know that I believe it completely, it is nice to hear. Holly's words affect me much differently: *You make things beautiful.* They pour over me like christening water, consecrating me to the task of beautification, or at least helping me recognize and put into words my inmost calling. Yes, yes. This is what I do, this is my greatest delight, to take things and make them beautiful.

"Thank you," I say with a catch in my throat.

"You know what? You should come to the fund-raiser. When people see these for the first time, you should be there. It will be fun. You can get dressed up, enjoy the food and the music, and get to see the look on their faces when we put *these* into their hands. Come on, Sara. Say you'll come."

I've never been to a fancy fund-raising event, and the suggestion bewilders me. "I don't know," I say. "When is it?"

Holly laughs. "Sara, you made the invitation!"

"Oh, right. Okay. I'll come."

"Bring your whole team. I'll introduce everybody to Eric, and I'm sure after they see this, plenty of people are going to want to meet you—so bring some business cards!"

After she's gone, the whole studio is aglow. Diana comes over and Finn and Huey leave the Iron Maiden, all of them circling me for a blow-by-blow account. *Did she like it? What did she say? And* then *what did she say?* "And guess what?" I conclude. "We're all going to a party."

"Fun," Diana says.

Finn nods slowly from his desk chair, tilted back at an alarming angle. "Righteous."

Righteous?

"Party," Huey says, bracing his lower back with both hands, shaking his head. "When I want a party, I know where to find one. This sounds like work to me. I won't be wearing a monkey suit, I'll tell you that right now."

"A monkey suit?" Finn rolls his eyes, getting up and heading back to the Maiden. "Who even says that anymore? Just wear what you've got on. Everybody'll know your name."

Following him, Huey glances down at his chest, where his name is embroidered onto his blue boiler suit, which is flecked with drops of a thousand different inks. "What's wrong with what I'm wearing?"

A couple of days later I see a man in an oversized olive raincoat through the studio's big front window, cupping his hand to the glass to peer inside. A compact man, his thick salt-and-pepper hair sticking out from under a tweed cap, his boxy face belongs on a man twice his size. But somehow it makes for handsome.

"Daddy!" I yell, motioning him toward the door. Then I run around to the corridor to walk him inside.

I intercept him at the Firehouse entrance.

"It's cats and dogs out there," he says, removing his coat, water dripping all over the floor. Even his round wire glasses are beaded with water. "Hi, doll." He kisses my cheek.

"Here, let me take that." I take his coat. He looks as neat and tidy as his calligraphy in the camel blazer he's had ever since I can remember and a pair of neatly pressed gray slacks. "You should have called! I had no idea you were coming."

"Neither did I. It was a spur-of-the-moment thing. You don't mind, do you?"

"Of course I don't mind. Come on in."

"Hold on a sec," he says, taking my arm. "Is Bel here?"

"No. She's home, why?"

"Rita," he says with a tone of disgust. "She wants to know what's going on, but of course she can't do it for herself. You getting along okay?"

"It's okay. I mean, Aunt Bel is family. I don't mind. It was awkward at first, but she's kind of settled in."

"I want to see her," he says.

I nod. "Why don't I call her and have her come over? It's walking distance."

"No," he says, reaching to take his coat back. "If it's nearby, let's just go."

"Don't you want to come inside? Finn's here, and we've rearranged things since the last time you came. And I've got some new prints . . ."

He pats my hand absently, considering his options. "All right. Show me what you got."

"Come on." I loop my arm in his, taking him inside.

I show him some of my new prints, let him yuk it up with Diana a little bit, after which we find Finn sitting cross-legged in a pile of cast iron. Dad jokes with my husband and even bends down to test his strength against the flywheel, feigning a back injury when he rises in defeat.

"You've seen a couple of these in your time—eh, Walt?" Finn asks him.

"In my time? You mean back in Civil War days? I'm not that old." He steps away from Finn. "Huey. How are you?"

Huey comes over, wiping his hands on a clean-up rag.

"Still keeping the machines humming, I assume?"

"That's about right," Huey says, gracing me with a superior look.

"Let's show him what we're working on." I take my dad by the hand, leading him over to the Vandercook, where Huey has spent two excruciating hours mounting the polymer plates for Eric Ringwald's origami brochure (which is how we're describing it), locking up the form and running test prints to scrutinize. "We'll cut them along the guides—here and here—and then they fold up like this. See?"

He fiddles with the folds, then sets the proof aside. "Beautiful work, Sare," he says. "Now let's find Bel."

Somehow, all these years later, my mom can still lead him around by the nose.

"Let's have lunch first," I say, tucking my arm in his.

"Did I hear you say lunch?" Finn calls from his spot on the floor.

When she comes up the stairs at the Grove Street Artisan, Aunt Bel sees my dad and stops cold. "Hello, Walter."

"What happened to your hand?"

Finn supplies the details.

The lunch crowd has yet to disperse, so we have to squeeze around a table near the back. It is so tight that every time I scoot my chair, the woman at the table next to me gives an exaggerated grunt, like I'm squeezing her to death. Finn and I do most of the talking, leaving them to steal glances when they think the other isn't looking. Finally, after pushing his plate away with his sandwich half eaten, Daddy asks Aunt Bel why she came back.

Blunt as that. "Bel, why did you come back? What happened over there? Rita wants to know, and so do I. Sara and Finn deserve to know too."

My fork freezes in midair. "Dad . . ."

"I'm serious, doll." He turns to look at Aunt Bel and takes her hand and squeezes. And I can see them when they were young. The older brother-in-law and the little sister. Divorce might have driven the spouses apart, but those two were family. Are family. Watching them together, it's evident. "Really, Bel. We've given you a few weeks now. The mystery act is wearing a little thin, don't you think?"

The left side of her mouth rises.

Next to me, Finn looks into his soup as if an oracle resides at the bottom of the bowl, holding very still, as if the slightest movement might derail her answer. Neither one of us has put the question to her directly, as much as we'd both like to. I can tell that, like me, Finn is straining to hear.

"It was time to come home, Walter, that's all."

"You have to do better than that," Daddy says. "I've been thinking about it since you left the house. You had to have known your return would reopen–"

"Of course I did," she says. "Do you think I haven't lived with it every day? How could it have been any other way, Walter?"

"What are you two talking about?" I ask. "Lived with what every day?"

My father reaches into his pocket, pulls out a billfold, and lays a few tens on the table. "Bel, let's take a little drive. There's something I need to ask you in private." He kisses my cheek. "I'll see you in a bit, Sare."

They depart. Finn, cheek resting in his hand, looks at me. "Well, that sure cleared things up."

I smack my hand over my mouth and stifle a laugh. The lady behind me heaves an audible sigh.

———

An hour later Daddy drops by the studio. "We need to talk." He rolls a chair over to my desk. "There's a lot you don't know about Aunt Bel and your mother. I was hoping if I came down, I could at least see if there was anything left of their relationship, at least on Bel's end, to repair what happened."

"What happened? You can't just leave me hanging like that, Daddy."

"It's not for me to tell you, Sare."

"Did she tell you anything just now?"

"Not really. Just that Kazakhstan was filled with a lot of trial and sadness."

I click Save on my current design project and swivel to face him. "That's evident. What happened between her and Mom?"

"Did your mother ever tell you when Bel was in high school she'd run away–you were just a baby–she disappeared for almost a month? They reported it to the police, everything. When she came back, they could hardly get anything out of her. No explanation at all, except that she was back, and suddenly it was Jesus this and Jesus that."

I take comfort just then in the sound of Huey running the press like always.

"Bel was the wild one back before she first disappeared," he says. "Then she found Jesus, and suddenly she was the favored daughter. But for your mother, the disappearance was a nightmare. When Bel went to Kazakhstan, it was like she was running away all over again. But it was missions this time, so . . ."

"Grandmom must have loved that."

He nods. "Yep. I told them all when they let her go to Kazakhstan after the accident that she wasn't coming back. Rita denies this, but I knew. There are some things you have to be an outsider to understand. The family . . . they knew her, they loved her, but they never understood her. Not that I did. But I knew enough to realize where it would end."

"Wait. What accident are you talking about?"

"You'll have to ask Aunt Bel or your mother. I said I'd never talk about it and I won't. But I'm tired of keeping people's secrets." He reaches for my sleeve and tugs it. "I want to help her, doll."

"What do you mean?" This man is too much.

"Aunt Bel can't make a life in your basement."

"That's for sure." Not with all that mess.

"She needs more resources. You'll have to work with me, because I don't want her knowing where it comes from. She's gonna need money to get back on her feet. I don't want her to know it's coming from me. Can you make something up, some kind of story she'll believe?"

"You want to give her money?"

He slides a hand into his trench coat pocket and pulls out a box of checks and a debit card. "If you'll help me, yes. Rita's not in the position to help her, and it isn't your responsibility either. This is all I can do, but I'm determined to do it. I think this will solve a lot of problems for everyone."

10.

Say Cheese!

"Families suck."

The cracks in the ceiling stare down at me, lit by a chink in the blinds that lets the amber streetlights in. Next to me, Finn rolls over and rubs a hand over his face.

"You're still awake? What time is it?"

"Families suck," I say.

"Go to sleep, babe."

He adjusts his pillow and settles in. After a while, from the regularity of his breathing I start to believe he's out again. It's not fair he can sleep and I can't.

"Families suck."

The sound of my voice startles him awake again. His head pops off the pillow. Gazing around the room through half-closed eyes, he remembers where he is, then scoots toward me, coiling his arms and legs around me, resting his chin against the top of my head.

"That's why you start new ones," he says. "To get it right."

Not this again.

"I don't know why you think I'd be a better mom than mine's been."

"Are you kidding?"

"True. How can I *not* be?" I wish the thought comforted me.

He stifles a yawn. "We're gonna rock as parents. We'll have the coolest little kids."

"Kids, plural?"

"Yeah," he whispers. "Four or five, just to get going. Then we'll see."

I push my elbow into Finn's ribs, which only makes him laugh. He rolls back to his side of the bed, dragging the covers along with him, and tells me to go to sleep.

"Everything will be better in the morning."

"Nothing will be different in the morning. There's still gonna be a hole in my bathroom floor where the tile should be. There's still gonna be a rusty medieval torture device laying in pieces in the middle of my studio. And Aunt Bel's still gonna be here too."

"You want her to go?"

"No," I say. "I don't know. I mean, I knew my family was a little off, but why can't these two sisters even talk to each other? All these feelings generated by my grandparents and here they are, all these years later? I don't know. Something isn't right here. There's got to be more. Daddy mentioned some accident years ago in all of this. And do you know, when I last talked to Mom on the phone and invited her down to have dinner with the three of us, she made some lame excuse and said her good-bye about five seconds later."

"Sara, go to sleep. There's nothing you can do about it right now. And is it even your job? You take everything on your shoulders. Let the grown-ups figure out their own stuff."

As if it's that simple.

He drifts away into sleep and I let him.

I don't deserve him. Jabbing him about the floor and the Iron Maiden when he did absolutely nothing wrong. And he didn't even get a little bit offended.

I poke him. "I'm sorry," I whisper.

"It's okay," he says, voice so groggy I'm not surprised to hear a soft snort a few seconds later.

———

File today's Wedding Expo under the heading of necessary evils. Since letterpress is a fussy and labor-intensive process, much more expensive than today's digital printing options, the costs are considerably higher, which means clients come to us mainly on special occasions. The most special occasion of all is the blockbuster wedding. Tens, even hundreds of thousands will be spent, and a chunk of that change will go to fancy invitations. To get our share of the business, which goes a long way toward keeping the lights on, Finn and I started renting space at the major bridal shows—first in Baltimore and then branching out as far as Northern Virginia and Richmond.

If I had known that four weeks ago Holly Ringwald would walk into the studio with so much work and such a looming deadline, I would have bailed on the show this weekend at the downtown Hilton. We're up to our eyeballs as it is. After ignoring the schedule as long as possible, toying with the idea of letting Diana staff the booth alone, on this Saturday morning I set aside everything Holly-related and finally put my bridal show face on for the weekend.

"So you *are* coming?" Diana asks when I call her to let her know. "I thought you were going to leave me alone with all those bridezillas."

"Don't tempt me," I say. "Are you wearing the dress or pants today?"

"I don't know—how about pants?"

Since this is a smaller, off-season event, the doors don't open until noon, which gives me plenty of time to roll out of bed early, grab a couple of coffees and some croissants to go, and pick up Diana outside her Canton digs. She wears black slacks and a cashmere-blend V-neck sweater with sleeves down past her wrists, covering up all her ink. Since she chose pants, I'm in a charcoal gray wool dress with three-quarter sleeves and skinny black belt—we alternate back and forth for these events, variations in black. (Huey once suggested matching polo shirts as a company uniform, but no one took that seriously.) Down at the Inner Harbor, we sit down on a bench overlooking the water to have breakfast. The cold, gray funk that has enveloped the city for weeks seems to have lifted, bathing us in tentative morning sun that casts gold rays upon the brick walks and winks off the waters, rendering *The Constellation* even more worthy of a postcard. I've always loved that old boat.

At the hotel, we cruise the curtained aisles in search of our assigned booth, rolling two big cases behind us. We keep them pre-packed with all our display items, along with lots of sample invitations to give away. Our little booth is wedged between two larger ones. On our left is a bridal shop booth, its half dozen young attendants cinched into swishy white gowns, and on our right is a wedding photographer who's set his booth up like a studio, complete with backdrops and lights. He snaps photos of any woman he can coax in front of his backdrop, the images appearing on a bank of flat-screen TVs.

"Sign me up for that," Diana says, unzipping her case. "Like, right now."

I laugh. "Nobody should want to see themselves that badly."

Across the aisle a display of cakes prompts Diana to investigate, reporting back that they plan to give out free slices.

"That's going to be a problem," she says. "Don't let me eat more than two."

By half past eleven, we've arranged our invitations on the table we've covered in a tasteful black cloth and hung a wall of our posters to hide the curtained dividers. While Diana goes in search of food—she has one of those freakish metabolisms that keeps her thin no matter what she eats, and she seems to be famished in ninety-minute intervals—I wander over to the photographer's booth. He is a great example of a certain type the wedding industrial complex specializes in: a svelte fifty-something man trying to pull off rock and roll. Black skinny jeans and a tight satin vest, with an oil-black goatee and spiked black hair with yellow-gold highlights.

A real groovester.

"Want to help me out?" he says, motioning me toward his Tuscan villa backdrop.

"I'm not one of the brides, I'm your next-door neighbor."

"Go ahead anyway. My camera's always in search of a muse."

His showman's patter, full of false enthusiasm, is one of the things I hate about these events. So much obsequious fawning. Some people can switch it on and off, while others have been in the game so long that all the unjustified gushing and cooing has become second nature. I'm not sure which category he's in.

"You ever shoot film?" I ask.

"Not in ages. I still have my Hasselblad, though. I can't give it up, even though I haven't used the thing in years. Why, are you into film or something?"

"I've been playing around with medium format. I have a Minolta Autocord."

"One of the twin-lens jobs? Most of 'em are paperweights these days. Come on, let me take your picture."

So much for prattle between professionals.

Still.

I step farther into the booth without actually entering the circle of strobe lights. "I'm having trouble with doing everything manually—shutter speeds, metering light, all the stuff my digital camera does automatically."

"Even with a digital camera, you can shoot in manual mode," he says, beckoning me in front of the lens. "Stand over there."

"I like to be behind the lens," I say. "Not in front."

"Everybody needs to be in front of the lens sometime. Give it a try. I'll trade you some advice in return for letting me take your picture."

He motions me toward the backdrop. I find myself edging over. "Just one."

The strobes flare. I walk back, but he holds up his hand.

"You've gotta smile," he says. "Come on."

So I stand in front of the Tuscan villa, put my hands on my hips, and smile. The strobes flash once, twice, and then I drop my hands and get clear. "Now what's your advice?"

"Next time you're shooting with your film camera, take your digital with you too. You can use it as a meter. Focus your subject, get the settings, and adjust the other camera accordingly. See? It's a lot simpler than guesswork."

"But it's a lot to carry around."

He smiles to reveal a set of new-looking teeth. "We all have a lot to carry around, but only some of us are catching it all on film."

And . . . boom! The strobe lights pop.

What are you carrying, Sara?

I gaze over at Diana, who's tweaking the arrangement of our wedding invitation books. A woman full bloom in pregnancy steps up to our booth and I have to admit, she's beautiful, her belly encased in a cream-colored sweater dress, her blond hair pulled back into a braid.

There were a lot of such women at The Community where pregnancy was exalted to not just an art form but a state of grace. Thank goodness we don't attend The Community anymore, or any church that makes a woman feel like crap because she's not living up to God's intended state for all females. "So when are you going to start a family?" they ask, as if it's any of their business.

And I know what they think deep down. They think I'm the most selfish person in the world. But those of us who choose to remain child-less have our reasons.

I just don't know what my reason is yet.

The woman calls over what appears to be her sister, the bride, and begins to leaf through our books.

I walk back over. "Let us know if we can answer any questions," I say. But after a few minutes, and taking our brochure, they amble on.

Diana and I sit down.

"Have you always wanted to have kids?" I ask her.

"Have you?"

"Nope. Never."

"I've never been willing to settle for any old guy just to have them," she says, reaching into her purse and pulling out her Altoids. "But I guess, yes. Yes, I always pictured myself as being a mom someday."

"That's just it. I've never pictured that for me. Is that weird?"

"Not weird." She holds the tin toward me and I shake my head. "But not the average. Why are you so worried about it?"

"Finn."

"Ahh. Well, marital issues are definitely something I'm *not* equipped to speak to. But I will say, if someone were to be a father, Finn would be amazing."

I know. And how can I keep him from that?

But how can I do anything else at this point? Shouldn't you really *want* a baby to have one?

Despite being off season, the unexpectedly good weather brings the bridal parties out en masse. Soon we are slammed. Brides and bridesmaids, mothers, mothers-in-law, and a few dazed-looking grooms shuffle past us by the dozen, some of them pausing a moment to figure out our booth, others rushing past to ogle the wedding gowns next door. All afternoon, the strobe lights pop on the other side of the curtained divider and I hear the photographer plying his trade, treating every woman in front of his camera as if she were the goddess of beauty.

"*Work it, work it,*" Diana mutters, then cracks a smile. "They just eat that guy up, don't they?" She glances over at the cake display, practically licking her lips.

We give out a lot of cards and talk to a lot of women. By the end of the afternoon, we've filled our sign-up page and booked eight appointments over the next couple of weeks. As much as I dread working the booth, once we get busy and people start asking me about ink and paper, my spirits lift, reminding me that this is my passion, my mission in life. To take things and make them beautiful, as Holly said.

The traffic starts to thin after four, so I take a break and weave my way down every aisle in the hotel ballroom to check out the other booths. The best of them all is the tuxedo rental booth, three spaces wide, where two men in tails spin a couple of brides in an abbreviated, never-ending waltz. The ladies have their hair pulled back tight like ballerinas and they hold their dresses almost up to the knee, showing off midheeled Mary Janes and the sculpted calves of a dancer. There's no music—at least, none I can hear over the crowd—but they move in sync, holding their bodies as rigid as flamenco dancers, which is perhaps what they are. I don't know. I stand and watch them awhile, impressed by their unexpected elegance.

When I come to the end of the last aisle, I stop in my tracks as I see my mother.

She is floating on a cloud of worry, because if she's not out of her element here, she's not out of her element anywhere, and if there's one thing my mom is good at, it's being out of her element.

I sneak up behind her and lean over, closer to her ear. "The Universe is watching you," I whisper.

She jumps. "Oh, baby! Don't scare me like that!"

"What are you doing here?"

"Daddy told me about what happened to Aunt Bel. I have to talk to you."

"What's the matter?" It must be big for her to show up downtown.

"I don't want to rush the conversation, baby. We have to talk."

"Well, we've got another hour yet."

She nods. No surprise to her. "I'll drop by your booth when things wrap up," she says. "Let's grab a bite, okay?"

I return to the booth for the final stretch, contemplating the fact that Mom and Dad compared notes after his visit. So mysterious, the nature of their estrangement, resentments intertwined with lingering intimacies.

Why did they divorce? Really? They've never actually said.

———

My mother and I walk several blocks to the Afghani restaurant, Silk Road, on Charles Street. We order some kebabs—beef for me, tofu for her—and two beers, which, I assume, are from Afghanistan. I have my serious doubts about the tofu.

"Let's talk, baby," she says. "Now tell me about Walt's visit. He said Aunt Bel was hurt at the shop."

"I'm sorry about that, Mom. Finn was showing—"

"Oh no, baby. This isn't about casting blame onto you. She's a grown-up."

Like Finn says.

"He told me about her studio in the basement, and that she doesn't seem to be too set on getting a job, helping you all out with the expenses."

I shrug. "It's okay with me. She doesn't eat that much."

"You don't feel like she's taking you for granted?"

I shrug again, thanking the waiter who delivers our drinks. "Well, I do wonder where she gets the money for her cigarettes."

"See? That's what I mean. She can find the money for that, but doesn't help out with the groceries?"

I can't say the thought hasn't entered my mind, but I haven't wanted to be nitpicky, and family codes seem to be passed down. Aunt Bel gave her life on the mission field and I resent the food she puts in her mouth? Please. No. I'm negative enough as it is.

"He said he wanted to do something for Bel. Do you know what he was talking about?"

So that's it. Dad hinted at the money without saying anything explicit, and that's why Mom wants a heart-to-heart. She's fishing for more dirt. "They talked by themselves. I have no real idea what they said in their conversation."

She waves my words away. "He wants to set her up, doesn't he? Give her a little nest egg to start a new life. Unbelievable. I can see this man's moves coming a mile away."

"Mom, you're being ridiculous."

"Am I? Your father always had a soft spot for Bel."

"Well, he doesn't anymore. It's just the opposite. You know he couldn't wait to pawn her off onto me."

"Honey, you know nothing about men."

"And you're the expert?"

"Walt always had a wandering eye."

"No, he didn't," I say. "You're making that up."

She shrugs and sighs. "That was probably a little too much information."

"Are you saying Dad and Aunt Bel had a thing?"

She shakes her head. "It's all over and dealt with."

"Clearly it isn't."

"Your dad is a good man. He's an odd man, Sara. But he's a good person."

Did Dad and Aunt Bel have a thing? Was the "accident" more of an accidental slip-up between those two? One of those "We didn't mean for this to happen" sort of things? Is that what this is all about? This family confuses me. How can people who have all lived far apart for so long be tied so closely with the bonds of a shared insanity? Really!

"And there's another thing, baby."

There always is.

"What's that, Mom?" The food can't come soon enough, because as long as there's some in Rita's mouth, she's polite enough not to speak with it there.

"I hope you're not getting too attached to her."

So I'll actually have a consistent female influence in my life? "I don't think you have to worry too much about that."

"It does worry me. Because Bel can worm her way into your heart and then leave you when you need her the most."

"Is that what happened when she left for Kazakhstan?"

"That was years ago, baby."

These women!

"Don't worry, Mom. You taught me how to take care of myself."

Boy, did she.

———

Finn arrives home after midnight, signs of his assignation with the Iron Maiden in evidence all over him. "How did it go?" he asks.

He sits on the edge of the bed while I free my wet hair out from under the neck of my GOOD TASTE shirt, which I've just pulled on over my damp skin. As he watches, I towel dry my hair, rubbing hard enough to make my ears numb. I tell him about Mom showing up at the Expo and our hardly enlightening dinner afterward.

"Diana met Mom at the booth. She said, 'Your mother and Bel are so different it's hard to imagine them being sisters at all.'"

"I agree with that."

"I'm not so sure. They have some things in common. They both have these elaborate mental constructs that shield them from the real world."

"You think?" He doesn't seem convinced.

"All I know is, I don't want to be like them. I was sitting there in the restaurant, staring at my kebab, thinking, 'This is not my life. This cannot be my life.'"

"It's not your life. It's theirs."

"Before Aunt Bel came back, they all seemed so distant. I hardly ever saw Mom. And everything with Daddy was just nice and fun like it's been for years. Now they're back in my life in a big way, and I look around and I'm like, 'Is this it? This is my life?' All I do is work, and everything's falling apart all around me."

At times like these, Finn usually has good instincts. He'll coax me into his arms, reassure me, help me see that I'm overthinking things. But his instincts fail him tonight.

"You know what," he says, climbing off the bed. "I think you're being really emotional. If you'd just look at things calmly and rationally, you'd be a lot happier, you know?"

He pads down the hall to the bathroom, shutting the door behind him.

So that's my problem. I'm simply irrational.

He comes back in. "Sara, I love you. But you've never been happy. You know that, don't you? If it's not one thing, it's another."

"It's all I've ever wanted to be."

"Why?"

"How much time do you have?"

"I married you so I'd always have enough time for you, hon."

"Can we get out of here?" I hold out my hand and he pulls me off the bed.

"Let's take a walk," he says.

———

Finn takes my hand as we walk down Eastern Avenue. We're well past the Broadway Market, a large indoor market that's been in Baltimore for decades, where the smell of fish is fine and people come not just for the offerings but for the vendors themselves.

The people here make Finn and me look normal. Boring, even.

But the market is closed down and the pedestrians on the streets of Fells Point are the very last stragglers of an evening out drinking. Soon the delivery trucks will begin their rounds.

By four, we have made it back down to the Inner Harbor. I can't help it; it's one of my favorite places. Yes, it's touristy with its Cheesecake Factory and upscale souvenir shops. But some talented local vendors are tucked into the glass walls of the pavilions. Potters. Glass blowers. Weavers. And anyway, I like the water. I always have.

We walk past the Science Center, the chill of the evening finally succumbing to the dew of morning, settling on our heads and shoulders. Finn hasn't said anything, but he's active in his ways, telling me he's fine to let me set the pace.

Finally, we sit atop Federal Hill, looking at the lights reflected on the Harbor, the neon lights of the massive Domino Sugar sign up the water to our right.

Finn puts his arm around me and draws me close in to his side. "You all right?"

"Yeah."

"Sara," he begins, then takes my chin in his fingers and turns my face toward his. "I need to tell you something."

"Okay."

"I know you're not happy. There's been something dark inside you, something hiding. And it's been there ever since I've known you."

I nod.

"I've tried so hard to make up for it." He clears his throat. "To make life a really beautiful thing for you. To do for you what you try to do for others. But I always mess up, and instead of making things better, I make them worse."

"Finn—"

"Let me finish. But the thing is, I can't. I can't do that anymore. Because as much as I want to be the balm to your pain, the person whose love for you heals all wounds, I'm not the one who can."

"What are you saying?" I feel the heat of uncertainty and fear collect under my scalp.

"I'm saying I'm sorry."

"What? Finn, no."

"I'm sorry for thinking I had it in me in the first place. Sorry for raising your expectations, sorry for wasting time and effort." He rushes to add, "Not that I wouldn't have been there for you. I just think my efforts have been misguided. And it's not like I won't continue to be there for you."

He's right. I wish he wasn't. "If anybody else could save me, I'd want it to be you."

He leans forward and kisses me on the mouth. "I know. But maybe I just need to walk alongside you, not try and drag you to safety."

I hug my knees to my chest. I don't deserve this man. I lean my head against his shoulder and am filled with a feeling of gratitude unlike any I've ever felt.

"Okay. I'm ready to talk now." I get to my knees and crawl to sit between his legs, my back against his front. He circles his arms around me. Together, his head atop mine, we look out from our hill.

And I realize something. Finn and I. We sit here together and we watch the world, and sometimes it comes up to us like waves lapping against the abutments down on the harbor below, sometimes it blows upon us like the breeze coming through the branches of the trees. But it's always the two of us. He's my person.

"I've never told you about my imaginary friend, have I?"

"No." His arms tighten about me and he places a sweet, comforting kiss on the side of my neck. "What did you name him?"

"Jason. Although imaginary friends seem to name themselves. At least mine came with one."

"Jason," he repeats.

I nod. "I remember my father putting a stop to it. He said, 'I don't care if you have an imaginary friend, and it's okay with me if you name him Jason. But please, don't use that name around your mother. That's all I ask.'"

"That's odd. Don't you think?"

"I never thought about it before."

"So your little friend . . . is he still around? What is he like?"

Tears prick at the corners of my eyes. Finn and I, we were friends first. For over a year. And sometimes, like right now, it shows. He doesn't call me crazy or laugh at my childishness. He's totally on board, instantly in the boat with me.

"He's actually just a baby. But it's in his eyes, like he knows so much more than his size and age would tell you."

"Is he nice to you? Does he like you, Sara?"

"He's sad, Finn. And it makes me so terribly sad. I know he's around because I did something. I did something really wrong. And I don't know what it is."

There it is. I said the words out loud. I'd never even voiced them as words in my own mind, keeping it a misty feeling as deep as feelings will go.

"Then you need to find out."

"I don't even know where to begin. And there's more, I think. I think. I think it might have to do with my mom and dad's divorce."

"Wait. You think you're responsible for your parents' divorce?"

Tears overflow the bottom rims of my eyelids. "Yes," I whisper. "I do. I've known that since the day my mother told me our family would never be the same again."

"Babe, most children think that sort of thing, but it's never true."

I turn around in the circle of his arms to look at him. I take his beautiful face in my hands. "Would I even tell you that if I didn't think it was true?"

He shakes his head. "No. No, Sara. You're smart enough to know the difference."

11.

Image of the Invisible

A string of fine days is all it takes, days where the sun rises early, warm and clear, then refuses to be budged by wind or concealed by cloud, to make a distant memory of the gray rainy fog we have been living in for the last couple of weeks. Finn and I start sleeping with the window open, lulled by street sounds and early-morning birdsong into a state of dazed bliss. It's chemical, I'm sure, our bodies recalled to their umbilical link with the physical world, something I am more conscious of than he is, being tethered already to the cycles of the moon.

At the back of the house, right outside the kitchen door, we have a tiny wooden deck just large enough for a hand-me-down wrought-iron bistro table and some outdoor chairs. Finn built the platform one weekend after tearing out the charming, trellised nook that had been there before, promising something bigger and better. He left the project unfinished—the steps down to the minuscule patch of yard and the fence separating us from the house to our rear consist only of precariously stacked cinder blocks—but now that the weather has turned, it's a perfect spot to catch the morning sun, so we fall into the habit of having breakfast outside.

I see this deck differently now. I see the bathroom tile differently. As well as the gouges on the floor in Aunt Bel's room.

I come downstairs most days to find freshly ground coffee brewing and Finn at the stove, cooking omelets in the skillet. Aunt Bel, also an early riser, will already be outside, still in her robe with her legs tucked under her, smoking a cigarette and drinking orange juice. "Breakfast of Champions," I'll say, or something in that vein, and she'll give the cigarette an appraising look—not a twinge of guilt—before saying good morning and raising it to her lips for another drag. Her fingers are always covered in dry paint now, especially around the nails, as if she's been scratching at her canvas with her bare hands.

She smells of linseed oil too. I like that.

She hasn't opened up to me since Daddy's surprise visit. When I ask about the past, she's every bit as evasive as before. But we have become closer somehow. I like to come home and see what she's been doing down in the basement, to sit on the steps and watch her make an ugly mess on the canvas. She doesn't know how to draw, doesn't know how to create the visual abstractions with brush or knife that read to the eye as convincing detail. She isn't interested in learning either. One Sunday night after the Microchurch broke up, I mentioned her painting to Rick, who offered to introduce her to his painter friend, the one who'd created the mural in the church. Aunt Bel shut this down straightaway and seemed miffed that I would even mention something so private as her painting to Rick. Whatever drives her, it certainly isn't the desire to learn or improve. And recognition? Not even a little bit.

Maybe that's why I find the process so soothing to be around. It's the physical embodiment of white noise, affecting me just like the change of seasons. Some evenings I take my Autocord downstairs with me, and when she's not too absorbed in the process, she tells me how during her first years in Kazakhstan she snapped hundreds of photos with the 35mm camera my grandfather had bought her for a high school photography class. Since my chat with the photographer at the Wedding Expo, I've been taking a lot of photos, using my digital SLR along with the light meter app on my phone, trying to get the hang of manual settings. Aunt Bel, however, is as uninterested in the technical minutia of photography as she is in the technique of painting. For her the process is, from first to last, one of emotion.

The question I want to ask is about the little boy in the photo on her dresser. Did she take that picture? Who is the boy? I never quite bring myself to ask, though, because I'm afraid of pushing. Let her open up at her own pace. *There's no rush*, I tell myself. She will talk about the past when she's ready, and not before. Still, I do wish she would open up.

And she never talks about God either. That seems kind of strange for a missionary. If that's what she was. I don't even know that anymore.

One night, while Finn is working late at the studio with Huey, trying to rebuild the used motor he bought to replace the Iron Maiden's treadle, I realize that maybe I haven't opened up to her either. Maybe somebody's got to be the one to start that in a relationship. I mean, that makes sense, right? So I talk to Aunt Bel about Finn's desire to start having babies.

"Where does that even come from?" I say.

"I didn't really want to have kids," she says. "But as for Finn, maybe you can simply chalk it up to instinct. It is a natural desire for men to want to reproduce, Sara." Aunt Bel is working on something she started earlier, a crude face built on top of a gold-and-black checkerboard, a primitive asymmetrical grid of muddy gilt and grime. She runs her finger thoughtfully along the dried ridge of clumped paint that forms the chin. "You don't want to have children?"

I pause before answering. It's a complicated question. "I'm fine with it, in theory. But no. Not yet. Babies are fragile, Aunt Bel. I don't trust myself with a baby. And Finn, as apt as he would be to care for our kids at least fifty-fifty . . . I mean, you can't send them back, right? If you're not the parent you'd hoped you'd be, you're pretty much stuck with it, you know?"

Her finger pauses, and I can tell she doesn't like what I've said. The same thing happens when I'm too blunt with friends who have children. You speak in less-than-fawning ways about the reality of kids and they react like you've uttered blasphemy. Or maybe it's something else. Maybe I've revealed too much.

"'Stuck with it' is too harsh," I say. "But what I mean is, your whole life is changed." I was about to say, *Your whole life is turned upside down*, but maybe that's too honest for my aunt too. "Maybe it was different before you left, but these days, if you have kids, people think your whole life should revolve around them—especially if you're the mom. I mean, I have friends I can't even talk to anymore, can't have a serious conversation with, because they can't think anymore except in baby talk. They're choking for air, spread way too thin, no time to get together, and I'm the bad guy."

"Tell me," Aunt Bel says, still pondering her painting. "Why do you think you'd be such a terrible mother?"

"I'm not sure. I've just never trusted myself around kids. I don't even like to hold babies."

"Did you drop one sometime or something?" Her eyes bore into mine.

I shake my head. "No. Not that I can remember. There's nothing like that."

She picks up a paintbrush and points it at me. "Then you're just like ninety-nine percent of all women. You just admit it."

"Maybe. But it feels different."

"How would you know?"

She has a point.

"This isn't criticism," she says. "Only an observation. I look back at my parents, the things they thought were important, and I wonder if my choices—which I thought at the time were my own—were shaped too much by a reaction to them. To all the family, really. Coming home, it's been on my mind a lot. Why did I go, Sara?" She shakes her head. "But this conversation isn't about me. I think you're being too hard on yourself. You'll make a wonderful mother."

"You really think I'm hard on myself?"

"You seem very sure you're not worthy to have a baby."

Worthy.

Huh.

"But who's worthy to do anything, if you think about it?" she says. "You can only try. And even then, you may think you're doing the right thing, and it's so far off the mark. But yet, what else could you have done?"

My conversations with Aunt Bel often go this way—tentative observations put forward only to die the death of a thousand qualifications—but this is different. She's not just hinting at something now, she's saying it.

"My father mentioned something about an accident. Something that happened before you left for the field."

She stares at me, unblinking.

So we're going that route again. "Never mind. Forget I brought that up."

"Sure." The left side of her mouth rises. "If you say so, Sara."

I can't help but smile back.

Still, I might as well go for broke.

"Aunt Bel," I ask, "who is the boy in the photo, the one you keep on the dresser in your room?"

"Just a little boy," she says, "from a long time ago."

"What was his name?"

She thinks about this, but doesn't answer.

"Tell me about him."

"Well," she says, walking to the worktable, absently turning the pages of her sketchbook. "Like you said. Everything changes, and then . . . you're stuck with it."

"Was he yours? You never said you'd had a child."

Now she's reaching for her cigarettes, her hands shaking. She puts the pack to her lips, pulls it away with one stick between her teeth, then lets out a deep sigh and snatches it away.

"Oh, Sara," she says, "there are so many things I never want to think about again. But not him. I can't forget him, but it hurts me to remember."

To my dismay, her eyes shine with tears. Her shoulders slump and I go to her, enfolding her in my arms. She feels fragile and slight to the touch.

"Where is he now, Aunt Bel?" I whisper.

She pulls away from me, covering her mouth with one of her paint-stained hands, eyes bulging with grief. Shaking her head in a gesture of forlorn negation. Saying no to me, no to the idea of the boy, to his very existence. Maybe no to the world too, and to its maker above. Staring at my aunt, I gaze into a pit of inconceivable loss and find that I cannot sustain this gaze, not even for a moment. I have to look away, my heart swelling with kindred shame.

———

After that night in the basement, I treat Aunt Bel like a fresh wound. *Leave her to heal*, I tell myself. *Don't pick at the scab, or else.* I tell myself this is for her benefit, though it is probably for mine as well.

Is the boy her child? Her failure to deny my assumption seems to confirm it. And was the boy left behind in Kazakhstan? No, surely not. The distance between them, judging by the shattering effect of his memory, must be more than geographic. *Bel had a child*, I tell myself, *and that child died.* And there I was, complaining to her about my fear of motherhood cramping my personal style.

So I see her at breakfast each morning and make my flippant remark about her combination of orange juice and cigarettes. And when I visit my aunt in her basement studio, I am careful not to prod her anymore.

But we are linked. I know this now because in her eyes, I see something I put there. She ran away because of me.

I can't even talk to Finn about this one.

I've never believed in ESP or even highly developed intuition. I think most things are as you see them if you care enough to cut to the heart of the matter. And perhaps this isn't any different. Perhaps once I get the nerve up to talk to my mother . . .

But I know Aunt Bel came to my house for a reason. I am the reason. And she is the reason. You can call it ESP, intuition, or whatever else you'd like. But I know this to be true.

———

"Guess who's in town?" Finn asks, leaning against my desk.

"I don't know. Tell me."

"You have to guess," he says.

"I love you, baby, but you're working my last nerve." I've just sent the e-mail to Holly with a link to the website we've spent the last three weeks building from the ground up. What I want to do at this moment is sit quietly at my computer, hitting the Refresh button every few seconds for Holly's reply. I hit Refresh for good measure. "Just spit it out," I say.

"You're not going to at least try? Okay, okay. Ethan and Dora called.

They want to meet up. They're over at the Walters Art Gallery and want us to join them."

"You mean right now?"

"Yeah, right now. Let's get out of here. You could use the break— besides, it's Ethan and Dora, so you can't say no."

And of course he's right. I smile and offer him my hand and we whisk away as if suddenly invited to the coolest party of the year. Which, in a way, we have been.

Dora Katz and Ethan Lime own a Brooklyn lifestyle store, one of those über-curated bastions of taste that sells everything from high-end designer furniture and coffee table books to imported European toothpaste. When they decided to add a section of paper goods, instead of flipping through the Kikkerland catalog they went out and made their own discoveries, including an obscure line of letterpress posters and greeting cards created here at the Firehouse. It was only once our work showed up at Katz Lime that the retail side of the business became viable. Though it's still small—supplementing the income from local clients without threatening to replace it anytime soon—I have high hopes, thanks in part to the way Dora and Ethan have embraced us.

You don't meet the couple behind Katz Lime in the ordinary way for lunch or dinner. They don't show up at the office for a meeting. Instead, Finn will get a call from Ethan out of the blue, saying they're in Baltimore unexpectedly and inviting us to meet them at some artist's warehouse space, or at Edgar Allan Poe's house, or at the Walters, where we find them side by side on one of the brown leather sofas, looking at a nineteenth-century Spanish painting of a bunch of shawled women huddled in the rain on the steps of a church as a black-clad minister approaches beneath an umbrella. The doors of the church are framed in dark green wood, the baroque ornamentation of the tiny window beside them in stark contrast to the building's gray-white stucco plainness. Dora and Ethan watch the painting with rapt attention, the way people sit and watch movies, as if the figures might suddenly move and the scene change.

Dora wears black leggings and an amorphous dolman-sleeved top that's part dress and part cape, the loud pop-art print rather striking in a gallery full of eighteenth- and nineteenth-century paintings with their fancy gilded frames. Not my kind of thing, but it works for Dora Katz. Bright red lipstick, big smoky eyes, Dora's face is more of a mask than a face, as much an accessory as her hoof-like ankle boots or her black leather clutch. Small and squarish, without the advantages of height or natural beauty, Dora is one of those women who dresses for other women without reference to the taste of men, her look every bit as curated as her famous store. None of her attraction is inherited or genetic. It is entirely earned. I am in awe of her and always have been, because she is so utterly self-made.

Ethan, on the other hand, always looks like he's walked out of the Katz Lime look book, dressed in whatever the store is selling at the moment—in this case, the American workwear look, which his slight frame lends an innate irony. An immaculately tailored plaid shirt with snap buttons, Japanese selvedge jeans rolled at the ankle to reveal very expensive-looking shell cordovan work boots, the kind no actual work-man would dream of wearing to a construction site. He gazes at the painting through clear plastic-framed glasses I'd bet a thousand dollars were handmade by a luxury craftsman.

Their respective looks sum up their personalities well: Ethan is always on trend, and Dora is a trend unto herself. Ethan's money comes from Wall Street, though he had the good sense to retire early and pursue his true love. I'm not sure about Dora's background. She probably sprang fully formed from the forehead of Zeus, or emerged out of a bedazzled seashell.

"Isn't it magnificent?" Ethan says, motioning us over to see the painting.

We sit beside them, quietly observing. Finn gives me a subtle nudge, and I can imagine him regaling Huey and Diana with the whole story afterward: "We barely said hello, we just sat and looked at this painting! Talk about eccentric!"

After a few minutes, Ethan leans over and thanks us for coming.

"We thought you two would enjoy this," he says. "It's called *Coming Out of Church*, and it's not normally on display, so this is a treat."

"Did you drive down just for this?" Finn asks.

Ethan shakes his head pleasantly, as if the thought of doing anything for just one purpose seems baffling to him.

Dora reaches across for my hand, a stack of chunky bracelets shifting on her wrist, squeezes, then lets go. "Don't you just love it?"

I nod my head. I do. After spending so many hours watching Aunt Bel's idea of art, it's nice to see a picture again, with recognizable shapes and colors.

We take a stroll through the rest of the gallery, the four of us advancing and pausing based on Dora's whims, while Ethan murmurs about an idea he's just thought of. Suppose he were to put together a line of Field Notes–style notebooks exclusively for Katz Lime? Would printing the covers be something we could do for him, or would it be too much? This inspires Finn to give a blow-by-blow account of the Iron Maiden's restoration, implying that our capacity for large print jobs is ever-expanding. I stay out of the conversation for the most part, knowing that only a fraction of the ideas Ethan throws out ever come to fruition. His success, I suppose, is the result of thinking of everything, but only doing what makes the best sense. If I leave Finn alone with him long enough, perhaps the magic might rub off.

"You know what I like about you two," Dora says to me, taking my arm in hers. "You and Finn are young entrepreneurs. We're the same, though maybe not so young. Do you know how rare that's becoming, people your age or younger wanting to go into business? Our daughter goes to college in the fall, and you know what she wants to do? She wants to work for a nonprofit. When I was her age, I don't even remember that being a thing."

"It's a big thing now," I say.

"Right. This is going to date me, but I think it's the problem with the younger generation. I wanted to get out from under authority, be my own authority—but them, they're happy to go on taking money from authority and resenting it at the same time, just like they do their parents."

I'm not sure I follow this, but I smile and nod anyway.

"Which got me thinking, Sara. They need role models. That's what's missing. And when I told Ethan, he realized, 'We have the role models right here,' meaning the shop is full of them, Katz Lime is full of them. They're people like you and Finn, the ones that design and make all the beautiful things we sell."

"Ah," I say with what I hope is an encouraging tone.

"And Finn was telling Ethan about your photography."

My what?

I've been to museums with Dora and Ethan before, so I am not surprised when we end up in the gift shop, where they buy an armful of trinkets to haul into the café, where we have an afternoon snack and discuss how a Katz Lime gift shop would differ from what we've just seen. "That's what we should do," Dora says, "open a museum gift shop. We'd need a museum first." Across the table, Ethan starts daydreaming about the sort of museum that would suit them best, while Finn looks anxiously for a way to help, perhaps not realizing the castles being built here are in the clouds. I tap his shin under the table, and he responds with a wink. Maybe he does realize and is only having fun.

When a gap opens in the conversation, I hoist my shoulder bag onto the table and pull out the proofs Huey made of the new card line—the trash-talk literature greeting cards. I spread them out on the table without explanation. Sometimes it's best not to preface the experience with words: just let the client look at the work and have a natural reaction, good or bad.

"Oh, these are wicked!" Dora says.

She and Ethan take turns opening cards, handing them back and forth. I can tell they're charmed. The more sarcastic the lines inside get, the more Dora keeps glancing at me, as if to say, *I didn't know you had it in you to be so catty.* Oh yes, sister. I do.

"Did you tell Sara about our idea?" Ethan asks. Then he turns to me, staring very intently through his clear plastic glasses. "The thing is, we think you should be the one to do it. There would be some travel involved, obviously, because we need to capture each individual in his or her natural habitat. I like the idea of those classic portraits, you know? Where some navigator or explorer is standing there in his ruffled collar, with his finger pointing to the spot on the globe that we wouldn't even know about except for him. Literal and symbolic at the same time. But I don't want to box you in too much. The point is, they have to have layers, pictures you can look at more than once and find additional meaning."

I glance at Dora, then Finn. "I'm not sure what you're talking about."

They all laugh, then it dawns on them that I'm serious.

"He's talking about the portraits," Dora says. "We want you to do them."

"What portraits?"

Finn clears his throat.

"The young entrepreneurs! I want to see them at their printing presses and their computer screens. In their offices or their garages or their bedrooms—some of them are pretty small enterprises, intentionally. There's a woman who makes our candles, and you should see how she does everything—"

"You want me to take people's pictures," I say.

Ethan nods. "Not just for the website either. This is going to be a display in the shop. We're going to blow them up, some of them wall-sized, and make a storewide theme out of it. Promoting the artisans behind Katz Lime, that kind of thing."

"I'm not sure if I'm the right person. I'm not a photographer, really."

"Don't listen to her," Finn says. "She would be perfect for this. She has the eye."

Under the table I give him another tap, this time much firmer. A warning blow.

"She really does," he says anyway.

"I *know* she's the one," Dora says.

"It's like Holly said," Finn continues. "You have the talent for making things beautiful. That's what this needs."

I curse myself for making Holly's words a personal mantra—or at least for confiding that mantra to Finn. The approval is wonderful, and the idea of taking on something like this, having my work showcased so prominently inside Katz Lime, is truly exciting. But that excitement gives way almost immediately to fear. They must know plenty of photographers much better than me. What if I agree to the job and can't deliver? What if my work doesn't measure up? The same doubts that plagued me after Holly Ringwald's commission recur again, as they always do. I'm not sure how much affirmation it would take for me to believe in myself without reservation. I only know I've never come close.

"This is for real?" I ask, hoping it isn't, hoping it's another of Ethan's blue sky ruminations that will never get off the ground.

"When we get back to Brooklyn, I'll have our girl e-mail you the list. There are twenty-odd names—all of our artisans. Obviously, we're just talking about the artisan lines, but that's still a good portion of the business. A lot of them are on the East Coast, but you'll have to travel farther afield for a few."

"We love to travel," Finn says, which surprises me. Since we put out our shingle, I don't think I've traveled more than two hours outside Baltimore. The last time was Antigua, for our honeymoon in the sun.

"Then it's settled," Dora declares. "I'm so excited about this."

"Me too," I admit finally. "And a little scared."

"Sara, there's fear and then there's the desire to do as well as your standards are good. Don't confuse the two. You can do this."

Ethan leans forward. "I can't tell you not to doubt yourself, but don't doubt Dora. She's got the instincts of a newborn colt."

"What a lovely thing to say, darling!" Dora grins.

And I do feel a little better.

When we leave the Walters, I expect them to say good-bye, but instead Dora and Ethan express an interest in visiting the Firehouse. Dora in particular wants to see the "funky old camera" Finn told her about, the birthday present that takes such incredible portraits. They follow us in their car, and on the way back I unload all my doubts on Finn, who brushes them aside.

"You'll do great," he keeps saying. "In fact, you know what would be interesting? What if you brought Bel into this? She might enjoy working with you, and you remember those pictures she took of you? She's got an eye for it too."

I remember the photos. The one of me sleeping is pinned up in Finn's cubicle, which makes me feel flattered and vulnerable at the same time.

"I don't think this would be Aunt Bel's thing," I say.

"Try her and see. You never know."

So I call Aunt Bel from the car to ask if she'll bring the Autocord from the house to the studio so Dora can see it. "I left it on the night-stand, I think."

"All right," she says.

"We'll be about ten minutes."

"I'll beat you there."

When we arrive, the twin-lens camera is sitting on the counter next to Diana, who is just finishing up a consultation with one of the brides we scheduled at the Expo.

"Where's my aunt?" I ask.

Diana gives me a funny look. "I'll tell you later."

While Finn shows off the Iron Maiden to a fascinated Ethan, I show Dora the camera and a few of the photos I've printed out from the scanned negatives. I did one of Diana leaning against the Vandercook with her arms crossed to reveal her inked sleeves, the focus razor sharp against the blurred background. Dora exclaims right away that this is just what she has in mind.

"You're a role model, you know that?" she says to Diana, who, despite having received plenty of compliments in life, may just have experienced a first.

When Dora and Ethan leave, Diana's portrait goes with them. They promise to send the list by e-mail and to confer with me on the schedule, then they're gone.

The studio is quiet in their absence, everyone pleasantly shell-shocked.

"Wow," Diana says. "She's something."

"Yeah. So what happened to Aunt Bel? Did she just drop off the camera and go? Finn was thinking she might want to help with the portraits, so I wanted to introduce her to Dora and Ethan."

"It's kind of weird," she says, leaning over the counter and lowering her voice. "I think maybe something's wrong."

"What happened?"

"She came in while I was with the client, so she went and sat at your desk to wait. While she was back there, a man came in. He was foreign, with a thick accent. A loud-talker, you know? I met him at the door. He wanted to see you, Sara." She laughs. "It was funny the way he asked. He said, were you the one who made the bird that goes 'tweet-tweet'? I couldn't figure out what he was talking about. I could tell he was making the bride a little nervous—he was a scruffy-looking guy, kind of burly, with a big mustache, like out of a Bourne movie, and like I said, he talked too loud. So I told him you weren't here, and he wrote a message for you on a slip of paper. I could have told him to wait, but I had my hands full and really, I just wanted to get rid of him, you know? Anyway, he left the note and then he was gone."

"And Aunt Bel was at my desk the whole time?"

She nods. "I was kind of hoping she would come and talk to him, so I could focus on the client. But she stayed hidden until he was gone. Then she left the camera on the counter and snatched his note. She read it, then crumpled it up and took off."

"You said this guy had a foreign accent? What kind of accent, exactly?"

Diana glances at the ceiling, trying to capture the words in her memory. "I can't do a good impression," she says, "but kind of Russian-sounding. Eastern European, I guess."

"And he didn't say what he wanted?"

"You'll have to ask Bel. She's the only one who read the note."

12.

The Man from Uralsk

Aunt Bel should get a phone. In the weeks since her arrival, I've suggested the idea more than once. "Who would I call?" she always protests. "Who would call me?" When I give the obvious answer—*I* would—she brushes me aside. Whenever I want her, I can always find her. Call the house, call the office, and if she's not at either one, then I'll find her somewhere in between. Bel lives a small, circumscribed life, and she sees a mobile phone as an unnecessary intrusion. I should have tried harder, though, because she's not at the office, not at home, and nowhere in between.

A few minutes after I get home, as I'm ascending the basement stairs, Finn walks through the front door, dropping his messenger bag on the couch.

"She's not here," I say.

"Did you check upstairs?"

I tap on her bedroom door. No answer. Turning the knob, I peer inside. The bed is made and the room stands empty. As I pull the door shut, a sudden panic overtakes me. My father's voice rings in my ear: *She ran away in high school.* Back inside, I pull the closet door open, making sure her clothes are still hanging in a forlorn row that barely takes up half the rod. On the closet floor sits her crumpled duffel bag, and her framed pictures are still on the dresser. She's not here, but she hasn't gone away either.

"I'm worried about her," I tell Finn downstairs.

He has already kicked off his shoes and switched the television on, scrolling through the list of trending clips for the day on Hulu. Seeing my agitation, he puts the remote down and sits up straight . . . but he doesn't actually get up or switch the TV off.

"She's probably at the park. She takes her sketchbook and spends hours there during the day. Maybe having to run your camera to the studio threw her schedule off."

"You're not worried about this man who showed up? Her reaction to the note?"

"We can ask her when she gets back, Sara. Getting worked up isn't going to accomplish anything."

"Fine," I say. "Watch your TV. I'm gonna go find her."

He reaches for his shoes.

"No, really, Finn, you stay put. It's okay. Call me if she comes back. Seriously. I just think there's something weird going on, and I don't like it."

———

I find her sitting on top of Hampstead Hill, under the shadow of the Pagoda with its stunning view of downtown. If she sees me, she gives no sign. Bel is in her own world—wrapped, too, in the chunky cardigan her friend Katya gave her. She is perched on the observatory steps much as the women in the Spanish painting at the Walters sat perched, her arms folded around her bare knees, pulling them tight in a kind of upright fetal ball. The scattering of cigarette butts around her feet attests to how long she's been sitting here.

"Hi, Aunt Bel," I say.

She doesn't respond. I climb the steps and lean against a stone pedestal holding one of several ornate urns that circle the Pagoda. Some kids on skateboards scorch past us, kicking their legs for speed before they reach the downward slope. As the sound fades, I stare down at her, watching the wind play in the edges of her hair.

"I wasn't sure where you'd gone. I've been looking for you."

Aunt Bel shifts her weight and squints over her shoulder at me before glancing away.

"Diana told me about the man who visited the studio. What did the note say?"

She shakes her head.

"Can I see it? Do you have it with you?"

"I need to think," she says.

"Is that what you've been doing? This is a good place for it, I guess. Who was the man? Someone from Kazakhstan, I'm guessing."

"From Uralsk," she says.

The way she pronounces the word, it's like the last syllable has to be swallowed or else she'll choke. I repeat the exotic word, trying to imitate that sound: "Uralsk."

"A place in Kazakhstan," she says. "Near the western border. One of the places I lived."

"So he's someone you knew. What does he want?"

"He isn't someone I knew," she says. "Just someone I knew of. I don't want to see him."

"According to Diana, it's me he wants to see."

She looks up at me. "No, you can't. You can't talk to him or listen to anything he says. Don't call him and he won't come back—he has no reason to come back. He had no reason to come in the first place."

"I'm sure he didn't come here on a whim, Aunt Bel. So what does he want?"

"Promise me, Sara, that you won't contact him."

"How can I?" I ask, making a joke of it. "You took the note."

"This isn't funny. It would be very bad to talk with this man. It would be dangerous for me."

"Dangerous?" I crouch beside her, putting my hand on her slight shoulder. "What's going on, Aunt Bel? Are you *afraid*?"

"You can't tell him I am here. You should have nothing to do with him. Will you promise me that?"

"Tell me what he wants, Aunt Bel. Why does he make you afraid?"

She shrugs my hand off and gets up, descending the stairs down to the sidewalk. I follow behind, my mind racing with possibilities: human trafficking, smuggling, espionage, dark secrets that have followed Aunt Bel home, things too terrible to acknowledge. *All ridiculous*, I tell myself, imaginings that result from having no other knowledge of that part of the world except what I've seen watching crime shows on TV.

"You have to level with me, Aunt Bel. If he's dangerous, you're putting us all at risk. I understand your need for privacy. But when your privacy puts Finn and me at risk, I've got a problem with that. Either tell me what's happening or I *will* talk to this man."

She spins around on me. "What? What did you say?"

"Look, if you're not going to be honest with me . . ."

"But I've told you, this man is dangerous." Pleading now, her hands clutching at mine. "Don't even joke about him. Can't you see? This man will destroy everything. You have to promise me you won't let him into our lives. *Promise* me."

"You're hurting my hands," I say, pulling free.

"All right."

"All right, what? This is serious, Aunt Bel."

"All right, I'll tell you."

"You'll tell me what he wants?"

"I'll tell you everything. Just for you, Sara. You cannot tell anyone. Promise me that."

"Okay."

We walk down the hill side by side, and for a minute there's nothing between us but silence. Not an empty silence, though. On the contrary, this silence is full. I wait for her to speak, tingling with anticipation.

"What I have to tell you," she says, "is going to change things. I am sorry for that. I wish it could be different."

"It's okay," I tell her. "Nothing will change."

My aunt hears this and gives me a look that suggests just how little I understand about the world.

———

She goes back to the summer of her arrival in Kazakhstan, where she'd gone with four other young women and seven young men to serve the Lord. They had one backpack apiece, and most of the packing requirements had been spelled out in advance on a photocopied sheet. Their destination was the capital, Almaty, where they would work with a missionary group for four weeks before being divided into smaller groups to travel west, assisting smaller enclaves.

"You have to understand something about me," she says. "The reason I was there, the reason I'd gone to Bible college in the first place. It wasn't piety. It wasn't missionary zeal. No, my parents had become convinced in high school that I was a 'troubled' person, that without discipline and structure, I was going to ruin my life. In some ways I believed them, I guess. It's hard to reconcile this with the way I think now, because I look back at that girl and she seems so innocent and naive to me. But according to Grandmom and Grandpop, I had a wicked way in me, as the song says, and after I ran away as a teenager—scared me to death, by the way—I figured I might as well try the program and went off to Washington Bible College. They were thrilled with my apparent turnaround. Everybody figured I went to Kazakhstan for the same reason." She rubs the palms of her hands down her thighs. "Whatever the reason, it was exhilarating when we first got there."

She recounts how the initial weeks in Almaty fulfilled all of her expectations concerning the trip. Working side by side with the other volunteers, rolling out their sleeping bags on the hard floor of an old building, they spent their days renovating to host worship services. It was as if she'd joined a commune of Christian hippies, a selfless unit intent on loving one another and serving the strange and marvelous people they found themselves among.

Traveling behind the Iron Curtain so soon after its fall felt the same as traveling back in time. Surrounded by real deprivation, it was hard for a well-fed American girl to keep thinking of herself as troubled. It was hard to think of herself at all—and when she did, she realized she was blessed.

After the building work was complete, the volunteers fanned out into the surrounding neighborhoods, rounding up children for an improvised Vacation Bible School, where the language barrier resulted in much more humor than confusion as they talked to the kids about Jesus, made crafts, and ate the only snack the youth in charge thought appropriate, punch and cookies. The fact that they were Americans made them a popular attraction. They could hardly have been more exotic to the kids of Almaty if they'd come from outer space.

As Aunt Bel recollects these events, she channels some of the exuberance she must have felt then. The worry lines recede from her face and she seems quite young. "My sense of myself started to change," Aunt Bel says. "I had always thought of myself as a Christian growing up, because our mother took us to church. Then in my late teens, I'd become a Christian for myself, finally owning the faith for myself. But if I'm honest, I don't think I ever knew Jesus until I met him in Almaty, living in a musty old tear-down surrounded by people whose language I couldn't understand."

Part of the change was thanks to the missionary enclave in Almaty, men and women from a variety of organizations, most of them fresh to the work and fearless. When the Vacation Bible School netted no converts—an unthinkable outcome back home—instead of lamenting their failure, the missionaries took heart: "The country had been in darkness for so long that, regardless of the outcome, it was a good thing just to spread some light. For us, the fact they were even there after so many years of being kept out meant that God was on the move. They used to say that a lot: God is on the move. God is doing things, whether we see them or not. And it was exciting to be around that kind of confidence. The world had changed. You are too young to appreciate this, but I had grown up in a world divided in two, East and West, and now suddenly it was one again. Anything seemed possible."

Another thing that impressed her was how lax these missionaries seemed. Their work left little time to invest in perfecting their personal piety. At the Bible college, she had internalized a sense of spiritual competition, always striving to outdo the people around her in word and deed (though mainly in word). Here that seemed not only irrelevant but counterproductive. It required more attention to self than their labor allowed.

"They taught me so much there," Aunt Bel says. "The attitude they took was so different from what I was used to in America, where we have so much anxiety about people's souls. I remember being so worried about saying the right words, having all the right answers. The missionaries in Almaty never worried about things like that, because they thought God was doing something through them, even in spite of them at times. I never slept so soundly in my life."

When their month in Almaty ended, their hosts threw a feast. Everyone they had met over the past weeks was there, smiling and joyous. This was the happiest moment Aunt Bel could remember in her life up to that point, partly because she had finally lost herself in the group.

"It was like we were a family," she says, "and we all had the same calling, which was to serve."

"It sounds wonderful," I say.

"If only it could have lasted," she says.

After the feast, the plan was to divide the volunteers and send the smaller teams to several sites in other parts of the country for the rest of the summer, bringing everyone back together in the capital at the end of August. The missionary efforts in Kazakhstan were quite new, and while a cluster of families from various mission organizations had gathered in the capital, the volunteers would now find themselves working alongside much smaller groups—perhaps just a family or two. Most of the volunteers—four men and three women—traveled northwest to Astana, which would become the nation's capital in the late nineties. They left first.

Following some phone calls to the western part of the country, the rest of the volunteers were told they would be heading to Uralsk in western Kazakhstan. The morning of their departure, a change was made. The three young men continued to Uralsk, but Aunt Bel and the other remaining girl were shipped five hundred kilometers south to a depressing oil town at the mouth of the Ural River on the Caspian Sea, where they lived in a grim Soviet-era apartment building with a newly arrived family of missionaries named the Galts.

"You know the painting *American Gothic*, with the farmer and his wife in front of the house, holding the pitchfork? That was the Galts. They were an older couple who'd spent twenty bitter years on the field in Turkey before the Curtain fell. They were nothing like the missionaries in Almaty. Living with them was a trial."

They had more experience than the Almaty missionaries, but it had consisted mostly of failure. Things had been hard for them in Turkey, which had taken a toll. Now in a country that was sixty percent Muslim, Herman Galt resented the people, their religion, their food, their dress, and anything else he could come up with. He spent more time holed up in the apartment than he did among the people. There were no renovations to work on here, no children to sing Bible songs with. Instead, the Galts put their volunteers to work mailing letters home to their supporters. Anxiety about failing financial support was a common theme at the Galt dinner table.

Along with Aunt Bel and her companion (a solid, sunburned girl who had never adapted to the diet in Kazakhstan and was always struggling with intestinal maladies), the Galts had a twenty-year-old son named Alan who lived in the apartment with them and a younger son who lived back in America with relatives. The girls rolled out their sleeping bags on the living room rug every night while the Galts slept in the bedroom. Because the quarters were tight and Mrs. Galt wouldn't have Alan sleeping in the same room as the girls, Alan was forced to bed down at night in the bathtub.

"Every morning there was this elaborate ritual. Alan's mother would wake him up, the family would dress, and then Mrs. Galt would come into the living room to make sure we were covered up before the men went outside. They would walk three flights of stairs down to the street, then come back up when she signaled them from the window."

We have walked all the way from the Pagoda past the bandstand, and now we're following the lights of Eastern Avenue, largely unconscious of the surroundings.

"What was the point of helping the Galts if they weren't actually doing anything?" I ask.

"Oh, but they were," she says with a strange laugh I have never heard from her before. "The Galts were arranging a wife for their son."

"No," I said.

"Yep," she said, raising her eyebrows and shaking her head.

13.

Missionary Imposition

Mrs. Galt had weighed Aunt Bel and her companion in the balances and found the other girl wanting. In her defense, the girl was often sick. She would have rallied—as she had in Almaty—had there been something definite for the volunteers to accomplish. In her state, however, if the Galts were content to leave her be, then she was content to lie on the little sofa, to read, and to sleep. After the first week, she started running a fever and throwing up every couple of hours.

"Herman made some phone calls and the next day someone from Uralsk showed up to collect her. I heard later that they flew her home early. But me they left behind with the Galts."

The more she learned about the family, the more uncomfortable her status as sole guest became. Alan Galt, as it turned out, had rejoined his parents on the mission field after a profligate spree at a Christian college in Florida that ended with his expulsion. What the boy needed, Mrs. Galt confided regularly, was a godly influence in his life, and she could think of no influence godlier than that of a pretty young woman who aspired to become a missionary herself. While Herman Galt sat at the desk beneath his bedroom window drafting financial appeals to churches in the States and working on what he called the Big Plan, a stack of typewritten instructions to the missionaries who would follow him to the banks of the Caspian Sea (he spent a lot of time pondering the great work he would do once properly supported), his wife invented errands in the city for Aunt Bel and Alan to undertake.

The first time they were alone together, Alan Galt confessed quite freely that he didn't believe in God or the Bible any more than he believed in Homer or the gods of Olympus. He wanted to be a film director or, failing that, a novelist, and he'd only agreed to come to Kazakhstan for life experience. By this time next year, he told her, he would be heading to Western Europe. Either Paris or Berlin, he wasn't sure which.

"Alan was a skinny, dark-haired boy not much taller than I was," Aunt Bel says. "But you know something? He could talk. I could listen to him talk for hours. He had this way of building a world around you with his words, bricking you in somehow. It's not that I gave up my beliefs for his. What happened was, I divided myself up, so there was the real me, and then there was Alan's me. Two different people, and I liked being both of them."

"Maybe you were both of them."

"There wasn't room for that kind of thinking in those days."

This idea of Aunt Bel's dividing herself in two reminds me of the first day she arrived on my doorstep, when I'd had a similar impression—one Aunt Bel shy and innocent to the point of coyness, the other world-weary and intimidatingly dark.

Through Alan she made other friends, including an old lady in the building who'd been deported long ago during one of Stalin's resettlements.

"She's the one who gave me the porcelain doll," Aunt Bel says. "As a wedding present."

"A *wedding* present?"

"She was very sweet," she continues, ignoring my exclamation. "And the two of us had so much in common. We were both exiles making lives for ourselves far away from home."

"Are you saying you married Alan?"

"I didn't really have a choice," she says. "I knew I couldn't come home."

Mrs. Galt's plan had been to throw the two young people together, letting nature take its course. Unfortunately, her grasp of nature proved faulty. Where she had imagined sweet purity triumphing over licentiousness, what actually happened was that, after a graceless fumble, Alan managed to get Bel pregnant, which forced her into a tearful confession before the Galts.

"I thought at least *she* would be sympathetic, but they were both extremely cruel. They said terrible, terrible things . . ." Her voice trails off, leaving me to imagine the worst. "And by the end of it, the crazy thing is that when Herman said there was only one solution—he would have to marry us—I actually felt grateful to him. I was bawling my eyes out over his kindness."

"Oh, Aunt Bel, I'm so sorry."

"He could be kind in his own way, compared to *her*. Mrs. Galt got what she wanted, just not how she wanted it, but she could never get past how it happened. Why did it matter to me, being a disappointment to this woman? I still don't know. But it did."

"So you married Alan and that's why you didn't come home?"

She nods. "My dirty secret. The worst of it is, Alan didn't care. He liked the look of me well enough, and when we were alone he seemed happy, but he never stopped talking about his future, never changed his intention to leave. And this future he described never involved a pregnant wife, never involved dragging a baby across Europe. In his future, he saw himself as free. Eventually he was."

Before the child was even born, Alan Galt had left the country, ending up back in America after failing to become either a film director or a novelist.

"I begged him not to go. I was desperate not to be left alone with them. According to Alan, though, the marriage wasn't valid because his father had officiated, and the ceremony—if you can call it that—was performed in the living room of the apartment, with only the old lady from upstairs as a witness. 'What about your son?' I asked. 'What about your son?' He said—and I will never forget the words, because they seemed so strange and cold. He said, 'The baby is nonbinding.' Just like that. Nonbinding. An unenforceable clause in an invalid contract."

"That's horrible."

She shrugs. "That's what he was like."

Aunt Bel and her little boy lived in the cramped apartment with the Galts for almost three years. One of the responsibilities that devolved to her was typing, copying, and mailing the monthly support letters, which would include copious updates on what was happening in the field. While he never made things up wholesale, Herman had a talent for embellishing, for making his efforts sound much more considerable and much more successful than they in fact were. To pad the letters, Herman included tidbits about the family, usually phrased as requests for prayer. *Pray for Mrs. Galt as she struggles with her arthritis. Pray for our son James as he prepares for graduation. Pray for our son Alan as he pursues his writing career.* And Bel would have to type these notices up as if nothing were wrong. Never once was her existence mentioned in the support letters, never once was her child acknowledged.

Then the Galts went home on sabbatical and decided not to come back. They never called Aunt Bel, never wrote. She discovered the news when the building manager informed her that she would have to move out of the apartment. The lady upstairs took her and the boy in. That lasted until the lady became quite sick and, after almost a year, died.

"By this time, my Russian was pretty good, and so was my Kazakh. You never really attain fluency, picking it up so late, but I could get by all right. After the old lady died, I took my son and went to Uralsk, where there were still missionaries. There was . . . a cloud over me, but they were kind. They helped when they could, and I would translate for some of them."

"Aunt Bel, did you ever consider coming home?"

Her nervous laugh sounds just like my mom's. "I never did. This was no longer a place that existed for me. Maybe that's hard to understand, but no. I was ashamed of what had happened to me—of what I'd *let* happen—and I knew that Herman had made up a story for the missionaries in Almaty about why I wasn't going back, a story that didn't include unwanted pregnancies and shotgun weddings. I said before there were two Belindas, the real one and the one Alan made, but really there were three, because one of them I'd left behind here."

"So you really were a missionary, then."

"No, Sara. I was a runaway who found herself in the company of missionaries. That is a big difference."

We have left the park behind, and now we walk down the amber-lit streets past darkened storefronts and bright porches and lines of parked cars along every curb. All this time she has never mentioned the child by name, the boy in the picture she carries with her, or explained where he is right now, or what happened to him.

"Your son," I say. "What was his name?"

She tilts her head, listening to the sound of our feet tapping the pavement. "I called him Michael," she says, as if he might have been named something else on paper. My mind goes there, imagining the indignity of the Galts imposing a name on her newborn child. *Alan Junior. Herman II.* I don't even have the heart to ask.

We have turned a corner and now the Grove Street Artisan is in sight, and a few blocks farther lies home. Part of me wants to pass it by and keep walking, and part of me wants this to end. Aunt Bel's story sits across my shoulders like a heavy weight. I'm not sure how much more I can bear.

"Did . . . something happen to Michael?"

"Yes," she says, but she adds nothing.

She's told me so much, yet left so much unsaid.

But I keep my questions to myself. Asking any more of her now would be cruel.

"You were gone for hours," Finn says, plopping onto the bed. "And when you got back, it was like you were in a trance. Did you find out what the deal is with the foreign guy?"

I blink a few times, then pull my T-shirt down over my head, crawling under the turned-back covers. "Not really, no. She doesn't want me to see him, I know that. She said he was dangerous—"

"For real?"

I nod. "Finn, she opened up about her past, and it's much worse than I imagined. I knew there was something . . . but not like this."

He rolls toward me, propping himself up on his elbow. "What did she say?"

"I'm not sure I should tell you. She made it sound like she was telling me in confidence. But if you want me to—"

"No," he says. "That's probably for the best. If she wants to tell me, she can do it herself. I know *her*, so I don't have to know everything about her, if you see what I mean. Just go to sleep. You look pretty beat."

I am pretty beat. But it's hard to imagine getting any sleep.

Long after Finn snores contently beside me, I roll out of bed and go to the dresser, opening the jewelry box where I keep my grandmother's cocktail ring and the little porcelain figure Aunt Bel gave me her first day here. I hide it there because the face's pearlescent craquelure patina reminds me of the veins of a vampire, a dark web of lines visible beneath pale skin. Bringing it back to bed, I set the doll upright on my chest, letting her back rest against the crest of the covers. That's how I saw the doll when she first gave it to me. I imagined throwing it away and waking to find it sitting like a succubus on my chest.

"You don't scare me anymore," I say to the doll.

There's nothing frightening about the little voodoo doll now. She just makes me deeply sad, like Michael's photograph makes me sad, knowing all the pain those tiny eyes have witnessed.

"Sara, are you all right?"

Holly Ringwald sits across the table from me, her butter croissant broken in two on a plate. Introducing her to the Grove Street Artisan, she told me, was a blessing and a curse. I know exactly what she means. I have the glistening fingers and the flake-covered plate to prove it. After watching her warm up to Madge, I can imagine Holly telling all her society friends about this place. We'll be swarmed by suburbanites.

"Sorry," I say.

"Seemed like you were a million miles away just now."

I give her my self-conscious, apologetic smile, knowing I must have been staring out the window again, still processing the story Aunt Bel told me last night. Even though Holly liked the work I sent her yesterday so much that she insisted on a face-to-face meeting, I can barely take in the praise, or even reconnect with the anticipation I felt less than twenty-four hours ago when I clicked the Send button. Somehow, after a taste of Aunt Bel's history, making things beautiful doesn't excite me so much.

"That's a beautiful ring," she says. "May I?"

I slip my grandmother's cocktail ring off my finger—returning the porcelain doll to the jewelry box this morning, I decided to wear it today. Holly holds it up to the light and talks about her admiration of vintage jewelry. She loves Art Deco pieces especially, even though she doesn't wear them. Not her style.

"How do you like something if it's not your style?"

"What I appreciate is the architecture. The way the jewelry reflects the design ethos of the period, the same way the buildings did. I used to *be* an architect. You didn't know that? Must be why I love what you're doing so much. The design process fascinates me. You're working hands-on, you know, but with abstractions. It's the perfect combination of the head and the hand." She holds the ring out.

"Yes," I say, slipping it back on my finger.

Her eyes take on a dreamy look. "The thing I loved most in my architecture program was making models of everything. You'd start with nothing, then you'd have your drawings, your blueprints—but it was the model that made it start to feel real. I still have some of the ones I made. I couldn't part with them."

It's nice of her to keep this one-sided conversation going. Nice of her to let me sit here and listen, smiling, nodding, enjoying the company of a woman a lot like myself. I remember thinking when we first met that she was the anti-Bel, an assured, self-confident woman, a success. Now I realize it wasn't being Aunt Bel's opposite that drew me to her; it was how similar she is to me. Or at least, to my idea of myself. Holly is, in a lot of ways, what I hope someday to become. Holly Ringwald. What a name!

"Do people give you grief about the Molly Ringwald thing?" I ask.

"All the time. Thank goodness I like *The Breakfast Club* or it would drive me bonkers. Of course, I knew what I was getting into when I married Eric."

"The things we do for love."

"Amen, sister. But it worked out right for you, didn't it? The former Miss Sara O'Hara."

"Did I tell you that?"

"It was probably Finn. Or maybe Rick. You can see why it would stick in my head."

"What made you give up architecture? If you don't mind me asking."

"Honestly? I wasn't as good at what I loved as you are. When I met Eric, I was doing the worst kind of grunt work at one of the big firms. Designing suburban strip malls. *Design* isn't even the right word. It's assembly line work, pure and simple. In school, I always imagined myself doing skyscrapers and museums and public buildings. I could imagine whole cities in my head, everything laid out just so. But you'd be surprised how few architects get to do that kind of work. Eventually, I got to where I hated it. One day Eric looked at me and said, 'If you hate it so much, just quit.' And I thought, 'Is that me? Am I a quitter?' I really struggled with that. I'd always been raised with a *put-your-hand-to-the-plow-and-don't-look-back* work ethic. Work is like marriage. You don't stop just because you fell out of love."

"Marriage is work," I say.

"Exactly. Fortunately for me, I could never convince Eric that doing a job you hate just because it's your job makes sense. I finally quit, and after toying with interior design for a while, this thing opened up at The Community. An opportunity to give back."

The thing she leaves unspoken is, it's easier to quit your job when you don't need the money. That's a luxury not all of us can afford. But I don't like Holly any less for having a husband made of money. If Finn were rich, I'd probably lie on the couch all day eating buttered popcorn. Holly invests herself when she doesn't have to. I admire that about her.

But then I think, would I? Really? What kind of an existence would that be? People think it would be the key to happiness. But I'm not so sure.

Since we're mixing work and pleasure, she starts asking me about the Microchurch, how things are going, how I feel about the experiment. It's hard to know how to answer, since she works at The Community, the church that seems to have inspired so much of Rick's and Finn's thinking, though not in a good way.

"You should check it out sometime," I tell her, trying to be diplomatic.

"And how is your aunt settling in? I don't see her at the Firehouse much anymore."

"After the accident with her finger, we've been keeping her away from the machinery."

"Has she gotten more comfortable being back? I got the sense she was having some challenges getting back up to speed. After twenty years on the mission field, I guess that's not surprising."

"She has a lot to work through."

"Oh?"

"I've never actually met a real-life missionary before, so I don't know what experiences are typical. I'm pretty sure, though, that hers weren't. There's a lot of . . . unhappiness, I think."

"And that makes you uncomfortable."

I have to pause and think about that. Am I sending unconscious signals again?

"Not uncomfortable," I say. "But if you'd asked me before she came whether I was happy or not, I think I would have said, 'I'm on my way.' It's something you have to work at, you know? Like marriage. When I see people who aren't happy—the answer seems pretty obvious: they're not working at it."

"Bad choices equal bad results."

"Yeah, that's it."

"And now you're not so sure?"

I struggle to answer, not knowing how to put my feelings into words. "I guess what I'm saying is . . . I can understand happiness as something you possess, and I can understand the absence of happiness, like a hole of contentment waiting to be filled. If that's all it is—a hole to fill—I can get my head around that. The thing that worries me with my aunt is that maybe unhappiness isn't a hole, maybe it's not an absence. What worries me is that it might be a *presence*." The presence I've felt in the room with me—for how long, I don't really know. What if it isn't an imaginary friend? What if it isn't the Holy Spirit? Suppose the presence in the room when I'm all alone is a form of unhappiness? "Something with roots and a whole history, something you can't banish with a little behavior modification . . ."

I can tell Holly follows my meaning. She leans forward, holding her breath, nodding unconsciously as the words come out. When my voice trails off, she sinks back in her chair, looking spent.

"Something with roots," she says. "I know what you mean. As if happiness isn't something to be attained. It's more about banishing unhappiness, or at least the reasons for it." The way she says it throws all my assumptions about Holly into doubt, and I can see that the questions that kept me up last night have cost her many more hours of sleep than I could have imagined. This abstraction of mine, unhappiness, is something she has worked with hands-on, something she knows from personal experience.

"You know what?" she says, lightening the mood with a forced smile. "We're gonna be best girlfriends, you and I. I can tell already. We're on the same wavelength, Sara. I resonate with the way you think."

Her convertible is parked on the street outside, the top down in honor of the glorious weather. I watch her strap in, fire up the engine, and pull away, waving until she turns around the corner, her hair, red today like mine, blowing in the wind. And I can't shake the feeling that Holly doesn't have things together after all. *Of course she doesn't,* I tell myself. *Nobody does.* But once you've tried someone on as a role model, it isn't easy coming to realize they might just need a role model as well.

14.

Thy Hand, Belinda

Back at the studio, paint fumes thicken the air while my mind is still buzzing with thoughts about my conversation with Holly. We put the whole happiness equation on its head, and I'm wondering what to do with it. Huey stands across the counter with his hands on his hips, peering at the Iron Maiden's pieces arranged on the floor in a more or less symmetrical grid, a real-life exploded diagram. Stepping between them with a paintbrush in hand, Finn daubs patches of British racing green onto primed iron here and there, tapping the brush against the metal as gently as a queen dubbing a knight. The paint drips onto the plastic sheeting underneath—and where there is no sheeting, onto the studio's waxed wood floor.

"Is that the best way to do that?" I ask.

"I'm painting swatches to see if we like the color."

I didn't ask him what he was doing. But whatever.

Finn fumbles the brush and it drops through the curved spokes of the flywheel, landing on the plastic with a wet smack. He fetches the brush, sets it across an open paint can, and nearly kicks the can over as he picks his way back to the perimeter of the field of Iron Maiden parts.

"Well," he says, surveying his work. "What does everybody think?"

Huey looks my way. He doesn't have to tell me what he's thinking. I already know. He'll have stood there watching the whole process, inwardly cringing at Finn's every move. Even if he didn't lecture my husband on the right way of going about things, I'm sure the speech was running in his head. He is one of those perfectionists who can't abide any outcome, no matter how good it is, if the process of getting there wasn't to his liking.

I find the green swatches quite nice, though, much better than the bald iron. "I like it. Let's go with the green."

"Hold that thought, though," Finn says, bending down to open another can. He dips a fresh brush into bright red paint, leaving a trail of blood-like droplets behind as he works his way back, streaking new blazes of crimson next to the still-damp green marks.

"Kind of looks like Christmas," Huey says.

Diana hangs up the phone and leans across the counter for a better look. "The red's not dark enough. It looks kind of pinkish."

"It'll dry darker," Finn says. "I hope."

Huey smirks. "Or, hey, just go with that. Big ol' bright pink printing press in the middle of the floor. That'll catch a lot of eyes."

"Don't laugh," I say. "It probably would."

"What's wrong with pink?" Diana asks. "This place could use a feminine touch—"

"I'm not working on no pink press." Throwing his hands up, Huey stalks off in the direction of the Vandercook, then whirls around suddenly. "And lemme just say, we're getting the cart before the horse here.

Before we start painting the thing, we better make sure it'll even go back together."

Finn jerks himself upright, speckling the floor with paint. "Everything that comes apart can be put back together."

"Tell *that* to Humpty Dumpty."

I point to the brush. "Wanna watch where you put that thing?"

"Sorry. But we'll have it up and running in another couple of days. The paint needs to go on first, otherwise you won't get good coverage on some of the parts. We'd be further along if Huey was helping in more than fits and spurts. This is a two-man job."

"The brochures don't print themselves!" Huey calls from his post by the window, a broad smile on his face. "The broadsides don't print themselves, or the greeting cards, or the wedding invitations, or anything else we do up in here!"

"Yeah, yeah," Finn says, slapping more paint on metal.

While he's at it, Aunt Bel steps through the Firehouse lobby and into the studio, peering through the door first like she's afraid of interrupting. She wears a light blue summer dress and sandals, accentuating the slightness of her form, and keeps her broken finger tucked with a wing-like arm against her chest, as if it were suspended from an invisible sling. Just inside the door, she unhitches a canvas shopping bag from her shoulder, leaving it beside the coatrack. Seeing her, Finn calls her over for a consultation on the swatches. Instead of demurring, as I expect, she goes around the counter for a closer look, unfolding the wing arm to steady herself against the counter.

"What do you think?" Finn asks her.

"These are the choices? I wouldn't vote for either one. Don't be disappointed. It's just—if it were me—I would keep the pieces as they are. Leave them raw and unpainted. It's more honest that way, don't you think?"

"They'll rust if I don't paint them." Finn's slumped shoulders and his flat tone are brimming with disappointment, showing me just how seriously he takes Aunt Bel's opinion. I'm surprised he doesn't shrug it off, the way he would Huey's dissent or Diana's, maybe even mine. He doesn't, though. I can see the gears turning in his head. "Maybe . . . ," he says, pondering a new course. "Just maybe I could clear-coat it? Put a clear finish on that'll keep the rust away but preserve that honest, raw look you're talking about."

"I like the green," I say.

"I've seen it on bicycle frames where they leave the metal unpainted so you can see the welds and the bare steel. It's a pretty cool finish, but I don't know how it's done." He pats his jeans and produces his phone. "I bet there's a video or something . . ." He heads off toward his cubicle. "Let me do a little research on this."

Aunt Bel gets to her feet, using the steadying arm to pull herself up. Even though she's putting her weight on it, the arm remains bent at the elbow and turned slightly outward. The break that never healed properly. She didn't get far enough in her story last night to explain that, or the man who visited yesterday. Reaching Michael was like hitting an emotional speed bump, or maybe a brick wall. No going beyond it, at least for now.

All I can do is ask God, though I surely don't deserve it, to keep us all safe if that's what's necessary. I hope he's not in a hateful mood and prone to let us all learn a valuable lesson here. What that lesson is, I can't say yet.

As I look at her, Finn's words to Huey echo in my head. *Everything that comes apart can be put back together again.* This is not true. And the man who said life breaks you and you're stronger at the broken places wasn't right either, whoever he was. The breaks may fuse, as Aunt Bel's have in her arm, but that isn't strength or even healing. It's just damage. Some places, when you bend or break them, will not mend. And you'll never move in quite the same freedom as before.

And I am honest enough to admit that this terrifies me. It's a low-wattage existential terror, not a scream-girl fear.

"You're not mad, are you?" Aunt Bel whispers. "I like the green too. It's a pretty color. I should have thought more before I said anything."

"No, I'm not mad. It's his monster, he can paint it any color he wants as far as I'm concerned. Or no color at all."

"I thought it was *your* monster."

"It'll be nobody's monster if he doesn't get it working. You may have noticed there's a pattern here."

"He's very ambitious. And he has a good heart."

"Yes, I know," I say.

Finn returns from his online research, but instead of popping more paint cans and slathering on a few more samples, he walks right up to Aunt Bel, rubbing his hands together briskly, and says, "Did you bring it? I wanna take a look."

"Bring what?" I ask.

Back around the counter, she retrieves the shopping bag from under the coatrack, then hands it to Finn, who sets the bag on the counter with reverence. Reaching inside, he withdraws a framed canvas about two feet by two feet in size. Not one of the pre-stretched ones we bought for her. She must have rigged it on her own. The surface is layered in black paint and gold, terra-cotta and copper, a charred-looking mess of ridges that reminds me a little of burnt toast.

Finn lifts the picture by the corners and holds it up for inspection. "Wow. So this is it. I don't know why, but I expected it to be bigger."

"The other ones were," Aunt Bel says. "It needed to be smaller. It needed to be whittled down."

"Why?" I ask. Other than, perhaps, to save paint.

"I don't know," she says. "Do I have to?"

"No, Aunt Bel," says Finn. "It's art. You don't have to analyze it if you don't feel like it."

She places her fingertips on her chin. "I'll have to think about the why. It's intriguing."

He turns the picture toward me. "Have a look, babe."

I have seen the image before—many iterations of it, in fact, though until now I had no idea the pieces I've watched her work on down in the basement were meant to be different versions of the same thing. I didn't know she was whittling down. Aunt Bel's work has all the sophistication of a cave painting. There's a face, not so much painted on as built up, the contours thick enough to stand out from the canvas, as if someone were standing behind it and pushing his nose into the fabric. There's a sort of gash for a mouth, and crescent-shaped craters where eyes should be, and all around the face, like a fringe or a lion's mane, the metallics are brushed on in thin slices that make me think someone took a chisel to a piece of fool's gold.

"It has sort of a primitive vibe," I say.

"Yeah," Finn breathes. "Really powerful, right?"

I hesitate and then nod.

"Let's go have a look," he says.

Aunt Bel dazzles us both with her girlish, beaming smile. She might as well jump up and down. "You like it, then? You both really do?"

"I think it's flippin' amazing. Right, Sara?"

"Amazing," I say, adding a thumbs-up just to be polite.

"Let's see it on the wall, then."

I hate this painting. I've hated them all since the moment she started painting them and, like my aunt, I haven't analyzed why.

Finn takes the painting and the two of us follow, passing through the lobby and down the back hallway, through the double doors that open into the gallery. I haven't been inside since last Sunday night. The skylights throb with clear white light, giving the gallery a clean, ethereal glow. To my surprise, the walls are bare. All the paintings that were hanging before—eight or nine of them—have been taken down.

"What's this?" I ask.

He strides over to the table, setting Aunt Bel's canvas down so he can fiddle with one of the art lights attached to the center of the wall. Then he grabs a coil of wire and starts stringing the back of the canvas for hanging.

"You're going to hang it all alone?" Aunt Bel asks. "All alone calls too much attention to it."

"No, it'll be perfect."

Frowning, she looks to me and mouths, *Help me?*

I have nothing to add, though. It seems they've had a whole conversation about this and I was none the wiser. If Finn had floated the idea past me, I could have told him this was . . . premature. Now he's going to cause her a great deal of embarrassment, and there's nothing I can do.

"There," he says, hanging the picture on the wall, then stepping back. "Wait, wait." He jogs back to the entrance and flips the dimmer switch for the art lights. The burnt toast cave painting absorbs and swallows the light, a bit like a black hole. Walking back, Finn gazes at his handiwork for a long minute, then sighs. "Perfect."

But Aunt Bel doesn't think so. Standing with her wing tucked in and her right hand clutching her left elbow, she starts shaking her head. Shallow turns at first, increasing in violence until I half expect an *Exorcist*-style three-sixty.

"It's not ready," she says. "I thought it was ready, but see that it isn't. I need more time. It needs to be smaller, a lot smaller."

"But it's perfect how it is, Bel," Finn tells her. "Don't you see? The *eyes*. Look at the *eyes*. I'm not going to let you touch it. That's staying right where it is."

She giggles like a schoolgirl. "You really think—?"

"I'll be right back," I say, heading for the door.

I'm not trying to be rude, and trust me, neither of them takes much notice. They're so absorbed in looking at the picture I could start pulling my hair out in clumps and they wouldn't stop me until I was bald.

Later, when I have him to myself, I can suggest to Finn that hanging my aunt's amateur crack at abstract expressionism for everyone to see will only expose her to ridicule. I can imagine them dragging St. Rick over to comment—Rick, who offered to introduce Aunt Bel to a real painter only to be rebuffed. There's nothing I can do for now, though, after being blindsided by the whole thing.

I slip through the door, pop into the restroom, then go back to the studio.

Diana nearly bumps into me, walking out as I'm walking in.

"Oh," she says, backpedaling. Then, to a man over her shoulder: "Here she is. Sara, I was just going to get you."

The man at the counter reminds me of a large, friendly bear. Portly, his face half-hidden behind a bushy salt-and-pepper beard, his smile reveals a row of yellow teeth with a gap in the middle. His belly strains against the weave of his black pullover sweater, the elastic at the waist bagging on the sides where he must have overstretched it too far trying to make room for his midsection.

"Please to make your acquaintance!" he exclaims.

From the accent, I know exactly who he must be. The man from Uralsk who visited yesterday. Diana's eyes widen, conveying a private note of panic. She knows as well as I do that Aunt Bel has no desire to see the man—or to be seen by him.

"You're looking for me?" I ask.

"You are Sara, the niece of Belinda Novikova? The one who makes the bird that says 'tweet-tweet'?"

My brain takes a second to process the accent. He's referring to the greeting card that Aunt Bel somehow got her hands on in Kazakhstan, the one with the not-so-subtle Twitter reference. And what was the name he called Bel—Novikova?

"Sergei!" he says. He offers his mammoth hand and I give him mine. I mean, who needs their right hand, anyway?

"You came yesterday. I'm sorry I didn't–" My voice jolts with each pump of his hand.

"It is my last day here"–he breathes deep and lets go–"in your lovely city of Baltimore. So I come to see you again. Is all right, yes? Over the phone is not so good, yes?" He raises his arms, and for a second I fear he'll put me in a bear hug, lift me right off my feet. That's the kind of guy Sergei is, I can already tell. He's about as dangerous as Finn, unless, I imagine, he's protecting someone. I wouldn't want to be on the losing end of that struggle. But Sergei looks around, noticing Huey over by the window, glancing at Diana as he takes another breath. It must require a lot of breath to employ that many decibels.

"I think," he says, reducing his volume to a stage whisper, "it is not so good in public, yes? In private is better. We go in private, yes? I tell you there."

"We can go over there," I say, pointing toward my cubicle. "That's private enough." Then to Diana: "You can go take care of that . . . thing."

She doesn't have to be told twice. She pushes through the door, heading down the hallway to warn Aunt Bel and Finn.

"Right over here," I say, motioning him toward my desk.

Sergei lowers himself carefully into my guest chair–afraid it won't hold his weight–and rubs his big hand over his mouth until the lips form a frown. The effect seems quite theatrical. A man pretending to be sad, or affecting sympathy for the sadness of another.

"What can I do for you, Sergei?"

"It is very sad occasion. I am bearer of bad news. I come to you from very far, from lovely city of Uralsk in nation of Kazakhstan. They send me because I am coming already to America, to city of Washington, D.C., where we have the great conference. I am the only one of Kazakhstan, the only one of the shepherds, to be coming there."

Again, my mind has to process. "You're a . . . shepherd?"

"*Da, da.* A shepherd of the flock of Jesus Christ."

"Ah, I see."

He's come here while visiting the United States to attend some kind of event in D.C., perhaps a world missions conference.

"What is the bad news?" I ask.

As the words come out, my skin tingles with anticipation, though somehow I know what he is going to say. He must be here to tell me what Aunt Bel couldn't. He is here to share with me the fate of little Michael, the boy in the picture, Aunt Bel's absent son.

"Is terrible," he says, and now there's nothing theatrical in his manner. He reaches one of his big hands out and cups my shoulder, the warmth of his body flowing into mine. "I never had pleasure of meeting her, but by reputation I admire her very much. Many people come and go. She never goes, she always stays. She shows love to so many people. I tell you, there is no one like her, no one at all. You be proud." He says something else that sounds like *ocean gourd.* "It is honor to know you, because she is your mother's sister."

"You're talking about Bel. Belinda."

"Something happens to her," he says. "Something has happened. In the middle of the night she drives, in the bad weather, in the snow. She is going beside river. A woman is sick. She goes to nurse her, but the woman—" He shrugs. "Maybe she goes to Jesus, is for me to say? She is very sick, this woman. Sick in the head since many years."

"You mean Belinda is sick in the head?"

"No, no," he says. "Another lady. Katya Aslanova. The good friend of Belinda Novikova—who has *many* friends."

The name rings a bell. Katya, the friend who gave Bel the sweater she often wears. Katya, sick in the head. Maybe she goes to Jesus. In other words, dead.

"Is terrible, but Belinda Novikova, she is driving home beside river— is very far to go from Uralsk all the way to sea—and when it is snowing, and road is slippery, that is when her car goes down into water."

"That's awful," I say. "You mean she crashed her car?" That might explain the broken arm that wasn't properly set. A car crash in the snow, followed by some third-world triage in some former Soviet hospital. Then it dawns on me that you don't travel around the world and track down the niece of someone you never met in person just to tell her about a car crash. There's something more to this. Michael. That's it. Aunt Bel must not have been alone in the car.

"She crashed it, yes," he says, with an air of finality.

"But . . . she wasn't alone in the car. Was Michael with her? Her little boy?"

Sergei draws his hand back, cocking his big bearded chin sideways. "Little boy? Ah, I see, the little boy. Yes. I never meet her with little boy. That is much—no, many years past. But I am hearing of this boy many times, a lovely boy. Yes. Is sad, this life she lives. When I think of all the good things this lady does, and so much she suffers—well, if I did not have faith, I do not know."

"So Michael died a long time ago."

"Young lady," he says, hovering his hand over me again, this time in what seems like a gesture of blessing. "I am very sorry to the utmost. The great loss you suffer, we suffer with you. We want you to know this. When it happens—no, when it happened—" He smiles briefly at the correction, then recollects the subject matter. "—nobody in Uralsk knows who to tell. There is family in America, we know, but how to reach them? Is a mystery. But one remembers little card, which Belinda Novikova cherishes, because it comes all the way from here and is you who makes it. How to find you from only this card?" Sergei shifts in his chair, raising both hands in the direction of my computer screen. "On the Internet! There we look, and there we find. One says he will call and tell you, but this is not for telephone. And since I am coming here, I tell them I will do it. So here I am, yes? And I am telling you."

He keeps his hands up, a benedictory pose, and murmurs some

words in what I assume is Russian, or maybe Kazakh. Then he gazes at me, eyes half shut.

"Well," he says.

"You came a long way for this. I'm not sure what Aunt Bel was thinking—"

"She is very good lady," Sergei says. "No. She *was* very good lady, yes?"

"She was? You mean past tense *was*?"

He rubs his lips again.

"Sergei, I'm not sure I understand."

"My English. What a pity." He raises a big crooked finger. "Ah, yes! Almost I forget."

Digging through the pockets of his worn corduroy trousers, he produces a lumpy wallet made of cracked green leather. Opening it, he produces a photograph, handing it to me. In the picture, there is a stone cross maybe three feet high, with the slanted notch through the top half that denotes an Orthodox cross. In the background, down an icy slick, a wide gray river flows, its banks piled high with snow.

"Because there is no body, yes, when they bring up the car? Some of our people, they make a little shrine so she is remembered. They want you to see it, so you will know that no one is forgetting her."

"A shrine for Belinda?" I ask, the photo quivering in my hand. It falls to the ground and Sergei bends to return it.

"She was good lady," he says. "And I know—listen to me, I *know*—she goes to Jesus. You remember that always, yes?"

Sergei rises, but I am frozen in place. He draws a deep breath, gazes down at me, then smiles. "It is terrible, I know, but she . . . she finishes the race."

"You're saying Aunt Bel is dead."

He bends down and kisses me on the forehead, an ancient gesture. My chair reclines slightly, my feet leaving the ground. I feel weightless and numb.

"I am sorry. I would bring you something more of hers, but has nothing. And what she has, it is all swept away. Like she never existed, so we put up that cross. Like stake in the ground, to show her place."

He backs out of the cubicle, turning to go.

This is bad. Very bad. Much worse than anything I imagined.

What if he sees her on his way out?

I rise from my chair, so unsteady on my legs that I could have been sitting for hours. As I start to follow him, Diana appears at my elbow. She's been outside the cubicle, listening. Not that you'd need to be very close in order to overhear Sergei's voice.

"Did you hear that?" I whisper.

She clutches my hand.

"It's pretty bad. They think she's *dead*."

"Sara," she says, leaning close to my ear. "Are you sure that's the real Belinda? She could be some kind of impostor."

This makes me laugh. "Oh no. We've got the real Belinda. And from the sound of it, she's a regular saint. Is she still hiding in the gallery? I want to see what she thinks about all this. Look at the picture. They've built her a shrine and everything. I wonder what he'd say if he knew. I wonder what he'd tell the people back home."

"I'm sure she has her reasons," Diana says, her tone doubtful.

"For faking her own death? I'm sure. Let's go and find out."

The gallery is empty except for Aunt Bel's painting on the wall, another monument to the work of a woman passing through.

15.
Good Taste, Less Fitting

Aunt Bel's doing it now, the nervous cleaning ritual. I have noticed this before. Coming home after a long day, the mess we left behind in the morning will be tidied away. All the dishes washed and back in the cupboard, the furniture moved back into alignment, a pine-fresh scent on the air, or maybe a scented candle burning on the mantel. Down in the basement, the dryer will be churning, or else the clothes will be folded and put away.

I pause halfway down the basement steps, leaning down so I can see her moving a lump of wet clothes from the washer to the dryer.

"Aunt Bel," I say. "Are you okay?"

Her back clearly says no, as does her inability to speak.

"Can you come up here for a minute? We need to talk."

She nods curtly, continuing with her task.

Her worktable is a composition of spilled paint and balled up or torn paper. There are some paints on the floor, an overturned jug of what looks—and smells—like solvent. A fit has been pitched, I think, imagining Aunt Bel trouncing her little studio in frustration. After a pause, I head upstairs.

"I wish she wouldn't feel the need to do all the chores," I tell Finn. "She's not the maid."

"If it bothers you so much, just tell her. But talk about looking a gift horse in the mouth. Plus, I think she likes it. She wants to be useful."

"I'm sure you think that, but trust me, nobody likes doing that stuff. She's doing it because she feels bad, like she has to justify her presence here. So if you think about it, this is our fault for not making her comfortable."

"Your fault," he says, cracking a smile. "Bel and me are good."

Accompanied by squeaks, Aunt Bel's feet compress the treads as she walks up the stairs slowly, presenting herself in the living room like a naughty child who's been caught. Taking a cue from her downcast expression, I motion her to a seat on the couch but remain standing over her. She smoothes her dress over her knees, clutching the hem in slim fingers, kneading the fabric within an inch of its life.

"I talked to Sergei today," I announce.

"I'm sure you're happy to finally know." Her tones, soft and smooth, try to cover the mound of chagrin, to no avail.

Finn shifts his weight, making the floorboards creak. He walks a few paces toward the kitchen, like he's leaving, then pauses on the edge of the room. Available for peacekeeping, should it come to that, but also within earshot so he doesn't miss anything that's said. That makes me smile inside, the same way I smile when he makes fun of a girly reality show on TV and then sits down to watch it with me.

"Listen, Aunt Bel, I think this is serious. Please explain things to me. Here, look at this." I try to hand her the shrine photo, but her hands cling to her hem, forcing me to lay it on the couch cushion beside her. "Those people miss you so much, they've built a shrine for you. Do you think it's right, letting them think that you're . . ." For some reason, I can't say the word *dead* out loud, so I let the silence hang in the air.

Aunt Bel glances down at the photo without touching it.

"You told me a lot," I continue, "but you never explained who Sergei was, or why you didn't want to see him. Now I know. The thing I can't figure out is what purpose this . . . deception serves. What would be the harm in telling him the truth? He could go back and put a lot of people's minds at ease. And then you wouldn't have to carry the guilt either. I know there's something eating away at you, and I think this is it."

I pause to let her speak. She doesn't even look up. From the doorway, Finn gives me raised eyebrows and nothing more. *This is your mess*, he's saying, *and don't think for one second that I'm jumping into it. I've been fine with letting things unfold naturally.*

"Aunt Bel, you need to talk to me. You lied to me about being in danger, and now I find out all of this. There's been a huge breach of trust."

Without glancing up, Aunt Bel shrugs her broad shoulders in what I take to be an Eastern European way, a very expressive shrug, more a commentary on the bleakness of reality than any particular questions of mine.

"Did you fake the car crash?" I ask her.

A small snort of a laugh comes out. She shakes it off, running a hand down the side of her face, as if she's checking for fever. "That was real," she says. "All too real. The water rushing in was so cold I couldn't breathe, like a fist of ice closing around me." She extends her badly mended arm, rotating the limb until it won't go any farther. The white bandage around her braced pinkie appears dingy in the lamplight. "I did this trying to get the door open. The pain, I think, is what revived me. Otherwise it would have been easy just to shut my eyes and let it take me."

I walk over to an armchair and sit down. What do you say to a revelation like that? Across the room, Finn stifles a cough with his hand, then goes into the kitchen to pour a glass of water, which he brings to Aunt Bel, hovering over her with the glass extended until she finally accepts it. Instead of drinking, though, she sets the glass down next to her feet.

"Why let them think you were dead?" I ask.

"I didn't let them do anything. When I crawled out of the river, I had to pull myself up with only one arm. I was frozen to the bone. Exhausted. I thought maybe I would die. But if I didn't, I told myself, this is enough. Just like that. This is enough. After this, I am leaving."

"When was this?" Finn asks. "I always assumed you came straight back to the States, but that arm would've taken awhile to heal."

"Last winter. I didn't think at first to come home. I stayed with some friends, a couple of missionaries in Romania. Near Varna, with a view of the sea." This jogs a memory: my mother said she'd received a postcard from Aunt Bel, sent from Romania. "I thought at first I would stay there. But some kids came, college students from America on a missions trip. They made me feel very old, but also homesick. I decided to come back."

"And all this time," I say, "you never let the people in Kazakhstan know where you were? You could have said something. Sent a postcard."

"I never made a secret of leaving. The secret made itself. I never knew until later."

"But it was a safe assumption that when they fished your car out and you weren't in it—"

"It wasn't between me and them," she says. "It was between me and God."

The way she pronounces the word *God* is funny, with that same swallowed syllable as when she first said Uralsk. I don't like it any more on her tongue than I do in my own brain. Does she feel the same way about God that I do? After what she's been through, maybe she thinks he's even more capricious and mean-spirited than my Sunday school teacher let on.

"It's not too late to let Sergei know the truth. I'm sure we could track him down at this conference of his in D.C., let him know what really happened."

"Do what you want," she says.

"I think *you* should do it."

She shrugs. "I'm done with that place. May I be excused?"

Just like that.

"Nobody's chaining you to your seat, Aunt Bel."

She heads up to her room and I follow Finn into the kitchen. As I begin filing sliced cucumber in my mouth while Finn forms hamburger patties for the grill, I say, "So much for dangerous. I mean, thank God, but I'm not sure whether or not to be relieved Sergei isn't a criminal or upset that she lied."

"How about both? But just don't hang on to the second feeling for a minute longer than you have to." He rinses his hands, then grabs the plate of burgers. He turns at the door, "Right?"

I nod.

"Why don't you get changed, grab a beer, and sit with your he-man while he grills your meat?"

"Okay."

I pad barefoot down to the basement to retrieve my favorite shirt. The whirlwind did more damage to Aunt Bel's art supplies than I could appreciate from halfway up the stairs. The contents of the table are scattered across the floor as if she'd swept them off in a fury. There's the mop, tilted against the table, its straggly gray head now speckled and matted with paint. On the floor, I can see the lines where she pushed the mop along, skimming the paint and the thinner and some shards of broken glass into a pile near the easel. I have to step carefully to avoid the mess.

The basket where the dirty clothes are usually heaped lies empty on its side, the bottom glistening with spilled paint. What a disaster. Hopefully the basket wasn't full when this violence was done. The dryer is still churning, so I bend down and open the washer, peering into its steely insides. Nothing but the smell of summer fresh detergent. I lift the dryer door, cutting off the cycle, touching to feel whether the clothes are still damp. They feel crispy and done.

I dig through them for the familiar softness, the spongy gray cotton of my favorite shirt, yanking it out from the twist of clothes by one of the sleeves. But something is wrong. A streak of lightness against the gray cotton. Instead of pulling the shirt over my head, I hold it out for inspection. The front is fine, but the back is marred by bleach-like stains, two long slices like rays of sunlight across the gloom, one of them overlapping the first letters in the words GOOD TASTE. Whatever the chemical was—thinner or solvent or paint—it was strong enough not just to discolor the fabric but to burn off the letters. The G and the O cling to the cotton only in flakes, peeling sunburned skin that chips away when I rub my finger over the fabric.

A voice in my head starts rehearsing every ugly word I've ever heard before, stringing them all together in a vile cacophony, a depraved and glorious monologue I won't even try to repeat. My GOOD TASTE is reduced to OD TASTE now, my favorite shirt, soft and beautiful and now destroyed. As if the hole on the hip wasn't bad enough, now the wide discolored streaks are hard to the touch and unsightly. And they have turned the sentiment into a joke.

I ball the shirt up in one fist and take the stairs two at a time.

"Aunt *Beeeeelllll!*" I cry. And anger overtakes me further.

She's sitting like a gargoyle on the front steps, her heels tucked against the concrete, hunched over her cancer stick. When I burst through the door, she uncoils herself, looking up in surprise, the cigarette clutched in her right hand.

"Look at this! Look what you've done!" I cock my arm back and throw the wadded shirt at her. It whooshes past her face and clips the cigarette from her hand, sending it teetering into the night. The shirt smacks into her lap, then slinks over the side of her thigh onto the concrete.

How could she just up and leave like that? Those poor people. They didn't know. And my family? She up and left us too. She disappeared when I needed her. Because I did. Because I remember sitting in her lap crying and crying and she was the only one around to comfort me. "And then you were gone!" I cry. "You were *gone!*"

For an instant, frozen in shock, Aunt Bel stares at me wide-eyed, like a startled child. Then she starts to say something. Before she can get out a word, I turn on my heel and stomp back into the house, banging the door shut behind me. Up the stairs, I slam the bedroom door, the airflow hitting my back as tears escape my eyelids. I fling myself onto the bed and will myself not to get hysterical.

The house is quiet. From the bed, with my face buried in a pillow, I hear Finn's footsteps coming up the steps.

"Is everything all right?" his voice calls.

The house answers with silence.

16.

Far Away, So Close

I am already awake when Finn gets up the next morning, but I pretend otherwise and let him get dressed and go downstairs without me saying a word. The house is quiet enough that I can hear his morning ritual, even from upstairs. The buzz of the coffee grinder. The kettle boiling. The hum of baritone voices on the radio news.

Ignoring all this, I gaze up at the cracks in the ceiling, which begin to resemble a map of foreign lands, craggy ridge lines intersecting wide stretches of pampas, a sun-cast shadow undulating like a river through imagined geography. And I find myself after a sleepless night looking up into this map and willing myself to visit there, trying on Aunt Bel's life over my own, leaving everything behind for the unknown, and maybe chucking that too once enough time has passed for everything familiar to become foreign to my eyes.

Finn sets down a mug of coffee on my nightstand and sits down wearily, his weight indenting the mattress and tilting me toward him.

"She's gone," he says.

I sit up in bed. "What do you mean, she's gone?"

"Bel isn't here. I had a bad feeling about last night, and sure enough, there's no sign of her now. The room's cleared out across the hall. She must have left early this morning, or late last night. Did you hear anything?"

"Not a thing," I say. "And I tossed and turned half the night. I think I would have heard if she'd made any noise."

"Well, she's gone."

He kisses me on the head and leaves the room, depositing a melancholy miasma in his wake. I throw the covers back, test the cold floorboards with my bare toes. The reality still won't sink in. I walk across the hall, pushing the half-open door wide, confirming with a glance that everything Finn said is indeed so. The pictures are missing from the dresser, the closet mourning the hanging clothes and Aunt Bel's duffel bag.

All night I watched myself, over and over like a gif file, throwing my T-shirt in her face.

Throwing my T-shirt in her face.

Throwing my T-shirt in her face, and how could I have done such a thing?

GOOD TASTE. How about GOOD MANNERS? How about not being such a spoiled brat? How about blaming everybody else for my unhappiness but myself? Well, at least I haven't blamed God yet like the rest of the world as if they actually expect him to come to the rescue.

Why everybody is still around me is now a mystery.

Well, except for Aunt Bel. And I don't blame her for going. The same person who escaped a sinking car in freezing waters and simply walked away to make a new life would realize she didn't have to take the kind of disrespect I was handing out.

Downstairs, I hunt around in case she left a note. Nothing. It would have been polite to leave some kind of message behind. When you're running away, that is.

Stop it, Sara.

In the kitchen, Finn plates a pair of overcooked omelets, then kisses me on the head again. He steps back, looking at the ruined shirt I'm wearing. When he came to our room last night, without explanation he had tossed it to my side of the bed, and I'd slipped it on.

"It's not so bad," he says.

I sit at the kitchen table, the chair cool against the back of my bare thighs. I pull the shirt down my legs, stretching the fabric, and remember the way Aunt Bel would hug Katya's sweater against her skin. The same thing has happened to my favorite shirt. She's put her mark on it, and now I feel the soft cotton against my skin and I think of her.

"Where do you think she's gone?" I ask.

Finn shrugs. "She did leave this."

I look up, expecting him to produce a note, but instead he places a small box on the table. The box from the bank. Inside, there's a stack of checkbooks that go with the account where my father deposited the money he asked me to give Aunt Bel. I lift the lid to find the ATM card resting on top of the stack. Although he'd requested that I come up with some kind of story, in the end I couldn't think of any way to explain to my aunt where eight thousand dollars might come from out of the blue, so I told her it was from my dad and that he didn't want her to know.

"You think she just forgot this?" I ask.

He shakes his head. "It was on the table in the living room, right in the open. I bet she never touched a dime."

"She has to have spent some," I say. "Cigarettes aren't cheap."

"Why do you think Walter gave her the money to begin with?"

"Mom was wondering the same thing. Honestly, I think he views her as a little sister, Finn."

"Sometimes the most forthright explanation makes the most sense."

"Have you known my father to be anything but?" I ask.

"Nope. Still, there's a reason this is so upsetting to your mom, right?"

We eat breakfast indoors, not talking much. When we happen to catch each other's eye, we look away. Guilty people act like this, or hungover drunks with regrets about last night.

"I guess I'll shower," I say.

"I guess I'll head out."

After he's gone, I creep down the basement stairs for a look at the mess. But Aunt Bel cleaned up. The paints are all there, lined up along the table with her brushes and the sketchbook we bought her and some unusual canvas. All the pages she'd filled with drawings have been ripped out, though, and I can't find any of her attempts at painting. She didn't just tidy the space, she removed all signs of her having been here. Realizing this, I feel cold suddenly. I go upstairs and run the shower until the mirror steams up.

I peel off the ruined shirt, inspecting the damage once more. Then I ball it up again and scrub a patch of mirror clean so I can see my face reflected. As soon as the glass clears, it begins to frost over again, but not before I see the shadows under my eyes, the puffy skin, the clogged pores. *You look like hell.* And I feel it too. I stare at my face until the mirror fogs, wondering what kind of person I must be to have driven Aunt Bel out knowing she has no other home. I step into the shower, sit down in the tub, and let the water sluice over my head and down my neck, shoulders, and spine.

Some things you regret after the fact, some you regret as you're doing them, and some you regret in advance, knowing you'll hate yourself after the fact but doing them anyway. Calling my mom falls under the third heading. Thankfully, J. D., her boss at the farm, has a phone. With each ring in my ear, a voice in my head tells me to hang up. But I don't hang up. When he finally picks up, I ask him if I can speak to her and wait until she answers. And when she answers I tell her everything, not just that Aunt Bel has left, but why Aunt Bel has left.

"Did you know?" I ask her.

"Baby, I don't know anything. Aunt Bel and I don't even speak the same language anymore. You say she left the money behind? That's strange. That's something I don't understand."

"What do you think I should do?"

"She's a big girl," Mom says. "She knows her own mind. Look, you helped the family out of an awkward spot, which I appreciate. But I don't see how Aunt Bel is your responsibility any longer. You can wipe your hands clean and let the Universe do its thing, baby. That seems to be what she wants anyway, right?"

"I would at least like to talk to her, though. We didn't part on the best of terms."

"Maybe she's not gone for good."

"The way she cleaned everything out, it looks pretty final."

"If you ask me, it's for the best. I'll tell you something—and don't go repeating this—if you ask me, it would have been better if she'd stayed overseas. Or at least stayed away from here. She brings too much . . . tension. Bad vibes. Where did you say she went afterward?"

"Romania. Where the postcard came from."

"Okay, exactly what I'm talking about. That would have been fine. It was coming back here that caused all the drama. She got your father all puffed up, and it sounds like she did a number on you too, honey.

Whatever the reasons, running away is in my sister's blood. She left us all, she left her flock of Kazakhs, and now she's left you. You're taking it hard now, but give this time and you're gonna see it's all for the best. For everyone."

"I don't feel like it's for the best. I feel guilty."

"What do you have to feel guilty for, Sara? Guilt is the last enemy in the battle for your happiness. Get rid of your guilt and you'll be free."

"How do I do that, exactly?"

"Stop feeling guilty, that's a start."

"I've never been very good at not feeling what I feel. I need to just be me."

She laughs. "Baby, that sounds very Zen, but it's not."

———

I spend the morning at the computer trying to work on the last of Holly's projects while also answering e-mails from Ethan Lime about my schedule for the summer. He envisions a photographic road trip of several weeks' duration, living out of suitcases and shooting portraits every day. What would I need? he wants to know. Who would I like to bring along? The way he words things, it almost seems as if he and Dora want to tag along. I can't even imagine what a trip like that would entail. I conjure up old pictures of British nobility camping on safari in India, drinking tea out of a silver service, dining off of china.

My rumbling stomach lets me know I've skipped out on lunch. I'm surprised how quickly the hours have passed, and how much solitude my coworkers have allowed me. It's almost two when I push away from the desk, my limbs stiff, circling the side of the cubicle and walking along the length of the counter separating office space from the print floor. Diana is gone, but Huey and Finn are surveying the pieces of the Iron Maiden.

"Wow," I say.

The Iron Maiden gleams dully under the lights, a gloss of British racing green paint covering her cast-iron form. I cross the counter to admire the results up close.

"You like?" Finn asks.

"I always said I preferred the green."

"Your wish is my command. Now let me take you to lunch."

Finn disappears to the restroom to scrub paint off his hands, leaving me alone with Huey. He's wearing one of his older boiler suits, without his name embroidered, little holes opened up here and there, especially along the zipper. I sometimes imagine him sitting in front of the TV at home, a six-pack of Leinenkugel at his feet, still wearing his mechanic's outfit. Maybe he has a fluffy one with attached footies for wearing at home.

"So I heard what happened," he says.

"The whole story? Including what the guy yesterday had to say?"

He crosses his arms, gives a contemplative tuck of the chin. "You know where she ran off to?"

"I have no idea."

"Do you want to know?" he asks.

"Why, did she tell you?"

"Don't get so excited," he says, stepping back. "The woman hasn't told me a thing. I'm just asking, are you done with her or not?"

"No, I don't think so."

"Good," he says. "Then there's hope for you after all. Tell me something. You ever gotten what you wanted, only to find you didn't want it after all? Maybe that's what happened to her over there. The way Finn tells it, she pulled herself out of that water and decided enough was enough. She hit her limit. Me, I can relate, and I haven't even been through that much. You hear what I'm saying?"

"I hear. It's not that I can't sympathize, or don't want to. But how am I supposed to understand something if she's not willing to explain it?"

"That's your problem right there, thinking you're supposed to under-stand."

"Okay, maybe I'm not supposed to—but I'd like to. I want to understand."

"Well, good," he says. "Maybe you will someday. I just hope you don't understand too well, 'cause the only way to do that is living through it, which I wouldn't wish on my worst enemy, and especially not you."

"Thanks, Huey. That's nice to hear."

"Hey, anything happens to you, that would make me the only sane person up in here. I can put up with a lot of crazy, but even I have my limits."

The first day is the hardest, Daddy calling to find out what happened and why Aunt Bel, who's staying at his house again, is even more tight-lipped than before. Then the second arrives to find me sitting on the edge of the bed feeling like there is too much oxygen in the house for just Finn and me. On the third, Aunt Bel's absence begins to feel real, and by the end of the week nothing jars me when I enter the empty house, descend to the empty basement, or glance across the hallway into the empty spare bedroom where Finn has already rolled back the rug and started talking about borrowing that sander again. That means another baby discussion is coming.

That Friday we flip the switch on Eric Ringwald's new website. Holly drives down for the occasion, bringing a check and a bottle of champagne. There's a dicey moment when Finn pretends to break the bottle against the Iron Maiden's side to celebrate her reassembly—a feat pulled off by him and Huey in tandem working into the wee hours. The neck of the bottle slips in Finn's grasp and nearly gets away from him, skimming the edge of the press's cast-iron arm with maybe a quarter inch to spare. The close call leaves us feeling exhilarated. We watch as Finn publishes the files, refreshes his browser to confirm that the site is live, then clink our glasses together in a toast.

"To the most inventive, creative, and talented young woman I know," Holly says, and I feel my cheeks redden when I realize that she means me.

"I'll drink to that," Huey says, tapping my glass.

On her way out, still flushed and excited, Holly puts an arm around me and squeezes. "You're coming to the gala, right? It's all agreed. A formal night like this gives us girls an excuse for getting all dressed up. Does Finn have a tux? It's okay if that's not his thing–"

"He can fend for himself. What about me? I have no idea what to wear."

"I know what," she says. "The two of us should go shopping." Her eyes light up, and I get this vision of having two-thousand-dollar ball gowns flounced in front of my face. "We could make a day of it, just us girls. It would be fun."

"Okay," I say. "But Finn's gonna kill me if I blow that check on a dress."

"Don't even joke," she says. "We'll find something *perfect*."

I experience the same discomfort I felt when the photographer at the Wedding Expo coaxed me in front of his lens. Making things beautiful is one thing. To be the subject of the making, sized up in the eyes of another–a project, basically–that makes me nervous. Self-consciousness, sure, but it's something else too. I don't like not having control.

Once I've seen Holly out, I wander back to the studio door. Through the glass, I see my husband and my two closest friends circled around the Iron Maiden, smiling, laughing, looking very much at ease with each other and with the world. All together, the Maiden doesn't seem either as tall or as intimidating as she did at first, now that her rust has been whisked away and her new coat of paint is on. As I watch them, Finn pulls on the throw-off lever, opening the platen wide like a lion's mouth. Huey puts some bright red ink on the disk–Dutch Fireball from the look of it—which Finn distributes by cranking the lever, the motion spinning the disk and laying an even coat of ink on the platen. Diana bounces over to the paper rack and returns with some sheets of Mohawk Superfine, stacking them on the feedboard ready for use.

"We're gonna pull her first print," Huey calls, motioning me inside.

Diana places the paper and Finn brings the lever down. The whole mechanism gives a clockwork lurch, then opens to reveal the pristine print. Reaching forward, Huey lifts the paper free and brings it over for me to inspect.

"Not bad, not bad," he says, using his appraiser's voice.

We have a tradition going back to the purchase of our first press, the Pilot, of pulling the same print for each inaugural test. Finn must have dug out the plate earlier in the day, locking up the form while I was focused on entertaining Holly. I hold the paper close for inspection. The bright red ink covers just a small portion of the page, dead center, an illustration of a couple sitting on a couch, his and hers crossed legs, each holding a book in front of their face. I designed this based on a bookplate I found in an old cookbook of my grandmother's, thinking it would make a cute logo for our fledgling business, which at the time was just Finn and me. That plan never panned out, but we kept the plate around for good luck.

"You're right," I say. "Not bad at all."

We pull a few more, marveling at the Iron Maiden's steady glide, marveling that she even functions at all. Only now does Finn admit to his misgivings the first time he saw her. "I was worried I'd never finish it, and we'd have this lump of junk haunting us for the rest of our lives."

"You weren't the only one," I say. "But you did it."

Huey claps Finn on the back. "I have to admit, I thought your momma dropped you on your head. But it turned out all right . . . with a little help from me."

Diana laughs and Finn takes the congratulations mixed with ribbing in stride. For the first time in weeks, I feel truly lighthearted. When

I saw this thing arrive, I thought it would be another of Finn's unending demolitions. Now that one of them has finally been seen through to completion, maybe more dominoes will fall. A patched-up floor, a finished kitchen ... who knows where this new energy might lead?

My mother has her harebrained theory of happiness, and I know she's wrong. The world doesn't always give back what you put into it. There's a Bible verse somewhere that says time and chance happen to us all, and I believe that is so. The world, the Universe, whatever you want to call it, is an ugly place, a broken place. And if there's happiness to be found, I think the formula must be something like this: To take what you find, whatever it is, and to make something beautiful of it. To strip life down to the bare metal and build it back up again gleaming and fresh.

17.

The Universe Does Its Thing

We walk around the back of the Firehouse, unlocking the gallery entrance. The long, narrow space is so bathed in light that although I'm crossing from outside to in, the movement feels reversed, as if I have passed from the wide-open world into an even wider, more open space, only the volume has shifted from the horizontal to the vertical. This is the logic of ancient churches, which when you think about it are shaped like slices, up-and-down cross sections of space that concentrate our attention not on the expanse of the cosmos but on its height.

I have not entered this space since the day of Sergei's visit and it seems neither has Finn, who is surprised to notice the painting has been removed from the wall. Startled, rushing forward, he spies it lying on the table and comes to a halt, relieved.

"That's strange," he says.

Then he takes the picture and, after inspecting the back, returns it to its hook on the wall. Rick arrives just then and comes alongside him, leaning forward for a better look.

"So this is it."

"It's weird not having her here," Finn says. "I thought for a second she'd taken it with her. I'm glad she didn't."

Rick laughs. "Me too, or I would've had to scramble for a sermon."

While they confer, I wander to the far side of the gallery, where the bare walls and the flood of light from overhead create the illusion of walking into negative space. In one of those ancient churches I mentioned, the empty space where I am standing would contain an altar, approached perhaps by ascending some steps. Maybe it would even be screened by some kind of gilded wall or altarpiece, I'm not sure. The focus of attention would be here, at the far side of the room. Instead, Finn has moved the center of attention toward the center of the room, which probably says something about where we want our focus to be—not ahead of us or above, but here among us, close enough to touch.

At the back of my mind, as people wander inside and I move to greet them, to say hello to those I haven't seen all week and to be introduced to one or two I've never met, the sense of increasing presence in the room is counterbalanced by a single absence, Aunt Bel's, and I find myself wishing she would walk through the door.

My advice to Finn applies as much to myself. I, too, need to learn how to let things be, how not to take relationships down to the studs by force of habit, as I've done with her.

Having moved from one side of the room to the other, I linger near the door, letting the chairs fill up, content to sit cross-legged on the floor. Despite Rick cautioning us not to worry about numbers, I do a head count and come up with forty-two. I am the last to sit down, waiting until Finn has propped himself on the edge of the table and begun to strum his guitar. As I move toward the edge of the crowd, someone takes me by the elbow from behind.

It's Holly Ringwald, enveloping me in a cloud of lilac-scented perfume.

"You said I should come. So this is the place?"

"We'll have to sit on the floor," I whisper, apologetic. "Or I could go down to the studio and grab a chair."

"The floor is fine."

She teeters on her high heels a little bit on the way down, steadying herself on my arm. The others are singing already, lifting up a refrain from the psalms whose number I didn't catch if Finn mentioned it at all:

> *How long, O Lord? Will you forget me forever?*
> *How long will you hide your face from me?*

Now there's a happy thought. But easily recognizable.

"'I will sing to the LORD,'" Rick intones, reading from the Bible in his lap in between our refrains, "'because He has dealt bountifully with me.'"

Forgotten at the beginning of the psalm, and loved by the end.

As the psalm dies off, Finn pauses before beginning another one. "The thing I like about this is the honesty. We've written new songs that let us pretend we don't despair, but with the psalms, there's no pretending. You can admit you have an open wound, because the God of the psalms is big enough to take it."

Next to me Holly leans over.

"Goose bumps," she says. "I love this place already."

Would that make Finn happy or sad? I mean, Holly might actually start coming here and the Microchurch wouldn't be so teeny anymore. He's been complaining about how fast the church is growing.

After another psalm, Rick starts asking people what's going on in their lives, eliciting a few stories, then prays a long time, both for the ones who spoke and for the ones who didn't. When he's done, he sets his Bible on the table, looking around at us as if he's not sure how to proceed.

"A month or two back," he says, "instead of speaking or preaching, I just read you guys a story. Remember that? I had this idea that the story could preach as well as I could, or even better. This got me thinking about what else could preach. I don't know about you, but sometimes I feel like I can't hear anymore. You tell me the truth, I know it's true, and somehow I still can't receive it. My walls are up. It takes some new way of speaking to get through to me. To hear from an unexpected source, though, you have to learn how to listen. That's what I want to try tonight. This is going to be strange, maybe, but bear with me.

"The night I read that story, there was a woman here. Some of you have met her, others haven't. I'm talking about Bel, Sara's aunt. If you *have* met her, you know what an unusual and challenging kind of life she's lived, how outside the box her experience has been. For the last twenty years she was on the mission field. She only just came back. And she'd never read anything by Flannery O'Connor before, but after I shared that story, she took to O'Connor like fire to a haystack. That particular story I read fascinated her. The vision of a different kind of Jesus than we're accustomed to, not the smiling, happy Jesus who wants to make your every wish come true, but a transcendent and demanding Jesus . . . that really captured her imagination, because that was the Jesus she'd come to know overseas. Something funny happened after that. Bel had never tried to paint before, but she had it in her head she'd like to. I'll let Finn pick up the story here, because he saw it firsthand."

Rick motions to Finn, who is still leaning against the table with the guitar strapped over his shoulder.

"Well," he says, clearing his throat, pausing, not at all comfortable speaking in front of people despite having no trouble singing in front of them. "Like Rick said, she'd never done any painting, but had this crazy idea it's what she should do. We got her some supplies and she went at it down in the basement, over and over again, day after day. Sara would go down there after work and watch her at it. Bel was . . . obsessive, driven. And I realized after a while that she wasn't trying to paint paintings. There was just one painting she was working on, again and again. She'd get it wrong, not knowing how to translate the vision in her mind onto the canvas. Finally, she did this."

He leaves the table and walks over to the square painting all alone on the wall.

"If you remember the story, the guy gets a tattoo of Jesus, but not the smiling Jesus Rick just talked about. The story calls it the 'flat stern Byzantine Christ' and says the eyes are all-demanding. Kind of imperious, you know—you can't look away from them. They follow you, seeing everything. That's what Bel was seeing, and that's what she wanted to capture, and that's what you see here, her interpretation of that Christ."

This comes as a shock to me, as real as the breathless icy grip Aunt Bel felt when she plunged into the river. I stare at that black-and-gold muddle and know that my jaw has dropped. Under my nose, night after night, she had made this image of the face of Jesus, and I had never even recognized it as such, and have a hard time doing so now. And it doesn't make me like the painting any better. In fact, I hate it even more.

I strain forward, willing my eyes to see. But it still looks like burnt toast to me, reminding me of the person who saw the face of the Virgin Mary on his grilled cheese and then listed the miracle on eBay—because that's what we Americans do in the presence of the holy, sell it off. What had Rick said? *"To hear from an unexpected source, you have to learn how to listen."* I want to see this. I need to see it. The way things were left between Aunt Bel and me is wrong, and like I told Huey, I'm not done with her. I know that. If I could look at this painting and see what she saw, see through her eyes—

Rick is talking now, explaining what he wants us to do. Instead of listening to him speak, he wants us to look. "Everyone stand, everyone stand and line up, and we'll approach one by one. You get as close as you want, for as long as you want, and I only ask you to do one thing: let it preach."

We get up. Holly brushes her jeans off—force of habit—and gives me a conspiratorial raised eyebrow. The setting is new to her, I realize, but Rick is not. She's been a spectator to his journey for much longer than I have.

As the line forms, I hesitate, letting it get longer and longer before I finally join in. This is the strangest thing that's happened at the Microchurch. I can tell it makes a few people uncomfortable and leaves a few more confused. Maybe Finn will have his wish and half of these people won't be back. Or maybe, just maybe, the picture will speak to them as Rick hopes.

"You okay?" Holly whispers.

I nod, wondering what my face is giving away. This is the painting I saw Aunt Bel run her hands over, the one I snatched from the wall and nearly threw to the ground. I've had more opportunities to see it than anyone here, but did I ever truly look? How did Finn know about this—and Rick!—but I did not? I feel blindsided by this revelation about Aunt Bel's work. Or simply blind. I've been judging by the standard of skill what was done from devotion, however obsessed, driven, and dark. Born in that darkness of the basement beneath my feet and now radiant in the gallery's bright light.

It takes a long time for me to reach the painting. People are following Rick's advice, taking their time. When they've looked awhile, some up close, others distant (maybe afraid to advance too near), they file toward the far side of the gallery where I stood earlier, congregating in twos and threes to process what they've seen.

"You go first," I tell Holly.

To avoid looking at the painting, I watch Holly instead. She stands with one leg ahead of the other, hands on her hips, tilting her head slightly like she can't quite work out the right angle from which to view the image. I can't see her expression, but her body language reads as skepticism. She stands before Aunt Bel's Christ the way she would before a picture at the museum, sizing it up, perhaps wondering about its value.

"Impressive."

She turns and says this to me in the tone of a woman rendering her verdict on a piece of art, an informed opinion from someone in the know. She is also letting me know, because this is my aunt's work and she must have picked up on my inner turmoil, that there's nothing for me to be ashamed of here, no reason to think the picture is unworthy just because it was done by an amateur and a relative.

She doesn't see it either, I think.

Holly is as blind to Aunt Bel's Christ as I am, as insulated and cut off. As she steps away to join the others, I edge forward, watching my toes the way a high diver might, approaching a precipice and using all my attention not to move too far and fall.

Then I look up. The painting seems larger viewed head-on from maybe five feet away. Also more distant. I cannot imagine reaching for it, cannot imagine ever having touched it. It feels too far from me now, too inaccessible. I do see the face rising down the middle of the canvas like a ridge of volcanic rock, the cratered darkness of the mouth and eyes. He does not smile or beckon, but he is not imperial and aloof either. He is of the earth, even molten, as if he has stepped through fire in order to be seen. This is not the Jesus of O'Connor's story, or the temple-stalking Christ depicted in the Gospels.

Go back, the eyes said to Parker in the story, and I look to Aunt Bel's painting as if her Christ might speak too.

Aunt Bel's Christ looks back at me now.

Go back, he says to me. Go back.

Who are you? I think.

But I know the answer. This Jesus is my Jesus. Aunt Bel's Christ is mine. And she's realized the Good Shepherd we'd been told about was not the Good Shepherd at all. He was the flat, stern Byzantine Christ who loved selectively or not at all.

18.

The Flat Stern Byzantine Christ

My dad is not adjusting well to Bel's presence at his house. "Things are not going smoothly. Your mother's washed her hands of the whole thing. No surprise there. But I didn't think you would follow her example, doll."

Though he speaks in a calm, reasonable tone, he might as well be screaming. The rebuke hits me hard enough to push the phone away from my ear.

"I don't know what you're talking about. I didn't wash my hands of Aunt Bel. She walked out. You can't blame me for that."

"So you'd take her back?" A hot air balloon of hope raises his voice to a higher pitch.

"Is that what she wants?"

"How the heck should I know? It's not like if I ask her she'll give me an answer. You'll have to do that yourself. And my advice is to come in person. Don't try something like this over the phone. There's too much room for misunderstanding."

No kidding.

"Hey, what's that swishing sound?" he asks.

That swishing sound is from the voluminous pink taffeta dress Holly is adjusting around my feet. I'm standing on a carpeted pedestal watching a candy princess version of myself reflected in a three-way mirror, hating the look every bit as much as I said I would.

"It's horrible," I say, hanging up the phone, handing it back to the hovering salesgirl, who seems to share my fear of the dress. She places it on top of my bag, not sure who to pledge allegiance to here, and rightly figuring not to meddle. "Not only does it make me look like a cake topper, but they've put some kind of lining in here that'll flay your skin right off. Is it supposed to be so uncomfortable?"

Before the princess dress, there was the junior high prom number cinched tight under the bust, with frilly layers stopping half a foot short of my knees. The dress looked like someone had shrunk it in the dryer and hiked up my body too high.

"I was thinking something simple," I say, now back on the floor and sliding hangers across the poles from which they hang lifelessly. "Classic. Maybe black, and formfitting without being too tight?"

Holly throws her hands up. "Black? Did you say black? Girl, when do you even get an opportunity to dress up like this? And you're going to waste it on a little black dress."

"A lot of these dresses, they don't look right on me. I don't have the right kind of body for them."

"You have no idea what you're talking about," she says. "Girls like us, we're pretty lucky, you know that? Having kids just wrecks you, but we can wear anything we want."

Girls like us.

Childless, she means. I gaze into the mirror, trying to see what she sees.

"How do you stand it at church?" I ask. "Do you not get the same sideways comments I did about not getting with the program?"

"I did at first. But they saw how hard I tried. *We* tried," she says.

"So it wasn't exactly your decision."

"Adoption is very big right now. But Eric . . ."

"I'm sorry."

"What about you?" she asks.

I shrug, look at her open face, and figure, client or not, if she isn't safe, I can find that out right now. "I don't know if I even want children, Holly. How terrible is that?"

I stare into her eyes, my breathing halted as I wait.

She doesn't blink but takes my hand. "It's your decision to make, Sara. Not mine or anybody else's. Only you know what's right for you and there are too many examples of really good *people* who don't become parents."

Men too, is what she's saying.

She holds on to the dress pole in front of us. "Sara, you're a good person. And it may not mean much, but I'd never dream of questioning a decision like that on your part. First of all, like those women at The Community, it's not my business but yours and Finn's. And second of all, even if it was, I'd support you. Period."

"Why?" I ask.

"Because that's what we women should do for each other in the first place."

"Thank you," I whisper, taking her hand and giving it a light squeeze. "Let's find that dress."

She takes the hint that I can only take so much soul baring and sends me back to the dressing room. Two minutes later she shows up with a shimmery mermaid-bottomed number made of ombré silk, light gray on top and deepening into dark navy by the time it reaches the floor. Strapless too, because as I've learned, Holly has no qualms about showing other people's skin.

I try on the mermaid dress and a couple of others, trying to get into the spirit of the day—or at least to appear on board. My dad's words keep eating away at me. Does he really think I'm taking after Mom? That's absurd.

Too exposed. Too covered up. Too tight in the bust, too full in the hips. Too bright. Too somber. There's an objection to everything I try on, and I'm usually the first one to make it. At first I feel guilty raising objections, afraid of hurting Holly's feelings, but she turns out to be imperturbable. The more I say no, the more dresses I have to try on, which is apparently all the fun. I have a feeling Holly Ringwald doesn't have a favorite soft T-shirt, and I'll bet she wears heels around the house. Or maybe she knows that when something is special, it's a crime to settle for anything other than what you love.

"Less bridesmaid, more cocktail dress," Holly explains to the salesgirl.

Eventually they bring me another one in taffeta—dark purple this time, with a scoop neck and a full, flouncy skirt that hits just above the knee. I start to object, then stop. It's clean and modern, with a touch of feminine whimsy in the bow at the waist. When I slip it on, the dress could have been made for me.

"You have to go through a lot of frogs to find your prince," Holly declares. "I know you were doubting me, but *this* is the one."

"You think so?"

"Sara, look at you."

She's right. It looks good. I left the house this morning with advice from Finn that you only live once, the business is doing fine, and I deserve a little treat. So I take him at his word and give the shopgirl a nod. "This one."

"And it's not even noon," Holly says. "Lunch?"

"I have to bail on you, I'm afraid. That phone call was from my dad. He wants me to drive out and talk to Aunt Bel, see if I can talk her into coming back. She left my place and is staying with him."

"Is that what you want?" she asks.

"To be honest, yes. I think I do. My family's kind of a mess, Holly."

"Sara, that's the only kind of family I even begin to understand."

Holly drives me home with the top of her convertible down, the wind whisking my short hair into a spiky mess. As she pops the trunk and removes my plastic-sheathed dress, I can tell she's got something on her mind. She holds the dress out to me and says, "You know something? The best thing about this is, I think I've made a new friend. This was fun, right? I think it was."

"I had a blast. Next time, though, you can try on the dresses and I'll just watch."

She gives me a hug. "Deal."

I hang the dress up in the bedroom closet and head straight for my car. I'll relieve Dad soon enough, but there's someone else I need to talk to, and maybe she'll tell me the truth for a change. Maybe she'll tell me why her relationship with her sister was shattered in more pieces than seems possible to put together again.

Because in all of these relationships interconnected with filament as fine as a spider's silk, theirs seems to be at the center of it all.

My mother's "campsite" is on the back ten acres, across Deer Creek, at Happy Hideaway Farm in northern Baltimore County. She went to college with J. D. Rebel, the owner, a person who thoroughly lived up to his last name in his youth. Now he channels that energy into a place where small festivals are held and organic farming erupts in joyful fields bordered by flowers of all kinds. It's nothing short of a wonderland and maybe, just maybe, I'd live in a tent to be around it all the time.

Mom's tent, on the other hand, well, not so much.

The gold-and-red two-person dome tent sits on the other side of the creek and is accessible by a small footbridge. She does this on purpose. "If I can't carry it to the tent, I don't need it." She was, thankfully, able to carry two bright red Adirondack chairs that she's placed in front of the tent, along with pots of perennial flowers and herbs that are just coming out of dormancy. Bamboo poles driven into the ground dangle all variety of items, mostly found by her along the side of the road and repurposed into yard art. My mother's aesthetic is very different from my own, but in its ability to make do and turn the castaway into something that shimmers and moves and sometimes even whistles when the wind is right, she expresses herself beautifully and in a style all her own.

I pull down the gravel drive, past the main buildings of the farm, including J. D.'s small cob house, an octagonal structure that looks like a hobbit resides inside. Which maybe one does. J. D., five-foot-three and probably weighing in at 110 pounds, waves to me from the pump where he's getting water for his mule. He plows his fields with the mule, so the thought of having an old college friend on the back acreage of his land is probably nothing out of the ordinary.

They had something once. I'm not sure if it was just a spring break fling or maybe even a longer relationship, but from what I can tell, they both realized they were more suited to friendship without those sorts of benefits.

I like J. D. He may be little, but he looks out for her, and is more than capable of keeping her safe. Not to mention, he's big into generosity when it comes to his crops. I wave back.

I park beside the field where several of the horses he boards are lying in the sun. Mom is usually home from whatever job she's doing by four, preferring an early start. Good. Her bike is leaning against the railing of the bridge.

"Hey, you!" she calls, standing up from her raised garden bed where she's been preparing the soil for her summer vegetable garden.

"Hi, Mom."

"What happened?" My mom is highly intuitive. She just doesn't always choose to act on it.

"You tell me. It's why I'm here. I need to know what's between you and Aunt Bel, Mom. Really."

She nods once and jabs her shovel down into the dirt she's just overturned. "You know, when Bel was gone, I never had a thought this would happen, that you'd ask questions I never wanted to answer. I thought we'd buried it all for good."

I sit down in one of the Adirondack chairs. The sun is driving in at a slant as if it's stopping on its heels.

She bends over and disappears into her tent. I hear her setting her two cups on the small table that serves as a kitchen counter of sorts, then the pop of the lid on her springwater jug. She hands me a cup of water and eases down in the other chair.

"Okay. Go ahead. Ask. It's not going to be any easier in a few seconds, a few minutes, or a few hours from now."

For the first time, I look at my mother as though seeing another human being, not just the woman who gave birth to me. I see someone who's run from her sorrows, just like her sister. She just didn't go as far. But maybe she went just as deep. In fact, I know she did. Look at where I'm sitting. If this isn't another country, I don't know what is.

"What happened between you and Aunt Bel? Mom, I don't know why, but I feel like this is the linchpin to everything that's been going on between everybody. There's a tension running underneath the surface that's palpable at times. Daddy taking up for Aunt Bel, you keeping your distance. And while I admit she's eccentric, she's not disagreeable. She doesn't even have poor hygiene, for that matter."

Mom smiles at my joke. "No. Your grandmother made sure we were always extremely clean."

"So why all this?"

"She ran away and deserted us, baby."

"Yes, I've heard that. You know I have. And it's not good enough. Sisters get mad at each other, but they get over it. You and Aunt Bel loved each other once, right? So tell me *why* she ran away, Mom. Tell me why your sister ran halfway across the world and almost never came back. And even more importantly, why nobody cared enough, or was angry enough, to go over and bring her back. How did you and Grandmom and Grandpop come to care for her so little?"

Mom flinches, then finishes her water in four gulps and sets the cup beside her chair. "You were four when Aunt Bel left. Do you remember much about her?"

"Just flashes here and there. I remember this young woman with beautiful, long blond hair. And she had these flashing eyes, so blue, and, Mom, I just remember that they always lit up when I came into the room."

"It's true. She loved you more than we realized she would. Both your father and I remarked that we'd never seen that kind of devotion in an aunt to her niece, at least not at that age. I mean, she was only fifteen when you were born." She laughs a little. "I remember one time I couldn't get ahold of her and had to ask a neighborhood girl to babysit. You would have thought I did everything I could to dishonor and offend her. On purpose."

We laugh together.

"She seems so much more subdued now, Mom. Maybe that's part of my problem. I'm having a hard time reconciling this Aunt Bel with the old one. I almost don't know what to do with her. It's kind of like biting into a piece of cake, only somebody forgot to put in the sugar."

She screws up her face.

I stretch my legs out in front of me, the sun warming my bare shins and the sides of my calves.

"Okay." She grinds her palms against her thighs and drags them down toward her knees. "I don't know how to go about this in any other way than just to say it. There's no gentle way to say it, I suppose."

I lean forward.

"Aunt Bel killed your brother."

"What? What brother?"

"You weren't an only child, baby. You had a little brother. His name was Jason, and he was only three months old when he died."

Jason!

"And Aunt Bel killed him? I don't understand. Was it an accident?" Was this *the* accident?

"Yes. A careless accident, which makes it all the more hard to bear. It was so unnecessary."

And my mother, my crazy mother who never made sense to me, comes into a focus so sharp, is bordered by a line so crisp and perfect, Huey might have pressed her. "Oh, Mom," I say. "Oh, Mom."

She leans forward into her palms, the backs of her hands slowly coming to rest on her knees, and she crumbles into the person she's been trying to escape, the person we all seem to be, the person who fears to look on herself in this state, because if we do, in the recognizing and the greeting, we will never escape who we really are. And if we are never who we are, we can never truly be rejected, or to blame.

Some things hide in corners and don't matter. Crumbs that make their way between the sides of the stove and the countertops, hard-to-reach fuzz under the bed. Even a dead bird in the attic, if undisturbed, won't harm anyone.

But what we've got here is a case of black mold. It's not going any-where and in fact, it will someday take over with its cancerous spores and "I will not go on being ignored" attitude. I don't know how to proceed. And I remember what Huey said. We've never really suffered. Not like this.

So I kneel by her chair, rest my forearm along her back, and run my fingers through her white hair. My mother, all this time, was only being a woman who had lost a child.

I wait as the evening shadows lengthen and she does not move. Twilight approaches and she does not move. The plum of dusk ripens into the fruit of the night heaven, bursting with stars that carry the seeds of who we are. I move her hair off her neck, kiss its nape, and whisper, "I love you, Mom. I'll be back tomorrow."

She looks up. "I love you too, baby." And returns to her grief.

———

"She was only doing the best she could," I cry into Finn's shoulder.

The thing is, he's never had to console me, not really. He married a basically nonemotional woman who took care of her own stuff, who experienced marriage as the icing of an already baked cake. And now, here I am, basically adrift for what seems like no real reason that's mine to claim.

"It's only part of the story," he says after I calm down, after I comment about what pain does to people, how unfair it seems.

"I know. But here's the thing. It's enough. My aunt has been harboring this guilt and fear, enough guilt and fear to keep her away for almost three decades. My mother, on the other hand, has been keeping this secret down inside of her where her wound lies, and the two together fester. To be honest, I can't believe how well she's done with this all these years."

"Amazing how your opinion of someone can change once you know what the load is they're carrying."

"I had no idea. Poor Daddy too. And he continued to try so hard."

"So what's your next step?" he asks gently. "Talk to Aunt Bel?"

"Yes. And then, somehow, we'll have to get those two back together."

"Were they close before, your mom and aunt?"

"I can't even answer that question. I have no idea."

"Wow."

I try to sleep that night, but my brain won't slow down, I keep seeing all sorts of accidents, car accidents, leaving the baby in a hot car (ugh), maybe a choking incident where something solid was fed to the baby too soon. My dreams aren't much better. Why have I heard the truth and it doesn't make me feel any better?

Isn't that the way it's supposed to work?

I peek way down inside me at my imaginary friend. My brother. My brother Jason.

After leaving a message at Happy Hideaway for my mom the next morning to tell her I'm thinking about her, I head out to my father's place in Timonium, a drive that takes me about thirty minutes, mainly because I'm in no hurry. I pull my car up in a driveway that's had its macadam recently refreshed and cut off the engine. With the window rolled down, I can hear the wind blowing in the trees. Otherwise everything is quiet. At the back of the property, the waters of Loch Raven sparkle through trees just starting to sprout their leaves. It smells like the lawn has been freshly mowed too.

The kitchen screen door of the small home, lacquered in a dark brown and sporting a couple of stained glass windows, squeaks. I step inside a small, highly utilitarian kitchen, the place Dad makes his cakes and jellies. At the end of the room, in front of a large bay window overlooking the reservoir, rests his spacious drawing board and his high-backed stool. I loved watching him work when I was little.

He sits there now, swiveling around, a slippered foot resting on the footrest. "Hey, doll. Come on in. Cookies atop the fridge. Milk's inside."

Yes, he makes me cookies and milk.

"You mind if I go talk to her?" I ask.

He stabs his thumb at the backyard. "She took over my shed."

I head out the back door, down a slate path lined with lavender not yet blooming. Of course Dad made the shed beautiful, its siding the same as the house, but no stained glass windows. He got on a wood-working kick awhile back and is still threatening to make more than a hobby of it.

Aunt Bel is tucked into the corner next to a drill press, sitting on a folding chair with a paperback book open in her lap.

"Hello," I say.

She watches me enter, saying nothing.

"Look, Aunt Bel, I came out here to talk. I want to apologize for that night, for throwing the shirt at you the way I did. That was wrong. I knew while it was happening. You forgive me?"

She tilts her head. "It was your favorite shirt."

"Don't make excuses for me," I say. "The thing is, we want you to come back. Me and Finn, we both do. You don't want to stay here."

"Walt says I can stay in the shed if I clean it up."

"But you can come back to my place and not have to do any of that. Your room is still waiting."

"Sara, you're being very nice. I appreciate you coming. I don't think it's for the best, though. I think ... when I went away, there were conse-quences. Not that I intended them. I made choices, yes, but they didn't *feel* like choices at the time."

"You did what you thought was best."

"No," she says. "I went for the wrong reasons. I've told you that already. I stayed for the wrong reasons too ...." Her voice trails off.

"And you came back for the wrong reasons? Is that what you think?"

"I came back because I couldn't take it anymore."

"Come home with me, Aunt Bel."

"The funny thing is, that first month in Kazakhstan, I thought I'd found my calling. Remember, I told you: the life of service. They were so selfless, the other volunteers. When you put us all together like that, with a single purpose, we all became selfless. It made us better than any of us would have been on our own."

"There's nothing quite like finding your group." I think of that crazy crew at the Firehouse.

"And then they split us up and we became ourselves again—at least, I did. It took a long time after that before I finally realized the calling on my life. And when I found it, I tried to be faithful, Sara. From the outside, I'm sure it looked like I was. But in here—" She puts her bandaged hand against her breast. "In here I was always fighting. It was too much, Sara. Too much for me to take."

"The service?" I ask.

"No." She beckons me closer. "I said I *thought* my calling was to serve. Such a noble purpose! To put others ahead of yourself, to forget yourself. I wish it had been that, Sara. I could have done that. I proved it at the beginning. I needed to."

"Then what?"

"My calling was not to serve. The longer I was there, the more things that happened . . . I began to realize that the Lord had called me to *suffer*."

"Aunt Bel, don't even say that."

"It's the truth. You don't like to hear it—well, I don't like to say it. But my child, Sara, my little baby boy. He had a father who didn't love him, grandparents who abandoned him, and he had me, a hopeless mother. And he was sick, Sara, right from the start. So small and underweight. Slow to develop. I knew there was something wrong, but once he was older the doctors said he would be fine." Her eyes narrow. "They know nothing, the doctors."

"What was wrong with him?" I ask.

"His heart," she says. She reaches out with her undamaged hand. I crouch beside her, clamping it against my chest. "When he was only five, just five years old, I went outside to hang the laundry and there he was in the grass. Like he was sleeping, with his legs drawn up, his back turned toward me. I knelt beside him and tried to wake him, but he was gone."

As she speaks her voice fills and empties itself, rocking with emotion then dry as dust, as if the words transport her back in time to the traumatic moment of Michael's passing and then fling her forward into the far, far future, where the death can be observed with chilling detachment. She channels grief the way a jaded veteran might channel violence, not devoid of passion exactly, but with too much experience to let it reign.

"It must have been terrible," I say. "I can't even imagine what you went through." I want to ask her about my brother, but how much can a person take in one sitting?

"That was only the start. Sara, I never opened my heart except to have it broken. I never loved without being hated in return, never understood anything without being misunderstood. I recognized what was happening to me, and where it came from. I thought of Job and tried to be comforted. Job did nothing, yet everything was taken from him. Why? For the glory of God, whatever that means. To prove a point. His family taken, his body broken, his friends turned against him—and I tried to tell myself, however impossible it seemed, this was good. No, not good. You should never call evil good or you'll soon find it impossible to tell the difference. Justified, that's it. I told myself what was happening to me was justified. That it served some greater purpose, and I should be content."

"You're so hard on yourself."

"There was Katya, eventually. She understood. She had her own suffering, you see, and marked people like us, we recognize each other."

"Sergei told me about her," I say. "He said she was 'sick in the head.'"

An icy smile twists her lips. "Sick in the head. Yes. Other pastors there would say she had a demon in her. A mental illness. Katya suffered from depression for a very long time. Who could blame her? I struggled myself. But with her, the situation was . . . clinical. Sometimes they gave her medicine that helped. Her illness was too strong; it always found ways around the medicine.

"She was always so fragile, Katya. Several times I expected her to slip away, to succumb to her madness, and then she would rally and I thanked God for it. She was the one thing God had permitted me to keep, you see. The one thing he had not taken or twisted or turned around on me. When you have nothing, you can be very grateful for just one thing. When you have nothing to love, you can give all you have to just one friend. I had made a kind of pact with him: You can do what you like as long as I have her. I don't care, just don't take her away."

"You really loved her."

"Oh yes. She was a widow, a few years older than me. She had been married to one of the local pastors—the man who started the church where Sergei is now. He died of leukemia—I barely knew what that was— and already Katya's troubles had started. She would seem normal, happy, and then . . . she would just let herself go. The dishes would stack up at the sink, the dirty clothes piled high, and her eyes would burn with this frantic energy. I had never seen anything like it. She seemed feverish, but was cool to the touch. One day I visited her apartment and she was shovel-ing earth into the bathtub. She was going to grow vegetables, she said.

"Then it would pass. I would say a prayer to God: *Don't go too far. You've done enough. You don't need to push her any closer to the edge.* And for a while, he would listen. I felt good then. All of the suffering I had gone through—and there are things I haven't told you, things I would never tell you or anyone—it didn't matter anymore. I could even tell myself it was worthwhile, because through suffering I had gained some influence. I could pray for Katya and he would have to listen. He owed me that much."

She straightens her spine and grips the arms of the lawn chair. "But he wasn't listening, Sara. Or if he listened, he did what he wanted regardless. He took her, and in the worst way, the most reprehensible way. When she seemed to be all right, I took her with me on a journey to the South. I had been living for years in Uralsk—Oral, they call it now—and this was the first time I went back to the Caspian, back to where I had first met the Galts. There was a couple there, young missionaries, and the woman was pregnant and struggling. I really felt for her. You can understand why. So I went down to help, and took Katya with me. She had never seen the sea. I thought it would do her good."

Aunt Bel rocks back and forth in her chair as she speaks, her expression distant, blank. This is not a story she's told before. This is still unprocessed grief. She tells it quickly, as if she's afraid we might be interrupted, afraid something will happen and she will be prevented from reaching the end.

"The young woman, her ankles had swollen and she could barely move without pain. It was her first child. She hadn't wanted to have it in Kazakhstan, she wanted to go home. The husband, I think, would have agreed, but they had this way of not telling each other their fears, not confiding. Like someone had told them to be an encouragement to one another and they had both taken the advice too literally. So she would tell him she didn't think it was too bad, and he would agree that she was probably right. I tried to talk sense into them, and so I was distracted. I didn't see how bad Katya had gotten.

"She turned suddenly. She grew very aggressive, very paranoid. That was a sign, you see, when Katya would suddenly hate everyone, suspect everyone. But they were getting on my nerves too, so I didn't see it. She left the apartment one day and said she was going to go walk along the water. I was encouraged, because I'd never heard such a thing from her before during one of her bad times. She'd barely leave her place. She was gone for hours, gone the whole night, and in the morning they fished her out of the sea. She had drowned herself, Sara. On purpose. I think she did it because I was not listening to her. I was paying too much attention to these other people who didn't mean nearly as much to me."

Hearing a tragedy like this, the only way to convey my feelings is through touch. There are no words, so I put my arms around her and squeeze her tight.

I pull back at the connections forming in my mind. I'm afraid to ask. Was the accident she walked away from really an accident? Or had Aunt Bel succumbed to despair too and plotted her own death?

"The funeral, of course, was to be held in Uralsk," she continues. "I was on my way there when I realized it would have been difficult. I would have said things, I think, that would have been misunderstood. Anyway, God had done it. He had taken her. We weren't on speaking terms at that point."

"How about now?" I ask.

"Silence, you know, is a two-way street."

"So did you make it to Uralsk?"

She holds up her injured arm and shakes her head.

"The river." I remember what Sergei told me. "Did you purposefully . . . ?"

"No." She shakes her head. "But there are days I wish I had, because then it would have all been over and done with."

That settles it. "Aunt Bel, I want you to come back with me. You don't belong here."

"I don't belong there," she says.

"That's not true. The house isn't the same without you. Even the Microchurch misses you. You should have seen it: your painting on the wall. Rick had us all line up in front of it, told us to look at it, really look at it. I can't speak for anyone else, but, Aunt Bel, it moved me. I should have realized before, but I didn't. I've seen that thing dozens of times, but it never even dawned on me what you were trying to represent."

"I'm not much of an artist."

"You *are*," I say. "You have an eye, Aunt Bel. It's true. I knew it when I first saw those pictures you took of me. I hate myself in pictures, even self-portraits. I can never get the me on film that I see in the mirror. But you did. You have real talent."

"Sara," she says. "I appreciate your offer. Let me think about it. If I have to answer right now, then, I think I will stay here."

"Then don't answer now. Besides, I don't know if you've picked up on this, but that man in there, he's looking to unload you."

She smiles.

"Aunt Bel, we *want* you. Think about that if you need to, but when you're done thinking, then it's time to come home. You call me, okay? Day or night. I'll come and get you, or if I can't Finn will. And here, I brought this." Reaching into my shoulder bag, I hand her the box of checkbooks from the bank. "It's a gift and you have to accept it."

"I can't."

"You can write a big check and give it all to charity if you want, but the money is yours and there's nothing you can do about that."

She tucks the box under the book on her lap.

"By the way, you're not going to believe this: Finn and Huey got the Iron Maiden running. Can you believe it?"

"Oh yes," she says. "I never had any doubt."

"They painted it green, though, you'll be sorry to hear."

She draws my hand to her lips and kisses it lightly. "That's for the best. Now leave me here. I have some reading to do."

"And some thinking?"

"Some thinking too."

I cross the lawn in a pensive mood. My dad opens the sliding glass door, motioning me inside.

"No luck today, Daddy. But she's coming home," I tell him. "Just not yet."

19.

The Limits of Beauty

W_e clean up all right, the Old Firehouse crew. In the studio, where we've gathered in advance of the gala so we can all drive to the hotel together, I line everybody up for inspection, impressed with what I see. Finn looks sharp in his new velvet blazer and dark jeans. He bucked my suggestion of renting a tux for the event, and he was right: this looks more natural on him. Then there's Diana in a bright red vintage fifties number, sort of a Marilyn Monroe, Lady in Red look that bares her inked arms for all the world. I'm sure she'll raise a few conservative rich-person eyebrows, but raising eyebrows is a good thing for creatives like us. We're going there to get noticed.

"Huey, Huey, Huey," I say. "You're the belle of the ball."

For Huey hasn't followed through on his threat to show up in an ink-stained boiler suit. No, it turns out that somewhere in Huey's walk-up apartment, tucked behind all the zip-front jumpsuits with his name embroidered on them, there's been a secret lurking all these years. Who would have thought that this sartorial blank slate of a man possessed an impeccable vintage tuxedo in midnight blue, nipped at the waist with shimmery round lapels?

"Secret Agent Man," Finn says.

Huey pulls a pair of dark shades from inside his jacket and slips them on. "We don't look half bad, do we?"

Diana struts over to me. "*You* look darling." She turns to the others. "I'd buy good taste from this woman, wouldn't you?"

"Hear, hear," Huey says. "Now, if the fashion show is over, we better get on the road. I brought my truck so I'm driving."

Huey's "truck" is a big black Chevy SUV with blingy rims. He washes the thing every weekend and keeps vulture watch on the uphol-stery. Once Finn asked to borrow it to run some boxes across town, which earned him a full minute of incredulous stares. The fact that Huey's brought it along for tonight speaks volumes. He is proud of how the whole project turned out. It's some of the finest, most challenging presswork we have ever done. He opens the passenger door and helps me inside, motioning for Finn and Diana to hop in back.

"Watch your dress," he says, snapping the door shut.

The Marriott Waterfront is only a short drive away, but it feels like it takes ages thanks to my nerves. This is a big night, after all. The first time I'll meet Holly's millionaire husband, not to mention all his million-aire friends who presumably have occasional need for design work and the money to actually have it done right.

"Last time we went to a hotel," Diana says, "it was for the Wedding Expo. It'll be nice to be a guest for a change—and have some fun!"

"Not too much fun," Finn adds. "We're still working, you know."

She laughs. "I could work like this every night."

Something else bothers me about tonight, something I haven't spoken to anyone about, including Finn. The way Holly and I parted the day we went dress shopping put an idea in my head. Every time I've talked to her since, in person or on the phone, that idea has grown. She's tense about tonight, on edge, and the thing I never appreciated about Holly until recently is that, when she wants to convince herself, she overpraises. From the beginning, I've loved this woman because she's unstinting in her praise. I can do no wrong in her eyes. Only now, hitting rewind and reviewing those conversations, I begin to wonder what was actually going through her mind. Why would she need to convince herself the work I've done is good? Either she likes it or she doesn't.

I think I know the answer. What she likes isn't what matters. What matters is what her husband likes. This whole project has been Holly's baby from the start. She's been more invested in it than any client I've worked with, happy to see proofs day or night, willing to drive down and talk things over face-to-face, and always—*always*—approving of everything.

The others don't feel it. Looking over my shoulder at them, I can see this. Diana sits dazzled by the waterfront lights. Finn taps his knee in rhythm, distracted but relaxed. Next to me Huey hangs his hand over the steering wheel, humming along with the music playing faintly in the background. I listen closer and recognize the guttural crooning of Tom Waits.

> *Well it's got to be a chocolate Jesus,*
> *Make me feel good inside,*

Finn leans forward. "Chocolate Jesus? Is that a black thing?"

"A black thing?" Huey asks. "No, man, it's what it sounds like. Chocolate candy. Shaped like Jesus, I guess—I don't know."

Leaning back, Finn resumes his tapping. Black Jesus must be worth talking about. Chocolate Jesus not so much.

"You know something," I say to Huey. "This thing tonight isn't a done deal."

"What do you mean? She loves our work. Your work. There's no question about that. This here is just to show us off. It's a victory lap, and it makes a nice change from the way most of our jobs wrap up."

"I think the jury's still out until her husband gives his approval."

"If they're handing out the pieces tonight, I assume that's already happened."

"She doesn't talk that way, though."

"We'll see."

When we arrive at the hotel, an attendant opens my door. We all gather on the driver's side while Huey decides whether to entrust the valet with his keys. He finally relents and we head inside. Several older couples in evening wear slip ahead of us. As the ladies walk, I catch a glimpse of red-soled feet.

"You might need these," Huey says, holding out his shades. "Otherwise you'll go blind staring directly at some of this jewelry."

At the entrance to the ballroom, I find myself at the elbow of a very bejeweled lady with a frosty white up-do. There's something sobering about standing next to someone whose accessories for the evening are probably worth more than my house. Finn loops his arm in mine, reading my thoughts.

"We are the youngest, poorest people in here," he whispers, "and, let's just be honest, probably the coolest too."

We both look over at Huey. "*He's* the coolest," I say.

"Then the pressure's off. So let's have a good time."

A string quartet off to one side plays, I kid you not, the theme song to *Somewhere in Time*, and a very busy bar off to the other side plays dueling bourbons. The room is packed already with people, but it doesn't seem crowded so much as clustered. We have to weave our way through, circling the edge of one group, turning to miss another. Instead of walking side by side, the four of us lapse into a single file line in the style of a *danse macabre*, with Finn up front, me trailing by the hand, Diana at my heels, and Huey in back, checking people out as he walks by.

"See if you can spot Holly," I call out.

Finn finds her at the opposite side of the ballroom, lovely in diaphanous pink silk, her high silver heels adding another half foot to her already towering height. Tonight's wig, a blond, short New York bob, gleams under the lights of the chandeliers. Instead of mingling with the guests, she fusses over a table with all our printed pieces laid out, mother-henning a group of servers who are ready to start handing out the goods at her say-so. Up close, I can tell she's frazzled.

"Take a deep breath," I say.

"Oh, good, you're here! What do you think?" She steps back so we can all admire the table. "I was going to have them given out at the door, but I thought it would make more sense to do it after Eric's speech so they have a little context."

"Everything looks wonderful," I tell her. "And that sounds like a great idea."

"Let me introduce you all . . ."

She takes me by the hand, guiding us back into the swirling crowd in search of her husband, who seems to be pressing flesh up ahead, always darting a little farther away before we can quite catch up. My first glimpse of him is in profile. Eric Ringwald is not as tall as his wife or as svelte, and at a glance I'd say he's a decade or more her senior, but he glows with the natural charisma of a man in his element. The smile seems genuine everywhere he turns. Everyone he faces is someone he knows, someone he can share memories with and joke with and pat on the shoulder and leave them beaming. His tux fits impeccably, but has a rumpled, slouchy quality, almost as if he'd slept in it. *Your idea of fancy is my idea of pajamas.*

"Eric, wait up," Holly says, catching him by the sleeve.

He turns toward us and the smile stays in place, the same light of recognition in his eyes, even though we've never met.

"Great to see you," he says, pumping my hand. "How 'bout this crowd tonight, huh? And it's for such a good cause."

As he leans past me to clamp Finn's hand in his fist, Holly frowns, pulling the sleeve once more. "No, Eric, listen to me a minute. This is somebody I want you to meet."

He recovers nicely, now giving me an expectant though somewhat bewildered glance. "Sorry about that. Eric Ringwald. My pleasure."

"This is Sara Drexel, her husband, Finn, and this is Huey and Diana. They're the ones who designed the new logo and website, and the new brochures."

"Designed and printed," Huey mutters.

"That's wonderful, wonderful," Eric Ringwald says. "So happy you all could make it. There's a bar over there, please avail yourselves . . . And enjoy the evening!"

He departs with a laugh, back-slapping Finn and Huey both as he makes his way to the next cluster of guests.

"He's very busy with all this," Holly says. "So caught up."

"Hey, it's all right." I try to reassure her, putting on a braver front than I feel. That was a bit of a brush-off, after all.

Huey slips into the crowd, saying he's going to take the man at his word and "avail himself," and soon Diana follows. If I could signal Finn to disappear, I would, knowing Holly would rather not have an audience just now. But my husband all of a sudden seems incapable of taking hints.

"So this is a pretty good turn-out, huh?" he asks, motioning toward the crowd. "You think that's because of the invitations or what?"

His joke falls flat and Holly, misunderstanding, starts to absolutely gush about those invitations, which are the best she's ever seen, assuring us that, yes, it probably was the invitations that ensured such a strong turn-out, lavishing Finn and me with all the praise she feels we are due, the praise we ought to have gotten from the man himself but didn't. Like a mother compensating for a father's oversight, the exchange is both reassuring and too revealing. I appreciate the kind words, but what they tell me about Holly's own insecurities, her standing in the marriage, even her perception of what we expect from her—well, all I can say is, my heart goes out to her. She's doing what we all do, giving others what she needs herself, and in the process revealing what is missing in her life.

"You know what?" I say. "*You've* done a great job. I mean, look at all this. This is you. I'm impressed."

"*Way* impressed," Finn adds, giving me one more reason to love this guy. Even when he's ripping apart my house, I have to remember, it comes from a good place.

Just to prove how right my instincts are, Holly blooms like a flower with just the faintest praise. The tightness in her brow lets go, her mouth unclenches, and she is momentarily (but truly) transformed. It's an interesting shift too: She doesn't giggle behind her hand and revert to a little girl. No, Holly grows. She stands up straighter and becomes radiant, as if all it takes to make this woman strong is a ray of sunlight, just a flash of acknowledgment. Give her that and you'll see a new person, the one she's meant to be.

In this place of opulence, I recall Bel's troubling words about the calling in her life. Not to service, as she'd expected, but to suffering. If there can be such a thing as a calling to suffer, then please, please let me miss my calling. A calling is supposed to fulfill you. It's what you're meant for. In the middle of your calling, how can you be anything but content? Who can be content with a life of suffering? Not me, I know that—and not Bel either, or she wouldn't have run away from it. No. The flat, stern Byzantine Christ calls us to suffer. Aunt Bel's Jesus goes deeper than that, back to the molten fires that forged us in the loving hands of our Creator.

And now Holly stands here, a beautiful woman with every advantage you can name: the face, the body, the brain, the rich husband with what I can only assume is a heart of gold (the man raises money for charity!), style, and class. The woman has good taste. But as she strides away to fulfill her hostess duties, I recognize that Holly Ringwald has missed her calling. This woman has been denied the one thing she needs in order to be who she ought to be. Praise? Respect? Simple acknowledgment? I'm not sure I have the right word. But I know this: it would be such an *easy* thing to give her, much easier to provide than the things she already has.

"That makes me sad," Finn says.

"What does?"

He gives me a look. "I'm not the blunt instrument you take me for, woman. I have eyes. I can see what's going on. She's not happy, is she?"

I shake my head as Huey, bless him, sidles up and presses a glass of red wine into my hand, then heads back into the throng.

"You feel out of place around all this money?" Finn whispers. "I can't help feeling like people are looking at us."

"We're not that different from them," I say.

"We're completely different." The passion in his voice takes me by surprise. "We're completely different," he repeats. "What do they do? They make a profit. What do you do? You make things beautiful. You're an artist, hon. You're nothing like them."

"Is making things beautiful all that different from making them profitable? Sometimes it's the same exact thing, don't you think?"

"No, I don't," he says.

"I think we agree, you just don't realize it yet."

At the back of the room, Eric Ringwald mounts a short flight of steps onto a platform. A spotlight comes on, picking out the wrinkles in his jacket. A moment later the chandeliers overhead begin to dim.

"Is this thing on?" Eric asks, tapping the mic with his finger, then laughing. "Seriously, people, I want to thank you all for coming out.

Thanks to you, the world is a better place tonight than it would have been without you. Thanks to you, there are children with food who would have gone to bed hungry, children in school who would have grown up on the streets, and children in hospitals where just a year or two ago there was no medical care, children who wouldn't *be* in the world tonight if there weren't people like *you* in the world tonight. So tonight is about you. Give yourselves a big hand."

The crowd applauds itself on cue, and there are even a few whistles from somewhere behind us. In the shadows beneath the platform, Holly stands at the table where all the printed material is arranged, a row of servers all in black lined up at her shoulder.

"I know, I know," Eric interrupts, raising his hand for silence. "Most of you know what it's like to be out on the ocean on the weekend, or down in the islands soaking up some rays, only to hear your phone ring and see my number on the screen. And you're thinking, 'What does he want?' even though you know exactly what I want—"

"Yes, we do!" someone shouts to laughter from the crowd.

"Believe me, I know what a pain I can be. But at the end of the day, this is what it's all about. You and me standing here, knowing we haven't done nothing with our lives, we've done something. Knowing we've done some good, that we've made a difference, that we found this place in a shamble and instead of walking by *we did something about it!*

"So tonight, let's give credit where credit is due. That call you answered, that line you picked up, that check you wrote—listen to me: ten other people, a hundred other people, they didn't answer, they didn't pick up, they didn't write the check, but *you did.* You think that doesn't mean anything? Of course it does. Together, the people in this room have done amazing things. We've built schools and hospitals. We've stocked the shelves with food. We have helped keep families together, we've given them a roof over their heads, and we've done something else: we've given them hope. And that gives *me* hope.

"Every person in this room—you're not just donors, you know; you're friends. Now a man can't always choose his friends, but I look around and I'll tell you, knowing these people, the people in this room, these *generous* people . . . are my friends . . . It makes me the happiest man in the world."

Eric waves and descends the steps to raucous applause, but there was no mention of the brochures. Finn casts me a glance easily interpreted as, *Wow. That's a shocker.*

As the spotlight winks out, the string quartet strikes up again, trading in the movie score fare of a few minutes ago for a jazzier beat. The drinks flow and the donors mingle and a few of them on the outskirts even dance. Looking around, I see Diana there, swaying happily with a much older gentleman who can't seem to believe his luck. Huey's propping up the bar, his shades back on, probably amusing himself with the thought that nobody in the room has read half the books he has. Finn takes me toward the front, toward Holly, who is whispering in her husband's distracted ear. He's nodding at her words without seeming to hear them, trying to slip past her without seeming to.

As we get closer, I can read his lips. *Go on*, he's saying. *It'll mean more coming from you*, or something like that. He's gesturing toward the stage, bidding her upward, all but pushing her toward the steps. If she wants something said about the printed pieces, she should do it—that seems to be the gist.

"Come on," I say, hustling toward her on tip-toes so as to not tip over on my heels.

We reach them just as Holly is mounting the bottom step. Eric disengages, flashes a smile, then disappears into the audience. I take Holly by the wrist, motioning her back to the ground.

"Eric forgot—" she begins, trying to frame an excuse.

"When I show clients a piece," I tell her, drawing her back toward the table, "I like to do it without a lot of explanation. Let the work speak for itself, that's the idea. What do you say we try that here? Instead of telling them, let's just show them. Here, we can help." I grab a stack of elaborately folded brochures from the table, placing it in Finn's willing hands, then take another stack for myself. For a moment Holly teeters on the brink, not quite convinced, and then she recovers some of the strength I glimpsed earlier, taking a stack for herself.

"Let's do it," she says to the line of servers.

Just as we begin to work the edge of the crowd, Huey comes up between Finn and me with some brochures in his hand. Diana, too, squeezes between two converging clusters that are close enough she has to raise her arms and turn sideways to slip by.

"I want in on this," she says, trotting back to the table.

It's silly, I know, but the sight of my people at my side, forcing brochures into the already crowded hands of old men in tuxes clutching cocktail glasses and plates, the sight of us strolling through the circles and breaking up conversations, making enough of a stir that women four and five rows away are straining to see what's going on, makes me glow inside. We're not handing loaves and fish out to the five thousand or anything monumental like that, but what we're doing, we're doing together without any of us having to be told. We're doing it as one mind, helping a woman who's never been anything but kind to us save face.

If I could say something to Huey, to Diana, if I could whisper loud enough so that even Finn could hear without my being overheard, I would say this: I am proud of you. Proud to be one of you. Because tonight wasn't about you and you didn't insist on tonight being about you. I'm not the happiest girl in the world; I'm not even sure what that means anymore or why it matters. If happiness isn't enough, that doesn't mean nothing is enough. Maybe there's something besides happiness to strive for, and if there is, you're the people I want around me as I try.

Glancing over my shoulder, I see the effect we've had. People are puzzling over the intricate folds, peeling them back like the petals of a flower. A few faces seem disinterested, preoccupied, even unimpressed, but there is wonder too—a lot of it. One lady who is cinched tight and spilling over the edge of her age-inappropriate strapless gown actually bounces with excitement as she figures out the folding trick, demonstrating it to the women around her again and again.

We're halfway through the room, already having run back several times to reload on brochures, when Eric Ringwald finally notices what's going on. He doesn't come over, doesn't say anything, certainly doesn't join in. But I notice he puts his hand on the shoulder of the man next to him and points our way. I don't know what he's saying, but I nudge Holly and point right back.

"I think he approves," I say.

She hands off a brochure, then glances over. Although she smiles, she doesn't light up like before. "If he approves, he should get off his butt and help." She laughs.

"You have a point."

Then, after the last of my brochures is gone, I gather my people together at the far end of the room. From there we can look back the way a farmer looks back over a plowed field. Holly comes over, putting one arm around me and one around Huey, nudging her way into the huddle.

"I want to thank you, all of you," she begins.

"We want to thank you too," Finn says.

I smile at them both. "All right, all right. Let's not go making any big speeches. Let's just enjoy the moment. Together."

The quartet plays and the glasses clink and here and there one of our brochures is unfolded, passed around, maybe even read. A lot of work went into this moment.

"You gonna be okay?" I ask Holly.

"I'm gonna be just fine," she says. "And . . . thanks."

After we say good night to her, the four of us exit the way we came in, a single file line with Huey bringing up the rear. When the door swings shut behind him, he takes the shades off and collapses against a convenient pillar.

"We left a lot of ourselves back there," he says.

"Yes, indeed, brother," Finn says, going for the fist bump.

For once Huey doesn't disappoint him. The two men bump fists and we disappear into the night.

———

I leave the closet door ajar so I can hang my purple taffeta dress up and keep an eye on it from the bed. Finn's jacket hangs from the doorknob, his inside-out jeans half standing in a stiff puddle at the foot of the bed. He's already sound asleep.

I'm not. I'm waiting.

Coincidence or serendipity, I don't know if there's even a word, but since we came home I've had a feeling, and I've decided to trust it and not go to sleep. So I lay in bed gazing up at the purple dress, holding my phone so I can feel the first buzz and answer before the ringer sounds. Aunt Bel's going to call. I know she is.

I wish Mom would as well, while the O'Hara sisters are making calls. I'm worried about her. Having something so painful exposed so suddenly has got to feel like being plunged down into a cave you thought you'd covered over for good.

And at a quarter to one, Aunt Bel calls. No apology for the late hour. She knows better than that. I pick up almost immediately and there's no surprise on her end. It seems natural to her that I would be waiting, as natural as it felt for me to wait.

"I've decided," Aunt Bel says.

"You want me to come now?"

"The morning is soon enough."

I glance at Finn. Still dead to the world. Then I peel the covers back and slide to the floor.

"Now, I'm leaving now," I say. "You need to come home."

I dress silently in jeans and one of Finn's old sweatshirts, then slip the car keys out from under his wallet on the nightstand. I leave the house, pausing to lock the deadbolt, then pad down the still and shadowy street to where our car is parked under the drooping leaves of the pavement-popping tree. It feels strange but special being out so late, alone behind the wheel of the car. The mission is energizing, though. It's time to bring Aunt Bel home.

Finn usually does most of the driving, so everything's set for him. I scoot the driver's seat forward, tilt the wheel down until it almost touches my thighs, fiddle with the mirror controls as I hurdle down the street. He's fussy about the mirrors, saying most people don't know how to adjust them properly—and by "most people" he means me. If I'd wanted to, I could have awakened him, could have asked him to drive. He would have complained, bleary-eyed and indignant, but in the end he would have done it. But I didn't want him. This is my journey to make.

As I leave the city behind, the hum of highway under my feet, my body fills with a sense of peace. Aunt Bel should be with us. We belong in each other's lives. Her history of loss doesn't threaten me anymore. It strengthens me. She has so much to teach me, I realize. So much still to share. And there are things I can finally tell her. That gives me peace too.

An orange light on the dash flicks on. The needle on the gas tank hovers at empty. I exit the highway and pull into a service plaza, driving underneath a vast corrugated awning to one of a half dozen well-lit fuel pumps. The storefront window proclaims "Open 24-7," and indeed there are several cars pulled up to the entrance and people walking around inside, poking their heads into the refrigerated units along the back end of the shop where the energy drinks and the sodas and the twelve-packs of beer are kept.

After unscrewing the gas cap, I slide the nozzle inside. I have to step over the hose to reach the passenger door, grabbing my purse off the seat. I fish around for my debit card, but it isn't here. Hours ago, as I was getting ready for the gala, I transferred my debit card, my driver's license, and my wadded roll of ones and fives from my purse to a tiny purple clutch that went with my dress. They're all back at the house.

I can't make it to my dad's without getting gas. Finn won't wake up to the sound of his cell phone. I could call Bel, who could borrow my dad's car—but that's a worst-case scenario. I can't see that going well.

So I crawl through the passenger's side and start hunting around for change on hands and knees. I empty the coins in the ashtray, dig some more out from under the floor mats, and find a stash of quarters Finn has hidden in the driver's door compartment for paying tolls. Counting up the total, I have five dollars and eleven cents. I transfer the money into a plastic bag from under the passenger seat, then go inside.

The attendant perches behind a thick Plexiglas partition. Up close I can see how scratched and filthy the surface is, as if a horde of people have tried to claw their way in over the years. The floors are grimy too, and there's a strange smell to the place, like milk that's gone off. I empty my bag of change into the hole in the counter that runs under the glass.

"You're paying with this?" the attendant asks. He's not much more than a kid, old enough to shave but too young to realize he should. He looks at the change through bloodshot eyes, as if he's never seen so many coins in his life.

"I lost my credit card," I say, smiling optimistically. I put a lot of effort into the smile too, trying to convey that, yes, I know it's a pain to count a bunch of loose change, and ordinarily I would never ask him to do it, but these are special circumstances and—

"You people kill me," he says. "Girls like you."

"What does that mean?"

"Nothing," he says, scooping up some of the coins. "At least you're paying. Some of them come in here and they smile and they think they can just stand there looking pretty and I'll turn the pump on for them."

"That is money," I say. "Legal tender."

"I know, I know. Like I said, at least you're paying."

I don't feel like getting into an argument with this kid. I'm embarrassed enough to be prepaying for $5.11 of gas in loose change. Some of the coins look sticky to the touch. They've probably been under the mat for months. At least he said something about looking pretty. I must be quite a sight, though, in my baggy sweatshirt with my face all made-up for the gala.

A line of people queues up behind me, waiting for the kid to finish counting all the change. I catch a whiff of pot coming off the guys behind me, who are clutching big bags of Funyuns and Cheetos to their chests.

"Okay," the attendant says. "Which pump?"

"I don't know the number. It's the only car out there."

He could just glance through the window, but instead he has to walk over for a good long look. I can hear the stoners fidgeting. One of them grows impatient and rips the Funyuns open.

"Want some, lady?" he asks.

I laugh and pluck one out of the bag. "Thanks."

"Pump #3," the kid says, then to the stoners: "You need to pay for that first." He sees the guilty Funyun in my hand and rolls his eyes.

Setback or comic relief? I'll take comic relief.

I rush outside, leaving the surreal world of the service plaza at night. Once my five bucks worth of gas is pumped, I screw the cap back on and get out of there, feeling strangely relieved. Putting distance between me and the gas station, I start to laugh at the kid attendant and the stoners with the munchies. I switch on the radio, still smiling at the absurdity.

Twenty minutes later I exit off the beltway onto Dulaney Valley Road, and as I head north, the lots of the houses I pass grow larger, and more trees push their way against the night sky. Finally, I pull into Dad's driveway, putting the car into park.

Aunt Bel is sitting on the front steps smoking a cigarette. Her duffel bag is at her feet. Over her head, a cloud of insects darts around the porch light, possibly agitated by the smoke.

I roll the window down. "I barely made it."

She takes a last drag on her cigarette, then moves to put it out.

"No, bring it. That's fine. It's such a beautiful night."

Aunt Bel glances up at the starry sky, as if she hasn't noticed any particular beauty. Perhaps she's right, but to my eyes everything looks beautiful just now, especially her.

20.

Default Divorcee

A package from Katz Lime arrives via the FedEx man, who shoots the breeze with Diana while I scrawl an electronic signature across his portable screen. Inside there's a fold-out map with the whole itinerary marked with striped washi tape and stick-on arrows, a stack of dog-eared tourist guidebooks in which Ethan has highlighted spots of interest along the way, and a beautiful book hand bound in teal leather with deckle-edged pages and thick raised bands on the spine. It was commissioned by Dora from a bookbinder in Vermont and inside it she's tucked a note instructing me to have every person I photograph on the journey write down a story, an idea, a memory, anything they like. When the portraits go up in a special corner of the Brooklyn shop, this book will stand on a display pedestal for everyone to see.

I unpack the contents on the conference table, savoring the thought of the journey and fearing it a little too. Two weeks on the road. Two weeks away from home. Two weeks living out of a suitcase, meeting up with strangers, taking photos. Although I've been practicing with the Autocord every spare moment and have the film developing bills to prove it, I feel less than confident in my skills, so I'm bringing along my digital camera as a backup.

Unfolding the map on the table, smoothing the corners down, I study the route and imagine what it might be like, the two of us together working side by side. "I'd feel better if you would come with me, Aunt Bel."

She's peering in the box, ignoring my comment. Every attempt I've made to get her on board, to elicit a firm commitment, Aunt Bel simply dodges. Give her time, Finn keeps telling me. You know how she can be.

"Look at this," she says, handing me a slip of paper she's found at the bottom of the box. One of them, Ethan or Dora, has copied some lines of a poem out by hand.

> *Mon enfant, ma soeur,*
> *Songe à la douceur*
> *D'aller là-bas*
> *vivre ensemble!*
> *Aimer à loisir,*
> *Aimer et mourir*
> *Au pays qui te resessemble!*

At the bottom of the page, a title is inscribed: *L'invitation au voyage.* "What does it mean?" she asks.

"I don't know. Let's go stump Mr. Literature."

Over at the Iron Maiden, which we've moved to a place of pride near the front window, Huey is pulling prints of the new line of trash-talk greeting cards, which Dora and Ethan are anxious to release alongside the unveiling of the portraits. He pauses to examine the lines from the poem, drawing out the suspense because he doesn't like being tested.

"If you don't know, just say so," I tell him.

"For real? You gotta try harder before it even feels like a challenge."

"Prove it."

"That's a famous French poem. 'Invitation to the Voyage.'"

"Obviously. Even I could figure that out."

"Charles Baudelaire," he says. "You want me to translate? Here goes. It's something like this: 'My child, my sister, think of the sweetness, to go down there, to live together, to love until we lose, to love and to die, in a country that looks like you.' That's more or less what it's saying."

"Huey, you're amazing."

"Please," he says.

Aunt Bel and I go back to the table, back to the journey that could be. She seems thoughtful, at least, meditative. Maybe she's trying to convince herself to come along. Since my midnight drive to retrieve her from my dad's house two months ago, I've tried to turn over a new leaf with Aunt Bel, not to pressure her or judge her, not to let her strangeness get under my skin, but instead to befriend her as I should have done from the start. Let her be who she is, not expecting more. The trip would be good for us, I think, and her presence would reassure me. I can't take Finn—the shop can't run without both of us for that length of time—and I don't relish the thought of going alone. Let's just say I need the company to keep me sane. Two weeks on my own is not my idea of fun.

"Come on," I say. "Think of the sweetness."

She laughs. "You don't need me to do this, Sara. You can do it on your own."

"I know I can do it alone. But I don't want to. Besides, it's not such a big inconvenience, is it? You can stand two weeks with me. It'll be fun. We'll meet a lot of interesting people too, see some places we've never been before. Looks like Ethan has managed to locate every eccentric, out-of-the-way bed-and-breakfast along the route. A road trip, Bel! And the client is picking up the tab. You can't say no to that."

"I don't know," she says.

"Listen, Aunt Bel." I lean closer so I can whisper. "I want to start over, okay? We have a lot to talk about. There are things you've never told me, you know."

"What things?"

"Sergei had a name for you. Novikova. He called you Belinda Novikova. What's that all about?"

"Oh, that." She dismisses the name with a wave of her hand. "Just a man I married once. Novikov. Nothing to tell."

"You married him and there's nothing to tell?"

She shrugs. "It's hard to be always alone."

"I'd like to know a little bit more about him than that."

"It was foolish of me. I make bad choices when it comes to men. Novikov was a bad man. There's nothing more to tell."

"Did you divorce him?" I ask.

She gives me a funny look. "Divorce him? I didn't need to, Sara. Remember, I died."

"Aunt *Bel*," I say.

"What?"

"You have a way of dropping bombs into a conversation."

"Two weeks of that," she says. "How could you stand it?"

"There are things I'd like to talk to you about."

She takes this in, nodding slowly. I remember the first time I saw her, unlatching her seat belt in my mother's car, looking at the thing in wonder like she'd never observed a seat belt in operation before. There's something similar to the look she's giving me now. Like she's standing outside our relationship as the buckle clicks shut, realizing belatedly how the whole contraption is meant to work.

"You don't have to talk to me about anything," she says.

"I don't have to. I want to."

"Maybe," she says, pausing before she continues. "Maybe it would be better not to. Knowing people is good, but knowing their histories and secrets, sometimes that's not so good. You ask me so many questions. I wouldn't know what to ask you."

"It's okay, Aunt Bel. You wouldn't *have* to ask. When people trust each other, the rest just flows. And we trust each other, don't we?"

"Trust is hard," she says.

I head back to the studio kitchen and pour another cup of coffee. Once more, I dial Happy Hideaway. "J. D.," I say when he answers. "Is Mom with you by any chance?" It's been a week since we've talked.

"Oh, hey, Sara. Naw, naw. She's on a staycation right now."

I almost spit out the coffee I just took into my mouth. J. D. and "staycation" should never, ever mix. It's the equivalent of Brian Williams saying "you know" at the end of every line in his nightly news report.

"Is she okay, though?"

"To shoot straight, I couldn't tell you. I haven't been over to the back fields in a couple of days."

"But she'd come over if she was sick or something, right?"

"Oh, sure. She's done this before."

"Will you just check for me sometime in the next couple of days to make sure she's okay?"

"Will do."

"I'm not sure what to do about Aunt Bel," I say to Finn the next morning.

Finn rolls over, propping his head up on his hand. "Why do you have to do anything?"

"Because I want her to come with me."

"She'll come around."

"You sound so sure."

I reach over and run my fingertips along the stubble on his jaw.

His hair is curled and tousled from sleep, the whites of his eyes looking milky and rested. Most mornings he's up and out of bed before I wake, but this time I've caught him before he can slip away to make breakfast. He regards me with an amused smile, the same way he would a child speaking in complete sentences or anyone else acting charmingly out of character. *Good for you, sleepyhead,* that curl of the lip says. *Up and at 'em.*

Since Aunt Bel's return, we've had a run of glorious mornings, which has made the revival of our back porch breakfasts all the more welcome. Hot coffee and bacon, street sounds carrying in the air—I'd even missed the smell of her cigarettes, something I never expected.

"Are you coming down," Finn asks, "or are you going to wait for the breakfast gong?"

"I'll come down."

As I slide my feet to the floor, he comes around the bed to inspect the state of my once-favorite T-shirt. Between the hole and the paint stains and the corroded letters, GOOD TASTE is on its last legs.

"I can get you a replacement," he says. "I know where to find them."

"It's all right. I'll keep this one."

"You won't be able to for much longer. You're not going to turn into one of those people who wears their old clothes until they fall apart."

"I'm not?"

"Not on my watch," he says, putting his arms around me. His bare skin is warm to the touch, a nice balance to my habitual coldness, which he'll only be able to endure a few seconds. Three, two, one . . . he pulls away. "Come on, let's go."

I don't want a replacement because the shirt doesn't mean to me what it used to. It's a good reminder now of what really matters.

Aunt Bel comes downstairs just as we're taking the plates outside. She's wearing an oversized set of men's pajamas that make her look like an emaciated child, albeit a child with a nicotine habit since her soft pack sticks out of the chest pocket.

"Morning," she says.

We eat outside to the accompaniment of public radio, which Finn streams from his phone when he's in a fancy mood. He even gets testy when we attempt to carry on a conversation over the announcer, who is sharing biographical nuggets about the composer Mahler. "I'm trying to listen," he says, and I'm tempted to repeat the words back to him in a high-pitched whine, letting him know just how he sounds. But Aunt Bel catches my attention. We share a knowing smile: *Let's indulge him.* She leans back in her chair, half closing her eyes, absorbing the Mahler life story as if it's the profoundest thing she's ever heard. I play along too, then start to wonder if Aunt Bel is actually playing. Maybe this interests her. Maybe she sees more in the gesture than eccentricity on Finn's part. Maybe there's some depth to him she appreciates that I don't.

I lean back too, closing my eyes, letting the announcer's baritone wash over me like a tide. Finn starts clearing the table. "Time for work. Time to trudge back to the salt mines and put in a twelve-hour shift."

"I don't think I'll go in today," I say.

He pauses. "Are you feeling all right?"

"It's not that. I thought maybe Aunt Bel and I could spend the day together doing girl stuff."

"While I'm in the harness. Nice."

"Take all this away," I tell him, sweeping an imperious hand over the dirty dishes. "We've got some planning to do."

He makes an especially tall tower of plates, balancing them on his forearm, almost stumbling over the threshold as he staggers inside, calling over his shoulder, "Don't mind me."

"You want to do it?" I ask Aunt Bel. "Spend the day together."

"Sure," she says. "I want to talk. I was thinking . . . I want to talk to Rita too."

"Mom? I don't think she'd be up for a girls' day out."

"Maybe lunch."

"Are you sure? I was kind of wanting to have you all to myself."

"I think it would be good," she says. "If you don't mind."

Is it time to talk about the accident?

My breath catches in my throat.

———

Daddy shows up just after I get out of the shower. My hair still up in a towel, my bathrobe cinching my waist with its cord, I show him back to the kitchen and offer him some coffee. Truthfully, I could use another cup myself.

"Who's here?" he asks.

"Just me and Aunt Bel."

"What's she doing?"

"I don't know. Getting ready for the day, I'd guess."

"Can we take this outside, doll?"

I tilt my head. "Okay, what's up, Daddy?"

"There's something I think you're strong enough to finally know. I know something haunts you and you don't know why. But the truth is, there is something. I thought you'd be too young to ever remember."

"I don't remember."

"Something inside you does."

After I pour water in the French press, he grabs two mugs. "Have you heard from Mom lately?" I ask.

"Not for a little while. Why?"

"She's just not calling me back."

"Not completely unheard of," he says.

"J. D. said he'd check, but I haven't heard from him either."

"It probably means he checked, saw she was okay, and got so caught up in all his organic machinations, he didn't think to pick up the phone to reassure you."

Oh. "So it's that way. Got it."

Dad shrugs. "Don't get me wrong, I like the guy. It's just that him letting your mother stay there hasn't been good for her in the long run."

We head out to the deck. I feel nervous, my insides coated with anxiety. This is it, I realize. This will change everything. I'll know the truth.

"So you know about Jason."

"Mom told you about our conversation?"

"Yep. Just after it happened."

His pain of silent years flashes like the reflection of the sun on a mirror and disappears just as quickly.

"Rita doesn't know the whole story," he says.

"You mean it wasn't an accident?"

"Oh no. It was an accident all right."

"And so she's still unable to forgive Aunt Bel, right? I mean—"

"Sara."

"What happened, then?"

He reaches across the table, gathers my hand in both of his, and squeezes gently. He looks into my eyes as tears form in his own. And I know. It wasn't Aunt Bel's recklessness that killed my baby brother. It was mine.

I cannot speak; maybe I'm wrong. Right? Maybe I'm just jumping to the worst of conclusions.

"It was me, wasn't it?" I whisper.

He nods. "Yes, boo, it was." He hasn't used that term of endearment since I was a child.

"What happened?" I can barely hear the words myself.

He keeps hold of my hand and I place the other inside his grip. "You were three years old," he begins.

Looking up at the back door, he makes sure Aunt Bel isn't in the kitchen.

"Well, your mother had just finished bathing Jason. You and your aunt were playing in your room. She was always drawing things for you, or you'd put blocks together. Only you wouldn't build them, you would arrange them flat, in a composition."

I nodded. "Yes! I remember those!" The hysteria inside me threatens to bubble over.

"Your aunt helped shape your ability to compose a picture, scene, poster, what have you."

So many of my interactions with Aunt Bel start flipping through my mind.

"So, that day you were playing dress-up and she had you looking like the prettiest fairy princess. With the baby still dripping a little, your mother exited the bathroom and was walking by the top of the stairs when you came running out of your room to show her your costume. You slipped on some water and slid into her."

"Oh no . . ."

"She wasn't braced for such a collision. She pitched forward, head-first down the steps. Jason flew out of her arms and landed at the bottom of the steps. His neck broke. They say he died on impact."

"So it really was an accident?" I feel a little girl inside me looking out of my eyes. "Daddy, please?"

"Yes, honey." He squeezes my hands. "It truly, truly was."

How can someone truly forget something like that? How does such a tragedy not etch itself into the heart of the one who caused it, no matter how young?

"Your mother was knocked out, so she never remembered what actually happened. But when she came to, and our faces were hovering over her in the hospital, your Aunt Bel took the blame."

My heart fills with even fresher grief. And I realize the way she looked at me when she first arrived, with such wonder and pride, and hope, was evidence of her thinking, *It was worth it. Every hate-filled thought directed at me. Every casting of blame upon my shoulders. Sara, you were worth it.*

"How do you know about it, Daddy?"

"I saw it happen."

"And you let Aunt Bel take the blame?"

"It happened so fast. I was looking at your mother and I thought, *How much more could one person bear right now?* So. Yes. I agreed. Bel said she couldn't bear the thought of her sister having to look upon her own child as the killer of her baby. And I agreed, honey. I still do."

21.

Travels with My Aunt

I was going to try to have a good day with Aunt Bel anyway. But once Daddy leaves, I go to my bedroom, climb in between the sheets, stuff an extra pillow between my legs, and assume the fetal position. *What do I do now? Where do I go from here?* I ask my baby brother. He doesn't seem to know.

Aunt Bel taps softly on the door. "Sara? Who was that?"

I don't answer.

"Are you okay?"

I don't answer.

Ten seconds lapse. Twenty.

She taps again. "If you're in there and you're all right, make a noise."

I knock on the nightstand.

I hear her footsteps retreat down the hallway and the door to her room click shut behind her.

Does she know?

Maybe a little, although she probably doesn't realize it. Aunt Bel and I are connected in a way two human beings rarely are. She made sure of that years ago. I'm just now realizing how much.

Oh, who makes that sort of sacrifice for a little child?

Someone who sacrifices her life in Kazakhstan, that's who. She may perceive herself a missionary by default, but she's been a missionary, a person of sacrifice . . . no . . . she simply is a person of sacrifice.

She makes sense now. My mom makes sense. My dad makes sense.

And I make sense.

About an hour later, my eyes glazed from staring at the doll on my nightstand but not really seeing her (a good thing), Aunt Bel emerges from her room and walks down the hall, the flapping sound of sandals on wood stopping in front of my door, hesitating for a few seconds, then moving on.

But I know this now. Even if she kept going, walked her way back to Kazakhstan, she wouldn't really be gone. She's always been with me. Like Jason. I couldn't see it then. But I can see it now. And I'm grateful.

Despite my shock, despite the sadness I feel for my family, my brother, for a little child who was forced to wander in an unvoiced guilt and shame, transferring it onto everyone around her, not knowing to look inward, I feel lighter. I wasn't looking for happiness, because happiness isn't a matter of getting what you want. It's knowing what you need, realizing you have it, and being thankful.

At 3:16, according to my bedside clock, Finn comes home.

I'm still in bed, sitting cross-legged in the very middle, smoking one of Aunt Bel's cigarettes.

He bounds up the steps two at a time, clearly composes himself, then gingerly opens the bedroom door, whispering, "Sara?"

"Come on in."

He takes one look at me. "Sara? What are you doing?"

"Just smoking a cigarette." I tap the ash into my morning coffee mug, long emptied.

"Have you ever smoked before?" If confusion could be written over a person's entire body, it would be written on Finn's right now.

I nod. "Middle school."

"Really?"

"Yep." I inhale on the half-smoked cigarette, willing myself not to cough. Middle school was awhile ago.

He sits on the edge of the bed and holds out two fingers. "Pass it over."

"Really?"

"High school." He takes a drag, then exhales a stream of smoke worthy of a laundry vent.

"Whoa. That was a serious puff of smoke there."

He shrugs. Hands me back the cigarette, then pulls a small packet of baby wipes and a tin of Altoids from his jacket pocket. He places them on the bed. "You know that tool box I keep behind the driver's seat of my truck?"

I nod.

"Yeah."

I giggle. "You *still* smoke?"

"Yeah. Confession time. It's why I always drive with the window down."

Speaking of confessions. "When I was three, I killed my brother by accident."

The words hit him visibly. "Oh, Sara."

I nod again. "Can we talk about it?"

"Of course. Wow. Wow. Yeah. You want to do it here?"

"No. Let's take a walk."

Forty minutes later we sit atop Federal Hill, looking over the harbor. And I can tell we've found our new sweet spot. Right here. I sit between his stretched-out legs, lean back against him, and tell him everything I know.

———

We arrive home at six, both Finn and I carrying a sack from the Broadway Market. I'm going to tell Aunt Bel tonight that I know the truth. I know she'll want to run when she hears the news, but I don't want her to run away for good. Never again.

And here in the unfinished work-in-progress we call home, we're all going to figure it out together. I'm just not going to have it any other way.

My bag holds a Pinot Noir, three small beef filets, and a packet of fiddlehead ferns. Finn's bag is filled with a container of the biggest scallops I've ever seen, some fingerling potatoes, and—because Aunt Bel is my mother's sister—three pieces of tiramisu, homemade chocolate fudge, two cannoli, and a dozen chocolate chip cookies.

He can tend to go a little crazy at a bakery stand.

As soon as we unpack our bags in the kitchen, I open the bottle of wine to breathe, cross my fingers, and head up the steps to find Aunt Bel, thankfully, in her bedroom.

"You were smoking," she says with genuine disapproval from where she sits in a chair by the window. A chair I don't recognize.

"Where did you get that chair?"

"Somebody pitched it to the sidewalk."

"And you carried it all the way here?"

"It was terrible." The disapproving look fades. "Carrying it all the way from next door was one of the most grueling things I've ever done."

I laugh, leaning my shoulder against the doorjamb and crossing my arms. "I won't keep smoking. I had my reasons for trying one after all these years."

"Okay."

Just like that.

"I like it. The chair. Actually, it's ugly. But you're making the room your own, and that is definitely beautiful."

"You can say it. It's not exactly in 'good taste.'"

"I don't care about that."

She runs a hand over the upholstered, threadbare arm. "I don't either."

"I know. We're having a nice dinner tonight. Finn's getting started down in the kitchen."

"To celebrate that you made it through whatever happened in the bedroom today."

"That. And more." I push off the door frame. "You're in, right?"

"Yes." She looks out of the window, then back at me. "I'm in."

I turn to go.

"You know what, Sara?" she says, still looking out the window. "Finn really knows how to make things taste good, doesn't he?"

"Yes. He does. Maybe he's always known the words *good taste* are better when switched around."

———

In the kitchen, Finn has just put the scallops into a marinade of orange zest, soy sauce, and garlic.

"Let's do these on the grill," he says, leaning down into a lower cabinet to pull out the pans he'll need. Finn is a very methodical cook, the opposite to his contracting. He gathers all his supplies and ingredients in advance, every step prepared for in his mind.

"You should have been a chef." I sit at the kitchen table and reach for the jar of peanuts someone must have placed there earlier.

"I am a chef," he says. "I cook good food that everybody loves to eat."

I can't argue there. Some chefs are born, not made. Honestly, I can picture Finn taking a bath as a little boy and making crab soup out of a Sebastian tub toy.

I unscrew the lid. "Let me ask you a question. You and Aunt Bel. I knew there was something between you two that bonded you together. Smoker's bond, right?"

"Yep."

I laugh. "Isn't it amazing how most things are rarely what they seem?"

"Yes. And usually in a good way. I mean, you're almost always pleasantly surprised that what you were thinking was far worse than what it actually turned out to be."

"Usually."

I think of my baby brother. He doesn't fit into the pleasantly surprised realm. Not at all.

But he fits.

He is the missing, final piece of the puzzle. And now he's been placed where he should be. At least in my mind.

I tip the jar and shake some peanuts into my palm.

"Sara? I was thinking." Finn sets a sauté pan on a cold burner, then slides a cutting board down from atop the refrigerator.

"Uh-oh. Always dangerous. Does that mean we're going to start another church?"

"Uh . . . no. Your thoughts about having a baby."

Crap.

"Do you think your fears are coming from what happened with Jason? Like, you just don't trust yourself with a child?"

"I haven't thought much about it yet." And I still don't really want to. "But I will think about that."

"Really?" I hear an edge of hope to his tone.

"I'll think about your theory. Not anything further. Finn . . . I just can't. Not yet."

"I get it, hon. It's okay." *It's a start,* I can practically hear him thinking.

Aunt Bel enters the kitchen with a camera I've never seen. "I've decided something," she says, sitting down opposite me and setting the camera between us. Whatever brand it is, it isn't written in English. "I'm not a painter."

Finn starts to argue.

"No, Finn. I needed to do a painting. But I'm not a painter."

"I get what you mean, Aunt Bel," I say.

"And I know I'm not a photographer in the usual sense. But what I'm reasonably sure of, is that I can take pretty pictures."

Finn raises the wooden spoon he just plucked out of the drawer. "Hear, hear."

"How long until dinner?" she asks.

"An hour. So a little after seven."

"I'll be back."

She pats the pocket on her skirt, making sure her cigarettes are there, then heads out the front door.

I tell Finn about the chair.

"It's like her soul knows and she can come home now."

The new chair should make me feel a little better about the upcoming conversation, but there could be a host of other reasons my aunt chose to bring it up to her room. She won't run. No, she won't. Why would she?

Finn acts like our carefully constructed plan from this afternoon just hit him out of the blue. "Look, you two ladies. Get out of my kitchen and leave me to clean up in peace and quiet. I've got a podcast I want to listen to." He's cute when he's pretending to be a curmudgeon. "Why don't you two walk down to the harbor and take a paddleboat ride?"

Aunt Bel looks at me, completely fooled, if I have to guess. "That sounds really nice."

"I think so too." I stand up and kiss Finn on the cheek. "Shall we?"

So now we paddle in silence to the middle of the harbor. "There's something so chummy about paddleboats, isn't there?" I ask. "Watching both sets of knees rise and fall together."

"Yes, I suppose that's true."

"Let's stop here, Aunt Bel."

The two pavilions of the Inner Harbor, now that the dusk has settled in, are lit from inside, their glass walls glowing and casting their reflection on the water. Four places for the price of two.

"So what is it you have to say to me, Sara?"

"I should have known you weren't fooled."

She doesn't say anything.

I don't either. What if she's become so used to this role she's played for all these years that telling her removes a part of her she's become so accustomed to that she won't know how to exist without it?

"You're ready for me to move on, is that it?" she asks. "Because, I mean, I understand if I've overstayed my welcome."

"No!"

"Because, I swear, Sara. I'm going to get a job or find a way to bring in money to help. I'm not thinking I can stay here forever without sharing the load."

"That's not it either."

It seems without a moment's notice, the sky has blazed to life and surrounded us in the little place that has always been just me and Aunt Bel. All of the sadness with which she gazed at the picture of her son, all of the anger and fear she felt toward God, all of the squashed hope, the lack of love and security, bounces out from her heart, up against the sky, and into my own. In some ways, in her carrying the load of my action, she became me. She became me for me.

She took my place.

And I feel it.

Oh, Aunt Bel.

"I know it was me who killed Jason."

The yellow of the sky begins to deepen to orange. The red to plum. Cerulean descends into indigo.

She takes my hand, saying nothing. And there's nothing left for me to say, other than, "Thank you."

The whispered words cause her to squeeze my hand.

The minutes slip by.

Finally, she begins to paddle toward the dock, so I paddle alongside her. Looking forward she says, "There were times in Kazakhstan I wondered if all that had happened had been worth it."

"Is that why you came back?"

"Not just that. I just knew I needed to. It felt like a calling in some ways."

"Did you know it had something to do with me?"

"If I hadn't, I would never have come back, Sara." She lays a hand on my arm. "Sara. Promise me you won't tell your mother. Please. The reasons I did what I did still stand."

"I can't promise that, Aunt Bel. But I will say I won't make any extra effort to tell Mom. I'll play that by ear."

She steps forward. "That's all I should have asked of you in the first place."

"Then that's what we'll do. What we'll always do."

"But any of the other secrets . . . ," she begins, and I think of her first husband, Alan, Mr. Novikov, her escape from Kazakhstan, and most likely more revelations that will follow.

"Will stay just that."

"I think it will do me good to trust in you, Sara."

Aunt Bel's profile is cast into silhouette by the golden beam of our house light. When the front door opens, her features are illuminated to their fullness. And she is beautiful.

Odd, yes.

But all the more beautiful for it.

———

The next morning, all three of us with a food hangover, we practically stumble into Grove Street. Madge takes one look at us. "Just coffee?"

"I couldn't eat another bite," Aunt Bel says, laying my old lavender backpack, now holding my digital camera and lenses, a healthy snack, sunglasses, and an aluminum water bottle clipped to a hook on its side, on an empty chair.

"Same for me," I say. "Just the coffee."

"You." She points to Finn. "Don't disappoint me now, boy."

Finn caves. "A toasted bagel? Plain?"

"Ah, now that is what I want to be hearing." She turns from the counter to assemble the order.

We sit and stare at each other for another ten minutes, sipping our drinks until Finn's bagel arrives. Then we sit and stare at each other some more, Finn chewing the bagel he doesn't want.

Aunt Bel gets up, grabs a paper napkin, and holds out her hand. Finn hands her the rest of the bagel and she wraps it up. "See? Lunch. Thank you very much, Finn Drexel, for buying a girl lunch." She stuffs it into the front pocket of the backpack.

I see the missionary in her now. In fact, she's been everywhere since our conversation.

It was almost as if Aunt Bel was afraid to act like she loved me as much as she did in an effort not to give anything away.

Just as we're ready to head to the Firehouse, Holly Ringwald pulls up to the curb in her convertible. All of our jaws drop a little as she gets out of the car in jeans, a pair of sneakers, and an old hoodie. Her hair, a regular old medium brown, sprouts in a short ponytail from the nape of her neck. She unlocks the trunk and pulls out a leather suitcase, tanned a golden brown, with a pink bow attached to the handle.

"Hi, guys!" she cries, coming through the door. "I was hoping I wouldn't miss you. Huey said you would probably be here." She holds up the suitcase. "Look! For your trip, Sara. As a thank-you for all the hard work you did. The fund-raiser was the most successful one yet!"

"This is beautiful." I stand up and hug her. "Thank you! You know—"

"—I didn't have to do it. Yes. But . . . well . . ." She scoots out the fourth chair and sits down. "I'm really somewhat jealous and I was thinking if I couldn't come along, I'd get you a suitcase that could."

"So there's no hidden camera in that thing, then?" Finn raises an eyebrow.

She laughs.

I tell her how happy I am that her husband's event was a success.

She nods. "Yes. I was so pleased!"

Was Eric? Maybe not so much. But maybe that doesn't matter.

Holly turns to Aunt Bel. "So. Have you made up your mind about accompanying Sara on what could be the most amazing adventure of your life?" She holds a hand up to her mouth and stifles a laugh. "Wait a second! Who am I talking to? A lady that's lived in Uzbek—"

"Kazakhstan," I supply.

Aunt Bel shakes her head. "And no, I haven't. I've been looking for a sign. Now that my life has slowed down so much, I have to be a little more careful about my decisions. Back in Kazakhstan, I usually went from one thing to another, but everything always a reaction."

"This is much nicer," I say.

"Well, I've got just the sign for you." Holly jumps to her feet, hurries back to the car, and pulls another suitcase out of her trunk. Same pink bow, but made out of dark, walnut brown leather. She runs in and places it next to Aunt Bel's chair. "Done."

Aunt Bel, for the first time since she's come home, looks truly astounded. "Well, no kidding? Huh!"

But she isn't talking to me, Finn, or even Holly, for that matter.

"Well, okay!" she says. Then looks at me. "Okay. I'll go. But there's something I want to do. It's going to be a big surprise."

And why not? It's Aunt Bel. Whatever she wants to do should be fine with me.

22.

Communication Breakdowns Aren't Always the Same

The next Saturday, standing in front of a long line of shoes at a discount shoe warehouse out in Hunt Valley, Aunt Bel picks up a sandal that should be labeled a contraption, not footwear. "I know these are supposed to be good for your feet, Sara, but I just don't want to wear something that looks like this."

"Me either." I pick up a pair of Keds, little navy blue slip-ons. "How about the old tried and true?"

We're assembling a small traveling wardrobe for Aunt Bel. Two pairs of shoes, three dresses, and a sweater does not a wardrobe make, and this trip is a good excuse for her to purchase what she needs.

"How about in white?" she asks.

"You're the natural fashion maven, not me, Aunt Bel."

"White it is." She tucks the box under her arm and we head toward the checkout counter. "Your mom always wore white Keds when she was young, Sara."

"What was she like back then?" I stop in front of the sock rack.

"Not the hippie-type person she's become, but she was more of a free spirit than the world gave her credit for being. She and your dad were such a cute couple. One of those little couples."

"I guess all they went through made them seem bigger."

"I can see that." She reaches out and slides a package of footie socks off the hook.

"I still haven't heard from her," I say. "I'm starting to get a little worried. Daddy hasn't heard from her either."

"Well, you've probably rightly assumed I haven't."

"Yes."

I think back, realizing it's been a couple of weeks. "What do you say we drive over to the farm, just to make sure everything's okay? It's not that far from here."

Aunt Bel hasn't seen her sister since my mom dropped her off to stay at our house. "I think that's exactly what we should do."

As I pilot the car farther north into Baltimore County onto Falls Road, I try to make myself feel better. "I mean, if something bad happened, surely J. D. would have called. No news is good news and all that, right?"

"That's usually the case."

"Are you nervous about seeing her again?" Now that I know the dynamics of my family, I have no trouble seeing why she should feel that way.

"A touch. But I've lived with this for so long, Sara."

"Wouldn't it be nice to have your sister back? Were you all ever close?"

"She is almost seven years older than me. But yes, we had a strong sisterly bond that I assume would have grown into friendship had I not felt the need to leave."

When I pull onto the farm, I drive straight to the little bridge. Mom's bike is tied to the railing, which seems like a good sign. We park the car and as we emerge Aunt Bel says, "So it's true. She really does live in a tent."

"Yep."

She takes in the flower pots and chairs and spinning sculptures. "This is nice!"

"What?" I whip my head around to look at her to see if she's kidding. She's not.

"I love this!"

"You'd live in a place like this?"

She shrugs. "I've never had occasion to think about it before. But she's sure made this little campsite homey, hasn't she?"

I look through Aunt Bel's eyes. The precise, artful arrangement of Mom's garden gear and furniture, the tipi trellis of morning glories to the left of the tent, the pots of ranunculus and dahlias, the garden behind everything where sunflowers will grow, keeping watch over zinnias and cosmos.

"It really is beautiful, isn't it?"

"She always knew how to make things beautiful. Like you do, Sara."

I smile. "I come from an artsy-fartsy family and I didn't even real-ize it."

We stop just short of the bridge. "Aunt Bel? Remember when you almost made me promise I wouldn't force the reunion of you and Mom, that I'd just let the Universe take its course?"

"Yes. But I have a feeling all that's about to change."

I lay my hand on her injured arm. "Only if you want it to."

"But what about *your* relationship with her?"

"It can't hurt it. We're already too distant as it is." I set my foot on the bridge. "Maybe the truth is what we all need to bring us together. Maybe the truth deserves its chance to make a difference."

She pats my hand and holds it in her fingers as we walk forward. "Maybe you're right."

"Let me be the one to tell her what really happened, Aunt Bel."

"Oh no, Sara!" Her protests come from the place that sought to protect me in the first place.

"Yes. I think the message will be better heard coming from me."

Oh, hi, Mom. Yes, just wanted to stop by and drop this bomb on you. By the way, your sister didn't kill your son; your daughter did. Isn't that grand?

I suppose some truths are so terrible, there's no compassionate time to make them known. But in the end, I'm doing this for a woman who lives in a tent, and for another woman who spends her time wandering around the streets of Baltimore like a homeless person, armed only with a camera and a water bottle. And I'd be fooling myself if I didn't say I was doing this for myself as well. We O'Hara girls deserve to be together. Not again. But for the first time ever since I can remember.

We step off the bridge. "Mom?" I call.

No answer.

"She must be here," I whisper. "Mom!" I call again.

"She won't answer if she doesn't wish to," says Aunt Bel.

"Like sister, like sister?" I ask.

"If you'd like."

I approach the small vestibule of the tent. "Mom?" I unzip the flap and peer inside. "Nobody's home."

A few minutes later we approach J. D.'s house, the mud slathered over the corncob walls baked by the summer sun. He's sitting on a handmade bench by the door, feeding scraps of meat to his thousand-year-old German shepherd.

"Have you seen my mom?"

"Yeah, sure. She came by this morning to borrow my car. Said she was heading downtown to see you."

I turn to Aunt Bel. "Let's go."

When Aunt Bel and I slide into the car, she looks as pale as her new Keds. "You don't think she's finally come to have the confrontation she's been avoiding for years, do you?"

"I don't know. Maybe she just wants to see how I'm doing."

"Not by driving a car, she doesn't." Aunt Bel shakes her head. "No, I can't imagine it's that. She could have picked up J. D.'s phone."

When we get to the house, I see J. D.'s Toyota pickup parked halfway down the block, and not in a skillful manner. I feel as if my nerves have formed an external suit. I throw the car into park, breathe deeply, and look at Aunt Bel. "You ready for this?"

"I don't know," she whispers, grabbing handfuls of her dress.

"We don't have to," I say, backpedaling at the sight of her bloodless face. "Really, Aunt Bel."

She inhales deeply and grabs the door handle. "No. It's time, Sara. This has got to be the way now."

Mom and Finn are in the backyard. She's helping him rebuild a part of the cinder-block wall that's always been a wreck. Finn's actually putting something together without tearing it apart first. I can hardly believe my eyes.

"Hey, hon!" he says from down on his haunches where he's mixing cement in a five-gallon paint bucket. "Guess who showed up by surprise?"

"Hey, baby." Mom straightens up and approaches me. "I'm sorry I haven't called."

"You've had me worried, Mom. Like, really. We just dropped by your tent. J. D. told us you were here. Are you okay?"

She nods. "I will be." She turns to her sister. "After I talk to you, Bel."

"How about we eat first?" asks Finn. "Have you two had lunch? Because we haven't and it's almost three, and us Drexels always say difficult conversations are best had on a full stomach."

"Why? So you can actually throw up if it makes you feel nauseous?" I ask, already nauseous.

"Better than the dry heaves, Sare, and you know that's true."

Both my mom and my aunt nod. Great. First thing they've agreed upon in years is regarding the dry heaves. Well, it's a start.

"I'll make lunch," I announce, "while you two finish up. Aunt Bel? Want to help me with the sandwiches?"

She follows me back into the house without a word.

———

I assemble a quick chicken salad with the leftover curry chicken from a few nights before and lay it atop some spinach greens. Aunt Bel is making wedges out of pita bread, brushing on a little olive oil, sprinkling sea salt, and throwing them into the oven.

"Not bad," I say, trying to sound normal.

"Will do in a pinch," Aunt Bel responds likewise.

As Mom and Finn wash up, we arrange the lunch on the deck. Finn returns with clean hands and a pitcher of Arnold Palmer he made earlier in the day.

They join us at the table and we begin to eat. Finn chitchats the tension away, or tries to, and I respond as if that will make everything smooth. Instead, we achieve the effect of a puppet show. Watch the young married couple for your entertainment. Free of charge!

Finally, I can't take it anymore. "Mom. I know you want to talk to Aunt Bel, but there's something I have to tell you."

"Sara, you really don't—" Aunt Bel interjects.

"Yes. Yes, I do."

My mom, holding her drink, freezes her hand. Looks wary. Sets down the glass. "What is it, baby? Are you all right?"

"I accidentally pushed you and Jason down the steps all those years ago, not Aunt Bel." The words crash land into the space between us.

"What did you say?" asks Mom.

The devastation on her face constricts my throat. I can't say a thing.

Finn takes her hand. "Mom, Aunt Bel has been carrying the load for Sara all these years. She didn't want you to resent your own daughter, so—"

"Is this true?" Mom looks directly at Aunt Bel.

She nods, grabbing the largest handful of skirt I've seen yet. "Yes." She casts down her gaze. "I'm sorry."

Mom rushes around to kneel in front of her sister. "You'd do that for Sara?" She takes her hand.

Aunt Bel doesn't pull away. "Yes. You know how much I loved her. And I'd do that for you, Rita. I'd do it for you all over again if you needed to hate the person who killed your son. Better that it be me."

Mom gasps, both hands coming down atop her white hair. She turns to me. "But, Sara, I don't"—turns to her sister—"Bel. I . . . I never held that against you!"

"But didn't you say—" I interrupt.

"No! I only said those things because I couldn't reveal that while I grieved your brother, it was Bel who broke my heart." She turns her face up to Aunt Bel. "You deserted me, Belinda. I was in the darkest place of my life . . . and you left."

"I thought you hated me, Ri. I would have hated me too."

"But you didn't do anything!"

"You didn't know that."

"Yes, Belinda. I did." She takes both of Aunt Bel's hands in her own. "You were my baby sister. It was an accident. Truly. I could see that. If there was anyone to blame, it was myself for not drying him off properly, and believe me, blaming myself is what I've done."

For over twenty-five years. Oh, Mom!

She leans over and pulls her sister into an embrace and her shoulders begin to heave.

Finn taps my leg under the table and I stand up. "Finn and I are going to get these dishes done."

We leave them on the deck.

———

The kitchen looks as clean as an old kitchen is able. Finn is already in bed, the sisters still haven't returned from their "we're going to continue this conversation at the park" walk, and I'm on the living room sofa working on a crossword puzzle, too keyed up and filled with the day's emotions to be much good for anything else.

Finally, the O'Hara sisters return.

Aunt Bel heads to the stoop to smoke. Mom sits next to me. "Baby," she begins.

"Mom. I'm so sorry."

Everything flows out of me, all the mysterious sadness I could never quite understand, all the yearnings for a happiness I'd never find, all the dissatisfactions, the superiority complex, the guilt. I crumble and the water table rushes out, stinging my eyes and nose.

Mom crumbles too. We find refuge in each other's embrace and cry together like we were supposed to have been doing for the past twenty-six years.

"I'm so sorry," I say again. "I didn't mean to hurt Jason. I loved Jason."

All the memories of my little brother come pouring back into my mind. His little red face when he cried, the tiny hands that I loved to put in my mouth and suck on. (I was only three.) How soft his skin was and those dark, little intense eyes that looked at you as if to tell you he'd just come with a report from heaven and the news was good. God still loved the human race.

"I know you did, baby. I forgave you a long time ago."

"You knew?"

"Oh no. But would I have felt any differently? Even then?" She places both hands aside my head. "Sara. I love you. You're my sweet girl. There's nothing you could do to change any of that, baby."

"Does that mean you'll come off the farm and live in a place with walls?" I ask.

"Not even a little bit."

I can honestly answer, "Good."

Time is ticking down on the big trip. Dora calls me at least three times a day now, and Ethan another two. Aunt Bel actually bought a new camera for herself. "I'm not going to take over or anything, Sara. But I'd be a fool not to take advantage of this."

She is so right. And she's enjoying digital, embracing the technology like a pro.

So when Aunt Bel runs into the studio, I'm thinking she's got some amazing captures from her morning out.

"You said I could spend the money on whatever I want, right?" she says, her eyes shooting off sparks of excitement.

"I didn't make the rules, Aunt Bel. It's your money."

"Okay. Because I bought something." She turns toward the floor where Huey is pulling more prints of the trash-talk card on the Iron Maiden. "Huey! Come see! You too, Diana."

What she's purchased is a 1985 Winnebago. "It only cost me five K," she says, ushering us inside. The entire gang fills the twenty-two-foot

RV. We stand smack up against each other, looking around. "We can take it on the photo trip, Sara."

"I don't know if Ethan and—"

"They're already on board." Finn speaks.

"You knew about this?"

"Uh-huh." He touches an overhead cabinet. "Ever heard of 'glamping'?"

Boy, have I! Tricked-out little trailer or RV.

"They're going to have it redone?"

"Yep." Aunt Bel is zinging with excitement. "And then after the trip, they're going to use it as a display in their store! After which it will come back to me. Isn't that amazing?"

"I'd sure like to use this during the fall when I go on vacation," says Huey, who heads down to the Gulf every October.

"Done," says Aunt Bel.

Diana sits at the dinette and slides her hands appreciatively over the, quite frankly, horrible brown laminate. "A girl could get used to living like this."

"Knock! Knock!" Mom peeks her head into the door, then steps up. "So this is it! I love it!"

"Wait until you see when it's done, Rita," says Aunt Bel.

Over the past couple of weeks, the two sisters have made up for lost time, and the love they shared as siblings not only caught up quickly but overtook them. Mom's been down to eat dinner several times and Aunt Bel's joined her for a campout on the farm, taking pictures and helping out around the place. They both glow with a golden tan.

Dad steps up into the camper as well. He's taken to being the women's driver, complaining about it with a twinkle in his eye. There's something about sharing a history like theirs that, with this new positive perspective, can go a long way toward shaping some perfectly acceptable relationships. Those three are doing a good job. Dad with his place on the water. Mom in her tent. And now Aunt Bel.

I think about it for a second. "This is your home, Aunt Bel. A place you can always take with you wherever you go."

She waves a hand. "I'm not going anywhere. Not really."

And neither am I. Everyone I adore is stuffed into this little space that's only going to get better and better. Happiness is right here, and I'd be a fool to be anywhere else.

Reading Group Guide

1. What preconceived notions do you have about what a missionary should look and act like? How did Bel reinforce those opinions or challenge them?

2. Finn apologizes to Sara for trying to heal her wounds and tells her "maybe I just need to walk alongside you, not try and drag you to safety." What did Finn's love do for Sara? Do you believe a person's love can heal another's wounds?

3. Bel says to Sara, "You may think you're doing the right thing, and it's so far off the mark. But yet, what else could you have done." Do you think Bel did the right thing in taking the blame for Jason's death? Was there a right or wrong thing to do in that situation? What were the consequences of that decision?

4. Describe the two sides of Bel and of Sara.

5. How did concealing the truth of the accident impact Bel? Sara? Her mom? Her dad? Finn?

6. Finn tells Huey that everything that comes apart can be put back together, but Sara says, "This is not true. . . . Some places, when you bend or break them, will not mend." Which philosophy do you think is true? What occurs in the story to support both these ideas?

7. Describe the different views the characters have of Jesus. How do you see him?

8. Describe the effect Bel's painting of the flat, stern Byzantine Jesus had on Bel, Sara, Holly, and Finn.

9. Why do you think Bel felt compelled to paint Jesus? Why did she keep making the painting smaller?

10. When Sara learns the truth about her brother's death and the accident, how does it change the way she views her parents?

11. How do the different characters view the role of suffering in a person's life and God's purpose for it? What do you believe about why God allows people to suffer?

12. How do each of the characters respond and relate to Bel's mysteriousness? How do you think you would respond to her?

13. Why do you think Sara's GOOD TASTE T-shirt was so important to her?

14. Do you think Sara will decide she wants to have a child?

Acknowledgments

Thanks to Chip for his ability to see solutions. My gratitude to all the good people at Thomas Nelson, particularly Ami and Jana who make every word better. And to J. Mark Bertrand who got things off to a great start.

Thank you to all of my readers, particularly those who have stuck with me over these past twenty years. You are more than appreciated!

Thank you to my family and friends who support me day by day. I couldn't do any of this without your love and care.

An Excerpt from
The Sky Beneath My Feet
by Lisa Samson

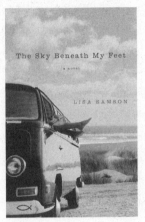

chapter 1
Jesus Fish

Every once in a while, I glance at the rearview mirror and see my own eyes staring back at me. It's disconcerting. *I'd forgotten you were in there.*

And then, blink, she's gone again.

Or I am.

Maybe it's the eighties music on the radio, or the breeze coming through the old VW van's rolled-down window, the warm sun on my bare arm. Maybe it's idling on the curb out in front of the high school, waiting as the kids tramp past in twos and threes, their backpacks slung over their shoulders. I don't know what summons her up. The old me. My former self.

The hatchback pops open behind me. Without a word, Eli shoves his bike in, cocking the front wheel over the backseat. He slams the hatch and comes around to the passenger door. Some passing girls call out to him and wave, then he slumps into the seat, pulling the door shut.

Unlike his older, bookish brother, who speaks with equal parts fear and condescension whenever the subject of public school comes up, Eli wouldn't have it any other way. He likes it. He's even popular.

"So what's wrong with your bike?" I ask.

Eli doesn't answer, doesn't even acknowledge my presence. He just reaches for the radio and changes the channel. "How can you listen to that stuff?"

"Hey, you don't know what you're talking about. My music's cool again."

"Whatever."

He flicks his hand in the air, beckoning me to drive.

"What's that?" I ask.

"Let's go."

"What was that thing with your hand?"

"What, this?" He does it again with an impish smile. "That's called a gesture."

"I'll show you another gesture if you keep it up. I'm your mom, not your taxi driver. So what's wrong with your bike, anyway?"

"Don't let the people at church catch you making rude hand gestures," he says. "Or the people on the road, now that we have the Jesus fish on the bumper."

"I told you the fish was ironic."

"Sure it is." He glances over his shoulder. "I bent the back wheel again."

"Again? You weren't doing tricks, were you?"

"Tricks?" He smiles at the word. "Yeah, I was doing tricks."

"Is that not what they're called? I can't keep up with the lingo."

"Don't try," he says. "I don't want to have the Cool Mom."

"Too bad." Reaching in the door compartment, I pull out my white plastic shades. "You already have the Cool Mom, so deal with it."

"Right," he says, dragging the word out and smiling at his reflection in the window.

"And stop admiring your own reflection."

On the verge of his sixteenth birthday, my younger son is becoming a narcissist. Born with the kind of languid masculine grace that pairs well with the square-jawed facial symmetry and thick, black hair he inherited from his dad, Eli is growing into his looks. He's handsome, in other words. Which explains both the girls waving to him from the sidewalk and his indifference to them.

"Try to be nice," I'm always telling him. Only, to be charming, Eli doesn't have to try—and consequently, he doesn't. Even at his surliest, Eli tends to get his way. That's not how the real world works, I try to tell him. But all he has to do is look at Rick's example. Whether he tries or not, everything works out for my husband.

Not that I have a problem with that. Except when I do.

At York and Ridgely, we get stuck at the red light. Eli looks around, realizing we're not heading straight to the house. "What's the deal?"

"I have a couple of errands to run," I say. "You remember the Shaws? No, of course you don't. They moved to Virginia when you were seven or eight—"

"I remember," he says. "Mr. Shaw had a silver Porsche."

Yes, he did, but that's not how I want a child of mine recollecting people. "They're coming over tonight. Your dad sprang it on me this morning, even though he's known for days—"

"I'm not gonna be there. I already told Damon I was coming over."

"Well, you can tell Damon . . . no, never mind. You made your plans, that's fine. You shouldn't have to drop everything at the last minute."

"What are they coming for, anyway? You haven't seen them in years."

"That's a good question, Eli. That's a good question."

Eight years ago Jim and Kathie Shaw moved three hours down I-95 to Richmond, saying they would keep in touch. At the time, the Shaws were probably our closest friends, Jim being one of the few people Rick could talk to about his job without fear of being judged. Once they left, the most we ever heard from them was a card at Christmas. It was a wrenching break, especially for Rick. And now they're suddenly on our doorstep again? I don't know what to think.

"So have you thought about what you want to do for your birthday?" I ask.

"It depends," he says. "Are we going to be here or out of town?"

"Your dad has the whole month of October off, and we thought we'd take a little vacation. Maybe we could go somewhere for your birthday."

"California?"

"Somewhere closer," I say. "How about D.C.? We could see all the sights."

"That's not a vacation, it's a field trip."

When Rick came home from the staff meeting over the summer announcing his four-week vacation—a *sabbatical*, he called it—he dropped the whole thing in my lap to plan. Figuring out where to go and what to do, scheming a way to get the boys out of school for a week or two without looking like delinquent parents—it was all up to me. Never mind that I hadn't known far enough in advance to put money aside. Never mind that Eli's idea of fun was visiting his cousins in California (something he's only done once before) and my eighteen-year-old, Jed, responds to every idea I come up with by saying, "Sure, fine, but you'll have to go without me."

Nobody wants to do what I want to do. Nobody can agree on anything else. And if I don't come up with something for them all—for my husband and my two teenaged sons, the men in my life—then they'll blame me for having failed in my most basic, primal duty. I just can't win.

"You know something—" I begin.

But Eli's not paying attention. He's already fished his iPod out of his jeans pocket and plugged the earphones in. He can't sit for five minutes without playing on that thing, and I've resigned myself to it. Now he taps his thumbs on the screen, absorbed in some game. I know better than to mess with the radio dial, though. He likes to blanket himself in white noise.

We pass a Greek diner, then a cluster of fast-food outlets. We pass the bowling alley and the office my childhood doctor practiced out of, then the Timonium Race Track and State Fair Grounds. I've never been to a horse race there in my life, or to Pimlico either. We pass gas stations and car dealerships, the sticker prices rising like mercury the farther north we get.

In the parking lot at Giant, Eli announces he'll stay in the car. Big surprise—I didn't see that one coming. With the door half open, I check my shopping list one last time to make sure I haven't forgotten anything. Mussels and scallops, Rick's favorites. When you're entertaining a Porsche-driving lawyer and his Ivy League wife, you have to keep up appearances. Not that I care about that sort of thing.

"Am I forgetting anything?" I ask aloud.

Eli looks over at me, but he isn't listening.

I'm positive I'm forgetting something. Maybe. Maybe not. I always feel like I've forgotten something.

On my way inside the grocery store, I say a little prayer. Not a pious prayer by any stretch.

Please, Lord, don't let there be anybody from church here.

Confession: There are things you want to do in private, anony-mously, and grocery shopping is one of them. When your husband works at a church of thousands, you're likely to be recognized in the most inconvenient places.

As I'm peering through the frosted glass at the seafood counter, I hear the screech of grocery cart wheels over my shoulder, followed by the high-pitched voice signifying the fact that, no, I have not found favor with my Father in heaven.

"Hey, *girrrrrl.*"

I put my smile on before turning. "Hi, Stacy."

"Hi yourself, Beth. I was just thinking about you." Stacy Manderville pulls to a halt next to my cart, her elbows propped on her own cart's handle, giving my shopping a once-over before continuing. "Got some big plans or something? I thought you'd be getting ready for the road trip."

"Not until next week," I say.

"The whole month of October, huh? What are you going to do with yourselves?"

"I have a few ideas."

"I bet you do." She looks me over now, blinking a few times, prob-ably trying to imagine the kind of ideas a pastor's wife can come up with. But then Stacy knew me long before I was a pastor's wife. We were in high school together. That was before Stacy married into the opulently wealthy Manderville clan. "That's what I wanted to talk to you about."

"You wanted to talk?"

"About this vacation of yours. A month is a long time."

"The timing couldn't be worse," I say. "Autumn is my favorite sea-son. With the leaves changing and the weather turning cool, our little neighborhood–"

"There's always Florida."

"Well, yes."

I wish we didn't work for such an affluent church, full of people who go wherever they want on vacation and stay for however long they want. Stacy married a doctor, so I'm sure it makes perfect sense to her that we'd pick up sticks and spend a month on Miami Beach. Sometimes ministering to the wealthy is counterproductive to attaining the peace of Christ that passes all understanding. Even if they do cut your husband loose for a month of paid vacation.

I mean, why are we having trouble raising twenty grand for the Habitat house we're cosponsoring with our sister church downtown when the parking lot on Sunday mornings is clogged with Mercedes and BMWs and Volvo SUVs, not to mention several Jaguars? (Okay, I can't help loving the Jaguars. But still.)

"Why do you have that funny look?" Stacy asks. "Did I say something?"

"What? No. Sorry, my mind was wandering. We have people coming over tonight and it was short notice. You remember the Shaws? They used to go to the church . . ."

Her eyes study the ceiling for a memory. "Doesn't ring a bell, but the place has gotten so *huge*. I remember when it was just starting out. I think there are more people on staff now than were even attending back in the good old days! Anyway, here's what I wanted to show you." She digs in her capacious purse for half a minute only to produce a set of keys attached to a bright yellow floaty. "Here they are. And here you go." She hands them to me.

"What are these?" I ask, turning the floaty over in my hand.

"You know we have a house in Florida," she says. "It's not a mansion or anything, but it's right on the water. Beautiful stretch of beach. I already e-mailed you all the details. Do you ever check your e-mail, girl? I was starting to wonder."

"I don't understand."

"What's to understand? You have a month of vacation coming, and

I have an empty vacation house on the beach. I don't care if you do like it when the leaves turn and it gets cold. When was the last time you had tan lines, Beth? And I'm not talking about on your arms either. You can go down there and soak up the sun and forget all about Lutherville and the church and the fact that we're not in high school anymore. Let your hair down and have some fun. Surprise that husband of yours."

"Are you serious?" I ask. "Stacy, this is too kind."

"It's not. You're my best friend, Beth. Of course I want you to have fun."

I wince a little at hearing her describe me this way. We're not that close, not really, but her voice sounds sincere. And it's such a sweet gesture, even if I'm ninety-nine percent sure Rick won't go for it. If nothing else, he'll object to taking the VW all the way to Florida with its broken air-conditioning and its crank windows and no power steering.

"I can't accept this," I say. "It's very sweet, but—"

"I'm not taking no for an answer." She tucks her hands into her armpits so that I can't hand the keys back. The yawning opening of her purse lies between us. I could toss them right in.

But I don't.

I mean, why shouldn't we?

✳

The Jesus fish is my own fault. I'm a Christian, but not *that* kind of Christian. Not the in-your-face culture warrior. Not the sort to plaster bumper stickers all over my car. I don't drive like a Christian, after all, and when I'm speeding or cutting somebody off, the last image I want to leave them with is that shiny faux-metal fish. But I shot my mouth off about the stupid fish and hurt the feelings of one of my study group ladies. You know the kind: she forwards e-mails to everyone in the group about liberal conspiracies and tries to sign us all up to march in front of clinics and boycott Hollywood and invest in gold.

But she's a sweet person who just never got the memo that God wants to save all types of people and not just her type. She can't imagine a decent, churchgoing person having any view other than her own. So she heard my offhand joke about the sort of people who slap Jesus fish on their minivans and she stored it away. By the time it got back to me that she was offended, I'd forgotten I ever said anything.

I went to her, because that's what you're supposed to do. I apologized. I managed to get through it without an implied reprimand too. Nothing about how she should have come to me directly and not told everybody else how upset she was. The next Sunday she presented me with the fish.

"What does she expect?" Rick asked. "You're not putting that thing on the car."

"I think she misunderstood the reason I was apologizing." I started to laugh, but Rick was still angry about the fish. Finally he gave in. "She's crazy, I know. But if I don't put it on . . ."

"I don't care what these people think about us," he said, though we both knew he did.

"When Pete Waterhouse had to shave his head, you and some of the other guys shaved yours too," I reminded him. "In solidarity. This is the same kind of thing."

"That was cancer. This is narrow-mindedness. I don't want to reinforce this kind of thing."

"What about your T-shirts?"

Rick had a closetful of kitsch T-shirts emblazoned with breathless religious slogans, most of them freebies from church-sponsored activities. "That's different. I wear those ironically."

"Right," I said. "And the fish will be ironic too."

Only nobody told the fish. Now, as I push my basket across the Giant parking lot, watching the Jesus fish glint in the afternoon sun, the fish looks awfully sincere. Earnest. He shines evenly in the sun, without so much as the hint of a wink.

Eli doesn't get out of the car to help with the groceries, naturally. Until I pop the hatch, he's not even aware of my presence. Eventually he does glance back, but just to make sure I'm not interfering with his bike. The rear wheel is distorted by an aggressive, curb-shaped bend. I fit the shopping bags in where I can, then slam the hatch.

Ordinarily I'd leave the basket in the empty spot next to the VW. But the Jesus fish is watching, so I walk it all the way over to the carousel.

When I get behind the wheel, I set my wallet on the bamboo shelf underneath the dash. (I refuse to drag around a purse because I like them too much. Get on the popular purse train and you never get off.) Eli takes no notice until the big yellow floater on Stacy's keys catches his eye.

"What're those?"

"Those are the keys to a beach house in Florida. How would you like to go to Florida for your birthday? The house is right on the beach."

He pulls the earphones out of his ears and sits up straight.

"For real?"

"For real," I say.

He slumps back down thoughtfully. "Florida, huh. Cool."

I'm not immune to the boy's charm, oh no. I put the plastic shades back on.

"Who's the Cool Mom now?"

The traffic on the way home is heavy and my luck is such that I seem to catch every red light. Eli's headphones are still dangling, still hissing his unattended music, while he contemplates the beach house keys in his hand. He sniffs the plastic floaty, trying to catch a whiff of salt water. I can tell the idea intrigues him, which is good. If the birthday boy's onboard, Rick will have to go along.

Stuck at the light, I start thinking of ways to say thanks to Stacy. I never would have expected something like this from her. And now that I know she thinks of me as her best friend, maybe when I get back I'll need to pay more attention to her. Maybe a girls' night out.

The light changes and we get a few cars ahead. It turns red before I can clear the intersection. On the grass verge next to us, there's a group of people gathered. On top of the noise of the radio and the traffic around us, they add another layer: chanting voices. Even with the window down, I have to pay attention to make out what they're saying: *"End the war, end the war, we can't take it anymore!"*

Some are standing and waving hand-lettered signs that say HONK FOR PEACE. Others sit in folding lawn chairs, shading themselves under wide-brimmed straw hats. They're an unlikely group of demonstrators, mostly plump, gray-haired white people with sun-pinked skin. Despite the signs, nobody is honking. The drivers all around seem, at best, indifferent.

One of them, an elderly woman with short white hair and a diaphanous sundress, reminds me of a woman I knew long ago, growing up with my Quaker family, before I met Rick and the whole course of my life changed. Miss Hannah, her name was, and she'd been a nurse in World War II and traveled the world afterward, one of those women who did amazing things back when women were expected to stay home with the kids, and subsequently didn't understand why women who didn't face similar barriers would do anything less.

Miss Hannah. I haven't thought of her in years. She'd taken my hands in hers once and fixed her hard, gray eyes on me and said, *"Do something with your life."*

And at the time, I thought I would. I couldn't even fathom why she'd think I needed the encouragement.

I look a little closer, and of course, it's not Miss Hannah, who passed away years ago. As I watch, a younger man walks among the group. He wears cargo shorts and a shirt with epaulets that makes him look like a

Peace Corps volunteer, and he has a scraggly beard that can't hide the fact that he's not much older than twenty-five. He has a drum tucked under his arm and starts beating it in tempo with the demonstrators' shouting.

This catches Eli's attention. I turn to find him shaking his head.

"Hippie losers," he says.

The light changes and we drive through the intersection.

"What did you say?"

The anger comes up on me suddenly, unexpectedly. I stomp the brake, then let up. I stomp it again and twist the wheel. As the car heads back toward the intersection, Eli stares at me, baffled.

"Mom, what's wrong?"

"That's what I want to know."

"I don't understand."

And to be honest, neither do I. The VW careens back through the intersection and pulls along the curb across the street from where the demonstrators have gathered. I turn the engine off.

"Come on," I say.

"I'm not getting out."

"I'm serious, Eli. We're going over there."

"What for?"

Good question. I can't think of an answer at first.

"Mom, what for?"

"To introduce ourselves."

He pauses, then smiles. "I get it."

"What do you get?"

"This is supposed to be a life lesson, right? Because of what I said? I'm supposed to see that they're not hippie losers, just normal people, and then I'll apologize?"

"Do you *want* to apologize?"

He thinks about it. "Are we going to do this or not?"

As we cross the street, I know I've lost already. Why did it make me angry? I know he was only joking. I *hope* he was, anyway. From his older brother, Jed, that line wouldn't have surprised me, but Eli takes life as he finds it. He doesn't judge. And besides, you can't teach life lessons to a kid who's two steps ahead of you. You can't teach a boy who's always willing to call your bluff.

*

"What am I doing here?"

"What *are* you doing here?"

Up close, I can see I was wrong about twenty-five. He's older, probably in his thirties. When we approached, he greeted Eli with some complicated fist-bumping handshake, and the two of them seemed to have an understanding right from the start. But not me. This is the story of my good intentions. I sometimes act on them but always regret it. Standing on the grass among all these strangers, all I want to do is get back in the van and speed away.

"I guess . . . well, we saw you guys out here, and . . . we just wanted to say hello."

"That's great," he says. "I'm surprised you noticed us."

"It's kind of hard not to."

"I don't know about that." He smiles sheepishly under his beard. "We're shouting at the top of our lungs, but nobody in this country is listening."

The line sounds practiced, something he's said a hundred times. It elicits a practiced nod from several of the demonstrators.

Eli grins at my discomfort.

"I know this probably seems a little bit out there to people in this neighborhood," the man is saying, "but you know what I think? Most people go through life disagreeing with the politicians, yelling back at the television set, but they never say anything, not out in the open. The way we're enculturated, we look down on people who care too much and aren't afraid to say so."

"We know this isn't going to change anything," one of the others says. "That's not the point. We're here so that they know—the people in charge—that we see what they're doing and we're against it. Even if we can't stop it or change it, we're not going to ignore it either." As he speaks, his voice grows louder, but not loud enough to drown out the roar of traffic. Behind him, several demonstrators start to fold up their chairs and put away their signs.

The scraggly-bearded man checks his watch and gives the others a nodded signal.

"My name's Chas, by the way. Like I said, this may not be your scene, but—"

"Oh no," I say. "I used to be a Quaker."

He pauses, cocks his head. "Okay."

That was a stupid thing to say, a stupid way of putting it. What I mean is, I know what it's like to be unwilling to ignore things just because you can't stop or change them, and while I might not forward mass e-mails or shout at intersections, I'm not . . . I don't know what I'm not, but I'm not.

"You know," Chas says, glancing at Eli, then back at me. "Here's what you ought to do. Come hang out with the Rent-a-Mob this weekend."

"The what?"

He smiles. "It's my little name for us. Not just these folks, but a whole bunch of us. We're not going to a demo this weekend, just working on signs, but it would be a great chance to meet everybody and see if—" He breaks off, gazing over my shoulder. "It would be a great chance—" Again, over the shoulder.

I turn around and see what he's looking at. On my bumper, the Jesus fish glows like molten silver, sparkling in the sun. A car rushes past, obscuring the fish for an instant, but then it reappears with an insistent flash. Refusing to be hidden under a bushel, or behind a passing vehicle. As I glance back at Chas, I feel my cheeks begin to flush.

"Anyway," he says, digging under the flap of his chest pocket to produce a card. "Take this."

I hold the thick card in my hand. CHAS WORTHING, it says. And underneath in red letters: ACTIVIST + POET.

Is that a thing? You can get business cards for it?

"Seriously, you should come this weekend," he says. "Every Sunday afternoon we get together. It's at my place this time."

"I wish we could. We're leaving town, going on vacation." I see Eli's smile widening. "In Florida."

"Well," Chas says, "if you change your mind, you know where to reach me."

❋

"You lied to Chas," Eli says.

"Don't start in on me."

"You told him we'd be gone, but we're not supposed to leave until next week, right? Did you not want to hang out with the Rent-a-Mob?"

"Honey, sometimes—"

"You just have to lie to people, I know."

"That's not what I mean."

"You were right," he says. "That was a life lesson."

He starts to laugh. I start laughing too. I can't help it. The whole thing is ridiculous.

"I'm worried about you, Mom," he says. "I think you might have some hippie loser in you."

"You bet I do."

We turn down our street and pull into our driveway. When I pop the hatch, Eli doesn't go for his fractured bike. Instead, he grabs some groceries and helps me bring them inside. Maybe he learned something back there after all.

The story continues in *The Sky Beneath My Feet* by Lisa Samson

Sometimes you have to go a little bit CRAZY to find the life you were meant to live.

Available in print and e-book

Biting and gentle, hard-edged and hopeful
. . . a beautiful fable of love and power, hiding
and seeking, woundedness and redemption.

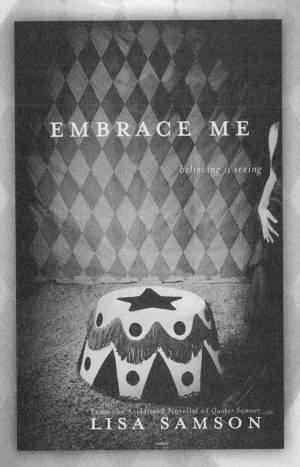

EMBRACE ME

believing is seeing

From the Acclaimed Novelist of *Quaker Summer*

LISA SAMSON

Available in print and e-book

THOMAS NELSON
Since 1798

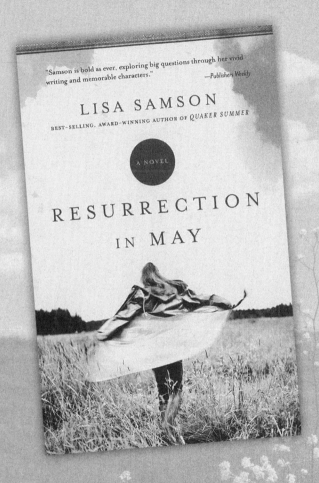

9781595545466-C

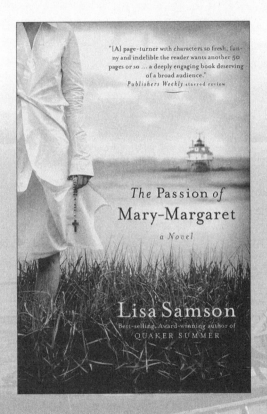

About the Author

The Christy-award win-
ning author of *Christianity Today's* Novel of the Year *Quaker Summer*,
Lisa Samson has been hailed by *Publishers Weekly* as one of the "most
powerful voices in Christian fiction."